DEPRAVED
DEVOTION

MORGAN BRIDGES

ORION

First published in Great Britain in 2025 by Orion Fiction,
an imprint of The Orion Publishing Group Ltd.
Carmelite House, 50 Victoria Embankment
London EC4Y 0DZ

A Hachette UK Company

1 3 5 7 9 10 8 6 4 2

A CIP catalogue record for this book is
available from the British Library.

ISBN (Mass Market Paperback) 978 1 3987 2921 6
ISBN (eBook) 978 1 3987 2922 3

Printed and bound in Great Britain by Clays Ltd, Elcograf S.p.A.

DEPRAVED DEVOTION

ALSO BY MORGAN BRIDGES

POSSESSING HER

Once You're Mine

Now You're Mine

THE OBSIDIAN ORDER

Vicious Secret

Vicious Society

DARK & DIRTY VOWS

A Match Made in Hate

I Thee Lust

To Have & to Hurt

To the reader who saw "obsessed psychopath" and immediately thought: "That's husband material."

AUTHOR'S NOTE

The contents of this dark romance book may be triggering to some readers. It contains explicit sexual content and a morally gray hero who is an over-the-top jealous/possessive stalker and is willing to do whatever it takes to have the heroine. A complete list of trigger warnings can be found below.

stalking/obsession
blackmail/coercion
breaking and entering
violence
murder
dubious consent
off-the-page rape set in the past
off-the-page murder set in the past
parental grief

DEPRAVED
DEVOTION

CHAPTER 1

GENEVA

GHOST IS CORPOREAL, A MAN OF FLESH AND BLOOD.

He's not the ethereal being the media has made him out to be. Or the elusive poltergeist the police think he is. As a criminal psychologist, I'd say that Ghost is barely human…if you consider the number of people he's admitted to killing.

I make my way toward the courthouse steps that are packed full with people. My skin crawls at the idea of unwanted contact with strangers, each touch brought on by pushing and shoving. But it's unavoidable if I want to witness this high-profile arraignment.

News reporters, with their cameramen right behind them, wield microphones like batons, nearly assaulting anyone who gets too close. Protesters carry their signs like badges of honor, hoisting the homemade signs into the air, their chanting loud and continuous. Some advocate for the death penalty, despite this being New York City. The other half pleads for mercy on behalf of Ghost, saying his crimes were justified.

Without a psychological profile on him, no one can know for sure.

I tuck my chin and ball my fists, prepared to do a little pushing and shoving of my own, if necessary. I'm almost at the top of the courthouse steps when someone slams into me from behind. My feet trip over themselves as I stumble. Before I can recover, I collide with a stranger.

A tall man with dark hair and medium build swings around to face me, his features twisted in a sneer. "You better watch where you're going, bitch!"

I step back to gain some distance, but I'm still surrounded by people on all sides. And close enough to make out the scratches on his wrist. They're not from a cat.

"I apologize," I say calmly. "Someone pushed me, and I didn't mean to bump into you."

"Save your story for someone who gives a shit."

"Fine." When he doesn't give me any indication that he's going to move, I clear my throat. "You're in my way."

The man glares at me. I glare back.

He leans forward, towering over me. "Who the fuck do you think you're talking to?"

I square my shoulders and lift my chin, unwilling to back down. I'm getting in that courtroom, come hell or high water. Seeing Ghost in person is an opportunity I won't miss out on because of some asshole with a complex.

I keep my gaze locked on the man in front of me, scanning his features for microexpressions and to analyze his body language for nonverbal cues. He crosses his arms, turning his torso away from me, indicating he's uncomfortable with my challenging him. Due to the curl of his upper lip, along with his use of the word "bitch," my intuition says he hates women. It's highly doubtful the deep scratches on his wrists were inflicted by a *man* he recently attacked.

His position on the stair above me gives him a feeling of superiority, so I even the playing field and get on his level, continuing to hold his stare. His brows lift in surprise.

"You may like to hurt women to gain a sense of control," I say, "but you only do it behind closed doors because you're a coward. So, either man up and hit me, or get the fuck out of my way."

My words have the intended effect. His mouth falls open and he blinks at me. Using his stupefied condition, I slip past him. The crowd of people closes around me, shielding me from his view. I don't stop until I'm in line for the security check.

I take a deep breath and release it slowly, trying to rid myself of the adrenaline coursing through my veins. Even though I was pretty sure the man outside wouldn't have hit me, there's never complete certainty when dealing with human beings. Like animals, their behavior can be unpredictable when they're in pain or mentally unstable.

The security guard waves a hand at me. "Ma'am, step forward."

I walk through the metal detectors, earn a nod from the officer, and retrieve my purse just as my cell phone begins to ring. While making my way down the hallway and navigating through a crowd—that's not as hectic as the one outside, but still too many people for my liking—I look at the screen.

Shit. It's Mason.

"Hello."

"Hey, Gen. I'm surprised you answered the phone. You haven't lately."

I pinch the bridge of my nose hard enough to hurt, and to

keep my thoughts about his "charm" to myself. "I've been busy. What's up?"

"I was hoping I could come over to your place tonight…It's been a while."

"Mason, you don't need to be coy about wanting sex."

He laughs, the sound airy and fake. Like our relationship. I only agreed to the term "girlfriend" to discourage the guys at the office from hitting on me. I'm more turned on by my work than by men. That's either really pathetic…or serves to exemplify the quality of males I've encountered.

"I'd love to take you to that new restaurant on Fifth Street," Mason says. "We can order a bottle of wine and spend some time together."

It wouldn't matter if he wined and dined me every night; our interactions are purely transactional. I let him have sex with me and he brings me sexual relief. *Sometimes.* If I don't come, neither does he.

"I'm busy tonight," I say.

"Let me guess: You have another serial killer to profile in order to save lives and whatever?"

"Yes. You know I love my job."

He huffs on the phone. I press my lips together as my annoyance grows. First, he insults my career. Then, he acts as though I've inconvenienced him. There's no way I'm having sex with him now.

"Fine, Gen. Why don't you call me when you're ready to have sex or dinner or both."

"Okay."

I pull the phone away from my ear just as he says my name.

With a shake of my head, I end the call. I don't have time for Mason's childish behavior. Not when there's a real man to study.

A murderer, to be exact.

Today is the first time the public will lay eyes on Ghost in person. The only glimpse anyone has had of him is the single mugshot that's been plastered across every news outlet.

His hair is pure white, making it hard to pinpoint his age, but his features place him somewhere in his thirties. His hazel-green eyes are bright with intelligence and his expression is confident. The way he looks at the camera in the picture displays a smirk filled with mockery, as if he's amused by the whole ordeal.

Even from a still image, Ghost exudes charisma, a raw magnetism that unnerves me. Then there's the scar on his right cheek, starting at the corner of his eye and slashing down to the edge of his mouth. It does nothing to detract from his physical appearance. If anything, it adds to his appeal. The mark speaks of violence but also survival.

What has he gone through?

He's refused every interview, denied every request to tell his story or explain his misdeeds.

People all across the country have heard about Ghost and started to romanticize him. They write letters to him, send him gifts, and post on social media about how they'd do anything to be with him. It's off-putting to me as a woman, but fascinating from a psychological standpoint to witness a whole contingent, made up mostly of women, viewing him as a tragic misunderstood figure, as opposed to the cold-blooded killer he really is.

Hybristophilia: the attraction to someone who's committed a heinous crime.

It's a twisted form of admiration that's borne from a desperate need to connect with someone powerful. Even if that power comes from violence. These people believe they see something in Ghost that no one else does, and that they can "fix" him.

Idiots.

Deep down, I understand Ghost's appeal. My education gives me the ability to diagnose behavior, label it, and distance myself from it. But as a woman, it's hard not to acknowledge reality. And the fact is that Ghost is ridiculously attractive.

I sigh with relief when I'm finally allowed entrance into the courtroom. Of its own accord, my gaze scans the room for Ghost and I find the defendant's table empty. I imagine him sitting there soon and anticipation swells in my chest. It's hard to manage my intrigue when Ghost is arguably the most interesting man alive.

Good looks aside, he's captured the public's attention in a way few criminals do.

He turned himself in.

Ghost has refused to explain why, after years of killing, he decided to accept punishment for his gruesome crimes. He's rumored to be remarkably intelligent, so why would he risk a death sentence?

The sound of my heels clicking against the polished marble is swallowed by the murmurs of those already present. I choose the first available aisle seat closest to the front, sliding onto the wooden bench and double checking that my cell phone is on silent. Once that's done, I retrieve my pen and notepad, placing them on my lap before rearranging my pencil skirt and straightening my sleeves. Then I wait.

More people file in, each one quickly grabbing their seats. A man with dark hair in a crisp beige suit takes the spot next to me. He gives me a curt nod that I return, my expression cool but polite.

A hush falls over the crowd as the bailiff stands.

"Ladies and gentlemen, as we prepare to commence with today's proceedings, please remember to turn off all electronic devices. There will be no talking or disruptions during the hearing. Anyone who fails to adhere to these rules will immediately be escorted from the courtroom."

The man beside me mutters a profanity in Italian and retrieves his cell phone from his pocket. I keep him in my peripheral vision, watching as he changes the volume on his phone. Once he puts it away, I relax a little and go back to scanning the room.

Anxious murmurs and quiet conversation circulate between the occupants, creating a buzzing sound that weaves through the room. The noise, the scent of polished wood, and the sunlight beaming through the clerestory windows tickle my senses, dredging up memories.

The last time I was in this building, it was one of the best and worst days in my life.

"All rise for the honorable Judge Pritchett," the bailiff says.

As a collective, everyone gets to their feet, eyes facing forward. The judge walks in, his full, black robes swishing with his measured steps. The man's forehead is creased and his mouth thin, as if he's already feeling the weight of the hearing.

The judge's voice rings out once he's settled in his chair with his gavel nearby. "Please be seated."

I sit, anticipation thrumming along my arms until goosebumps appear on my flesh. Any minute now...

Everyone freezes the moment the side door opens and the sound of chains clinking together echoes in the room.

Ghost has arrived.

CHAPTER 2

GENEVA

I STOP BREATHING AS GHOST WALKS IN.

He towers over the five guards surrounding him. His large hands are cuffed in front of him, the metal gleaming under the lights with every step he takes. Despite the extra security—overkill or not enough?—and restraints, Ghost moves with a deadly grace and an air of confidence that belies his situation.

He's devastating in person.

My lungs scream in protest, and I inhale deep as I run my gaze over his features. Features that no picture or camera lens could ever do justice.

His hair isn't just white; it's pure and blinding like the first snow of winter in Central Park. The man's face is gorgeous: the kind only found in romance novels and movies. His orange jumpsuit doesn't detract from his attractiveness whatsoever. Not when the black ink on his neck offers a sneak peek of the tattoos hidden underneath his clothing. His smirk—half-seductive, half-sinister—has me shifting in my seat.

Then there's his eyes…

Cold and calculating, but there's something else, too, something that's not quite right.

Intensity?

Insanity?

Inhumanity?

As I continue to study Ghost, his gaze slides across the room. And lands on me.

I stiffen, an involuntary reaction to the weight of his stare. Ghost stops walking, holding my gaze as a knowing smile graces his lips. If it wasn't for the way my skin heats, I'd believe I'm imagining the entire thing.

One of the deputies shoves Ghost, breaking our connection. I frown at the show of violence. Ghost needs to be held accountable for his actions but treating him like that isn't something I condone.

"Keep moving," the deputy says.

Ghost straightens to his full height of well over six feet, and cranes his neck back and forth before slowly turning around to look at the deputy over his shoulder. "If you do that again, I'll kill you."

The menace in his tone doesn't override the sensuality of his deep voice. A woman in the row in front of me hums appreciatively, and I have the urge to smack her upside the head. Yes, he could probably make someone come from murmuring sweet nothings in their ear, but he *literally* just threatened to murder a man in broad daylight with over fifty witnesses.

Ghost is not only deranged but delusional.

The deputy freezes before his brows snap together. "Shut up and start walking."

When he shoves Ghost a second time, I hold my breath again. The convict merely smirks.

"Deputy Wilson, I hope you have a notarized will in place."

Before the man can respond to the threat, Ghost faces forward and saunters away as though he doesn't have a care in the world. The security maintains their positions, keeping the criminal between them, until they reach the table.

Ghost plops down unceremoniously in the chair and lifts his hands. "Let's do this."

The deputies are quick to secure his handcuffs to a chain on the table. One of them breathes a sigh of relief once Ghost is fully restrained. I find myself doing the same. There's no doubt in my mind that Ghost would add to his list of crimes if given the chance.

"You are here today for your arraignment," the judge says to Ghost. "The charges against you will be read. Do you understand?"

"Yes, Your Honorship."

The judge doesn't react to the sarcasm, except for tilting his head away from Ghost. The microexpression of annoyance doesn't escape my notice. After Judge Pritchett gestures to the clerk, the man comes forward, document in hand.

"The court will now hear the case of the State of New York versus John Doe, case number 2025-CR-00567. The charges are twelve counts of first-degree murder—"

"Soon to be thirteen counts," Ghost says loudly, grinning at Deputy Wilson. "Thirteen is my lucky number."

Like a puff of smoke, gasps and whispers fill the room, permeating the space with shock and excitement. Judge Pritchett slams his gavel and silence reigns once more.

"Order in court." The judge shifts his attention to Ghost, a sheen of perspiration on his forehead. "You are to remain silent and listen as the charges are read. I will not tolerate interruptions."

The court clerk clears his throat and continues. "The charges are *multiple* counts of first-degree murder, multiple counts of aggravated assault, arson, use of a deadly weapon, theft, and one count of…"

The clerk frowns in confusion as he stares at the paper in his hand. "One count of bird-napping."

Ghost shrugs. "I had to save my cock from being caged."

My lips fall apart before twitching at his absurdity while people all around me snicker. The judge glowers at the crowd. "Order."

The convict places his boots on the table, reclining in his chair, an air of satisfaction enveloping him. I purse my lips when the deputies fail to instruct Ghost to place his feet on the floor, but a quick scan of their features offers mild relief. I suppose a relaxed serial killer in a non-threatening position isn't worth provoking. At least not *this* one.

In a rush the clerk finishes, "Presiding over this case is Honorable Judge Pritchett."

"Now that you've heard the charges against you, it's my duty to ensure that you understand your rights throughout these proceedings," the judge says to Ghost. "You have the right to an attorney, which you refused. Is that correct?"

Ghost shrugs. "Why would I hire someone dumber than me? Good help is so hard to find nowadays."

"Answer the question, Mr. Doe."

"I thought I did. I intend to represent myself." His grin returns. "Your Honorship."

The judge blows out a breath. "Given the results of your competency evaluation, I will allow it. Counselor?"

The prosecutor stands. He smooths out his blue tie and lifts his chin, eyes narrowed on Ghost before shifting his gaze to the judge. "Given the severity of the charges and the potential danger to the public, we request that the defendant be held without bail. The nature of the crimes indicates a high flight risk and further risk to the citizens of New York."

Judge Pritchett nods at Ghost. "Do you wish to respond to the prosecution's request for detention without bail?"

Ghost chuckles, his ever-present smirk still in place. "I have no intention to flee. I turned *myself* in, remember?"

The courtroom buzzes with suppressed laughter once again. Even I can't stop the smile that forms on my lips. Although I'm quick to erase it from my face and focus my attention on taking notes.

"I'll take your voluntary surrender into account, but you will be held in custody until your trial. With that being said, you have a right to a jury trial…"

The judge lists each and every one of Ghost's legal rights, his voice steady and resonant. Every so often he sweeps his gaze over the courtroom, but Ghost doesn't move. He stays reclined in his chair, nodding here and there as though aptly paying attention to the judge.

"It's crucial, Mr. Doe, that you fully understand these rights, given the severity of the charges you face. What is your plea?"

Every pair of eyes shoot to Ghost as he tilts his head, causing his pale disheveled hair to graze his shoulder. "Guilty, your Honorship."

The simplicity of the word "guilty" discredits the complexity of its implications. Which isn't lost on anyone present. As a collective, we stare at this enigmatic man. What reason, other than to plead guilty, would he have to turn himself in? Yet it's still a shock to hear him accept the charges and the loss of freedom that comes with it.

Judge Pritchett nods, his expression grave. "Mr. Doe, do you understand that by entering this plea, you waive your rights to a trial and to challenge the evidence against you?"

"I don't want a trial." Ghost shifts in his seat, removing one leg from the table. "That'd be a waste of my time. As far as evidence against me? I've provided everything you need. But if that's not enough, then—"

With a swift movement that's no more than a blur, Ghost swings his leg to slam his foot against Deputy Wilson's shin. The guard stumbles before slamming onto the tabletop, his upper body draped across the surface. As the deputies retrieve their firearms, Ghost slings his other leg over Wilson's neck, locking his ankles together.

The four deputies cock their weapons and aim them directly at Ghost's head, their stances rigid and their gazes wary but determined. I brace myself for the blast of gunfire, but it doesn't come. Not when there are innocent bystanders in the line of fire, located directly behind Ghost.

"Let him go!" one of the deputies shouts.

Wilson gasps and claws at Ghost's legs, unsuccessful in prying them away. The deputy to the left of Ghost, whose name badge reads "Tanner," presses the end of his pistol to Ghost's temple. "I said, let him go." This time the order is given without hesitation.

No one underestimates Ghost and his threats now.

He simply laughs in response. It's a bone-chilling, blood-curdling sound that frightens me more than the violence I'm witnessing. The noise echoes off the walls, the sinister notes filling the atmosphere like a poisonous gas.

This is a man who has nothing to lose…or he's already lost everything.

I sit there, eyes wide, my insides shriveling in horror. Wilson still tugs and scratches at the criminal's legs, his movements growing more frantic with each second that passes as he continues to struggle for air.

Ghost tightens his hold on his captive and turns to press his forehead against the muzzle of the gun, staring up at the deputy. From the set of his jaw and his focused gaze, Ghost isn't merely demonstrating dominance.

He's making a statement.

Ghost lifts his hands as much as the handcuffs allow, rattling the chain-links. "Look, ma, no hands."

He jerks in his seat and a sickening crack follows.

After that is silence, heavy with a chilling reality. Wilson's body goes limp on the table, his hands falling away from Ghost's legs.

The deputies freeze, their fingers tight on the triggers but none daring to make a move that could turn this standoff into a bloodbath. Ghost flicks his gaze around the room, taking in the faces of his audience, his expression unreadable. Except for that damn smirk on his lips. Then, very slowly, he unravels his legs and allows Wilson's now lifeless body to slide off the table onto the floor with a dull thud.

The sound of the body hitting the floor reverberates through the room, and then chaos erupts. Half of the crowd screams hysterically, people already clamoring to leave. I grip my notebook tighter to stop my hands from shaking.

Tanner yells an order to seize Ghost, and the men rush forward all at once. But Ghost is already surrendering. The sinister echo of his deranged laugh fills the air, a haunting reminder of the darkness that resides in the human psyche.

I was wrong about my earlier conclusion. This was not just an act of defiance. It was a message that Ghost cannot and will not be controlled.

CHAPTER 3

GHOST

"What's a man got to do to go to prison already?" I ask.

"Shut up, Doe."

"Just ignore him."

I grin at the guards flanking me as I sit on the medical exam table, one man then the other. Deputies Johnson and Garcia. From the way their gazes dart to and fro, they're more alert than the guys in the courtroom. Or they were told about Wilson's death, and that's why I have shackles on my ankles and they're watching me like I'm a bomb ready to explode.

Boom, motherfuckers.

"This med ward is boring," I say. "Blood pressure, blood sample, etcetera…etcetera…You'd think I'd be thrown in a cell by now. Killing with style is mentally exhausting, you know? I really need some 'me time.'"

Deputy Johnson stiffens beside me, but his gaze loses none of its focus. Deputy Garcia turns to look at me with a veil of hatred covering his features, and my smile widens. I swing my legs and wiggle on the parchment like a toddler, rattling the chains and wrinkling the paper underneath me.

"Doe, you—"

"Call me, 'Ghost,'" I interject. "The moniker is more accurate. Plus, it gets the ladies going."

When I waggle my brows at Deputy Johnson, his lips thin. "You won't be able to pull a disappearing act now, Ghost. After this assessment, we're throwing your ass in a hole so deep you'll never see daylight, or civilization again."

I clap my hands together. "An introvert's wet dream. Can't wait."

The door opens and I shift my gaze, keeping my amused expression in place. A man in his early fifties, with a trim salt-and-pepper beard and hair to match, walks in. His brown eyes land on my face, sharp and observing, giving him a perceptive air.

A psychologist. He's going to be fun to fuck with.

"I'm Dr. Richards," he says. "Before we begin, I want him confined to the chair."

Smart man, but I doubt he's more intelligent than me. Sucks to be him.

The guards roughly escort me to the metal chair that's bolted to the floor. After securing my shackles and my handcuffs, the doctor's forehead loses some of its wrinkles. He takes the unoccupied chair opposite of me.

"John Doe—"

"Ghost."

The doctor nods. "Ghost, I'd like to talk to you about your current state of mind and your history. Can you start by telling me your real name?"

"No. *Nein*. And in Spanish for Deputy Garcia: *No*." I wink at him.

"Do you feel safer hiding behind that name?" the psychologist asks.

"I don't struggle with feelings of insecurity. The name was given to me by the Feds, and since it was catchy, I decided to adopt it."

Dr. Richards adjusts his glasses, a flicker of intrigue crossing his features. "Names are powerful. They can define us. I want to understand you in order to help. Who were you before you became 'Ghost'?"

I lean back as much as the restraints allow, testing the give of the cuffs on my wrists. "Before my fame? Just a regular John Doe. Boring and predictable."

He smiles at my words, his gaze still analyzing every nuance of my expression and tone. "John Doe, the average Joe. But every man has a story. You turned yourself in to the police. That would indicate that you want your story told, Ghost. I'm here to listen."

"My story is simple: I love to kill people."

"Why is that?" he asks with a frown.

"It's fun. Duh."

Dr. Richards scribbles on his notepad before looking at me again, his gaze less indulgent. "What's fun about it? Is it the act itself? The fear in their eyes?"

"If you've never done it, you won't understand." I shrug. "The first time was my favorite. I've been chasing the high ever since."

"Feelings of euphoria can be addictive, but that rush of adrenaline can be achieved in other ways. Ways that don't involve taking lives. Have you ever considered them?"

I pause, debating how much to play along while my mind churns. Until recently, I watched people plan their lives to gain some measure of control. Then I would go about ruining said "plan" to wreak havoc and cause disruption, which happened to involve killing. A lot. It kept things interesting and my hands busy.

Idle hands are the devil's work, after all.

But then I saw the most unadulterated, wrathful, and fucking beautiful demonstration of chaos a year ago…and it made me higher than cocaine. I've been obsessed with the source ever since.

So, yes, I've considered other alternatives to experience feelings of euphoria. And she's it. The only thing that's made me feel alive since my first murder.

Dr. Geneva Andrews is my toy.

And I won't share her with anyone. Not this psychologist who thinks he can manipulate me. Not that fucking boyfriend of hers. Not even her profession and ironclad morals will stop me from playing with her.

Until she breaks into tiny little p

i

e

c

e

s.

CHAPTER 4

GENEVA

IT'S FRIDAY, BUT WHEN YOU'RE MARRIED TO YOUR WORK, EVERY day is the same. I guess my life is a compilation of Mondays then.

I sit at my desk, the hum of the activity outside my office completely muted by my noise-canceling headphones. With my back facing the wall, I'll be sure to notice if anyone opens my door. Although, everyone knows better than to interrupt me when I have my headphones on, unless it's urgent.

My notes from this morning are displayed on my computer screen, along with the stark images of the victim and the crime scene. Just like every other time, the details etch themselves on my memory. They'll stay there until the case is solved.

If the case is solved.

"Case #1025-0731, Crime Scene Analysis. Location: 1207 Maple Street. Victim: Julia Mills, mid-thirties, found deceased in her residence. Time of death is estimated between 11:00 p.m. and 1:00 a.m."

I type steadily, describing the scene thoroughly, noting the position of the body, the state of the room, and the lack of forced entry. The blood spatter is only in the living room, while the rest of the house remains untouched by the violent struggle.

"You put up a fight, Julia," I whisper to the victim. I stop to briefly run my fingertips over her gruesome image. "We'll catch this son of a bitch."

I move onto the profile development. The methodical arrangement of the scene suggests an organized offender, someone who plans and executes with precision. There's a ritualistic element to the positioning of the body, indicating a possible psychological compulsion.

"The suspect has a meticulous nature and possibly a background in forensic knowledge," I mutter to myself. "The lack of forced entry suggests the victim may have known the perp or was deceived into allowing them in."

I lose track of time as I continue adding to the report until I save the file and send it to the lead detective. A knock sounds the moment I remove my headphones.

"Come in," I call out, looking up from my desk.

The door swings open and Detective Allen Harris steps inside. His graying hair is cropped short, and a perpetual five o'clock shadow frames his square jaw. He smiles at me, then pauses, glancing around my office with a raised brow.

"You know, Gen, your office always feels like a morgue. There's no color in this room."

The walls are pristine white and every piece of furniture, down to the wall clock, is black. The starkness of the decor is only softened by the natural light coming in through the windows. The flooring is a polished concrete, the gray surface adding to the minimalist aesthetic. To me, my office is a haven of efficiency.

Inwardly, I sigh. "I find it easier to focus without distractions."

"Fair enough. But a plant wouldn't hurt."

I smile at him and gesture to the empty chair in front of my desk. "What can I do for you, Detective?"

He takes the proffered seat, his expression turning serious. "I saw your report hit my inbox. I'm sure it'll be just as good as the others."

"Thank you." I scan his face, noting the way he's clenching his jaw and the tension lining his mouth. How tightly he's clutching a folder in his right hand. "Is there something else you wanted to discuss with me, Allen?"

My use of his first name is a subtle tactic to put him at ease. It's a reminder that we're more than co-workers. We're colleagues, fighting on the side of justice.

Allen scrubs the back of his neck before his posture loses some of its stress. But only infinitesimally. Damn. I brace myself when he opens his mouth.

"Ghost refuses to speak to any of the professionals. We're talking about days of silence. For fuck's sake, we don't even have a psych profile on him yet."

"Where is he locked up?"

"Blackwater Correctional Facility," he says. "Usually that place knows how to handle people like him."

"Except he's not like anyone else."

My pulse kicks up a notch, just like every other time I've thought about Ghost. I assumed I'd get over my curiosity concerning him by burying myself in work and focusing on other criminals, but that's not been the case.

Like a ghost, he haunts me.

Allen sighs. "Before he stopped speaking, Ghost said he has information on the Riverton case."

My mouth drops open. I quickly snap my jaw closed with a succinct click. "Anna Lee, the eight-year-old who disappeared two days ago? But how would Ghost know anything about her? He was in prison before she was reported missing."

"I don't know. It could be a sick joke to mess with us, or..."

I thrum my fingers on my desktop. "Or he could have pertinent information."

"You know the first forty-eight hours are crucial. The chances of finding her alive decrease the longer she remains missing. We're past that."

"Damn it." I halt my fingers and tilt my head. "Why are you telling me this? Is it because I dabbled with the idea of writing an article about Ghost for peer review? If so, I'm not doing that anymore. After I saw him murder that man in court, I won't have anything to do with him."

"That's too bad because Ghost wants something from you. He's asked for you... by name."

"What?!"

My raised voice has Allen blinking at my uncharacteristic reaction. I clear my throat to regain my stoic composure, the one that keeps my emotions locked away where they're safe and can't hurt me. Or anyone else.

"I'm sorry," I say, gentling my voice. "You surprised me."

"Right back at you. Anyway, like I just said, Ghost refuses to speak to anyone but you."

Why *me*?

Dread coats my insides like molasses. Yet there's an unwanted spark lit inside me as well, one that I can't ignore. Despite witnessing Ghost kill someone, I remain captivated by him. His sense of twisted humor pairs with his devious actions to create a macabre allure that's hard for me to shake.

"How does he even know who I am?"

"I honestly have no idea, Gen. What I do know is you're the best in your field."

I wave a hand in dismissal. "It's easy to be successful when you don't have a life. But I can't do it." I shake my head for emphasis.

"You're our only in, and we're out of options."

"After the case involving Sarah, I don't want to work directly with criminals again. Especially someone as unhinged as Ghost. I can help catch the bad guys from *behind* the scenes."

If I'm around Ghost, then my fascination will only deepen. Which means he could do more than haunt me. He could possess me.

Allen nods in understanding. "Sometimes the only way to catch a criminal is to find them in the shadows where they dwell. If Ghost can lead us to her kidnapper, we might have a chance to find Anna Lee alive."

The truth of his words hits me like a fist to the chest. I suck in a breath, my nostrils flaring. I can still see Ghost's white hair hanging over his brow along with his cruel smile. However, I also recall Anna Lee's missing poster, her eyes full of innocence and joy.

Fisting my hands, I meet Allen's gaze. "When do I visit him?"

"Tomorrow."

Shit.

⌣

"Why?" I mutter to myself.

It's the question that I've asked myself for years. Sometimes

I find answers, but mostly I'm left with more questions and less clarity than before. Does that stop me from continuing to seek answers, to find closure buried deep in the minds of deviant criminals? No, I'll never stop trying to understand them.

My sanity depends on it.

The cab driver grabs my attention by clearing his throat. "Because you hailed me down, miss."

"I'm sorry. I'm talking to myself. Just ignore me."

"Whatever you say, miss."

The middle-aged man shifts his gaze from me to the road and turns up the radio a notch. I look down at the open folder resting on my lap before flipping through the scant information we have on Ghost.

Behavior

- **Name Preference:** Only exhibits a response to being called "Ghost." Identifies strongly with the alias given by federal authorities, possibly as a form of psychological defense.
- **Physical Movements:** Tests the restraints frequently, indicating discomfort with confinement but also possibly assessing escape potential or demonstrating his apathy.

Reading Dr. Richards's report is interesting, considering he's had the longest interaction with Ghost so far. However, I disagree with his conclusion that Ghost is assessing potential escape. He turned himself in.

So the real question is: What does Ghost stand to gain from it?

Psychological Indicators

- **Control and Power:** Derives satisfaction from the fear and control he exerts over others. This is a recurring theme in his speech, indicating a potential for antisocial personality disorder with traits associated with psychopathy. Further evaluation to confirm conduct disorder as a juvenile is required for a diagnosis of ASPD, and further tests such as the PCL-R may confirm psychopathic tendencies.

"Ah, fuck me."

I let my head fall back against the headrest and close my eyes, ignoring the driver's curious glance. Psychopaths are the hardest to deal with. The lack of human emotion is something I can intellectually comprehend, but even my reserved and strict nature isn't completely void of feelings.

No matter how much I try to ignore them.

The cab pulls to a stop, jolting me from my work.

"We're here," the driver says. "Have a good night, miss."

"You too."

I hurriedly shove the folder in my bag and exit the cab. In front of me is a modern high-rise design with a sleek glass façade and metallic accents. It stands prominently against the Manhattan skyline, with balconies for some apartments. Mine is one of them.

Lucky for me, a couple of years ago, my living room was a crime scene I was called in to analyze. I offered the landlord a reduced rate, explaining it'd be hard for him to find a tenant who'd be willing to overlook the homicide that took place there. Since then,

I've lived in an apartment that I otherwise couldn't afford without resigning myself to processed noodles for the rest of my life.

As I enter the grand foyer of the building, the familiar luxury envelops me. The floor is a glossy expanse of marble, reflecting the soft glow of the pendant lights above. Art deco pieces line the walls—curated spots of color against the neutral tones of the interior.

The concierge nods at me with a practiced smile, his presence a steady constant. He flicks his gaze and jerks his chin to my left.

I follow the gesture to find the last person I want to see.

CHAPTER 5

GENEVA

Mason leans against one of the marble columns, his figure casual but out of place in the meticulously designed space. At the sight of him, a knot of annoyance tightens in my stomach.

Uninvited and unexpected.

I mask my irritation with a practiced smile, the kind I reserve for suspects who think they've outsmarted the system. Or me.

"Gen, hey!" Mason pushes off from the column, his smile wide.

"Hey," I manage, my voice even. "What are you doing here? Were we supposed to meet, and I forgot?"

"No. I just wanted to surprise you."

He steps closer with his arms lifted, as if seeking approval for his spontaneous visit. He's not going to get it from me. Maybe on another night when I'm in need of physical relief my vibrator can't provide. But I doubt I'll be able to orgasm because of all the stress due to my impending interview with Ghost.

Although…his piercing eyes and muscular body might do the trick.

"Consider yourself successful," I reply dryly, moving past Mason and leading the way to the elevators.

We ascend in silence, the digital numbers ticking off the floors too slowly. By the time the elevator dings at my floor, I've mentally rehearsed how to cut this visit short.

Stepping into my apartment, my body almost relaxes from simply being back in my own space. The living room, once marked by tragedy, now boasts a tasteful minimalism, large windows casting light across the wooden floors, the city's pulse a backdrop. It's welcoming and my version of cozy.

Or it will be when Mason leaves.

Walking over to the side table, I set my bag down with a little more force than necessary. Then I head over to the kitchen to put some space between us and grab a glass of water.

He removes his jacket and tosses it over the back of my couch, as though settling in. I sigh internally, tapping my fingers against the countertop.

I'm of half a mind to fuck him just so he'll go, but I can't summon the energy.

"Look, Mason, I'm not in a good headspace right now." I turn to face him fully. "I have a ton of prep to do for a big interview tomorrow with a fucked-up inmate. It's really not a good time."

"Well, shit. I'm sorry to hear that. Are you going to be okay?"

I shrug off his concern, along with my twinge of guilt for being so distant with him. It's the only way I can do relationships. If you can even call it that.

"I will be. I don't have a choice," I say. "He won't speak to anyone else."

"That's weird. Why?"

"Wish I knew."

Mason comes around the counter, trapping me as he steps close and rests his hand on the curve of my waist. I go rigid at his nearness and immediately scold myself. Physical connection is all I've ever asked from this man. I can't be upset when he seeks me out for that very reason.

"You know, I'm more than happy to rid you of the stress you're feeling." After tugging me toward him, he grazes my ear with his lips.

My heart beats faster at his touch. Not with anticipation. With a vague sense of dread.

He presses his body to mine and kisses me, his lips firm. Insistent. It's a kiss of lust. Of a man wanting a woman.

Except I'm not that woman tonight.

I gently push him away. "I'm not in the mood."

He frowns at my sudden rejection. "What do you mean?"

"I told you. I just want to relax tonight."

"Are you fucking serious?"

I cross my arms. "Yeah, I'm fucking serious."

Mason studies me, his gaze narrowing. Intensifying. I scrutinize him in return, my brain rapidly firing data through my synapses, giving me insight in seconds. The slight furrow of his brow, an almost imperceptible crease, signals anger brewing beneath the surface. Then his eyes darken with intent.

This swift, but significant, change puts me on edge. However, I don't take a step back as instinct demands. I hold position, my stance challenging.

Mere seconds feel like hours as I wait for him to react.

Mason clears his throat in a deliberate effort to regain composure. A quick shake of his head follows as though he's attempting to dismiss troubling thoughts or aggressive impulses that have momentarily broken through his usual demeanor. I squint at him when he squares his shoulders and fists his hands at his sides, a clear sign of suppressed aggression.

While never taking my eyes from him, I grab my abandoned glass and take a sip. If need be, I'll chuck the water in his face to snap him out of whatever emotional state he's in.

Mason blows out a breath. "You're such a bitch, you know that?"

I shrug. "Maybe I am, but did you really think you could show up unannounced and try to fuck me? Because that's just what happened. I told you twice that I'm not having sex tonight, so you don't have the right to be pissed."

"I don't know why I try with you." He glares at me. "You're obviously not worth my time."

"Go home."

He grabs his jacket and stalks toward the door. I don't say goodbye. But I also refrain from saying "fuck you." A win in my book.

A few seconds later he slams the door shut. I roll my eyes and walk over to lock it.

Another "relationship" down the drain.

Not that I put much effort into it. However, I can't deny it's a pattern too familiar, too predictable.

I exhale deeply, the tension slowly draining from my shoulders as I retreat into the solitude that has become my fortress.

It's not just Mason, or the ones before him. It's a series of emotional barricades that I've meticulously constructed over the years. Men come and go, their presence temporary and their impact minimal. I find myself unable to forge anything deeper than superficial attachments, an emotional aloofness that I wear like armor.

Something I've both cursed and cherished.

As I pour myself a glass of wine, the bitter truth settles in: My inability to emotionally connect isn't just a facet of my personality. It's a scar, a deep-seated residue from the trauma of my childhood. The murder of my parents, a brutal and senseless act, left me orphaned and alone, thrusting me into a world devoid of warmth. That coldness settled deep within me, shaping my interactions, freezing the potential for genuine intimacy.

It also created my need to understand the criminal mind. To understand how someone could rape, torture, and then brutally murder two innocent people.

Living through such horror at a young age, I learned to shut down, to protect myself from the vulnerabilities that open hearts endure. The fear of losing someone else, the potential of another devastating heartbreak, has kept me at arm's length from anyone who might stir deeper emotions.

Except my best friend.

I grab my phone and my wine glass before settling on the couch. Then I dial Sarah's number. She answers on the second ring. Thank goodness.

"What did you do?"

I laugh at her greeting. "I threw Mason out."

"Again?"

"Again."

She laughs quietly, a mix of exasperation and amusement clear in her voice. "Geneva, what are you going to do? It's like a revolving door with you two."

I take a sip of wine, the rich flavor dancing on my tongue as I consider her words. "I don't know. It's always the same with him—or anyone, really. I get bored after a while. Then, I push them away."

"I know you're the one with a doctorate, but I hate to tell you that's unhealthy behavior."

"I know," I admit in a whisper.

My gaze drifts to the city outside, the myriad lights a stark contrast to the darkness that feels like it's creeping in around the edges of my mind. Did I project that same darkness on Mason? Wanting to paint him as an overly aggressive person so I could walk away without a backward glance? Sure, he could be an asshole but he'd never shown a possibility of violence.

"Every time I think I might be able to change, I end up right back here." I sigh. "Alone."

"You're not alone, Gen. You have me."

I smile, grateful for her understanding. "I know you're here. And I appreciate it more than you can imagine." I pause, gathering my nerve to give voice to my question. "How'd you do it?"

"What? Move on after being raped?"

I flinch. "Shit. I'm sorry. I just—"

Sarah cuts me off gently. "No, it's okay. It's not something I enjoy doing, but it's good to talk about it sometimes. Especially with you. If you hadn't gotten on the witness stand, that asshole would still be on the streets."

"I wish I could've done more."

There's a moment of silence as she gathers her thoughts.

"It's not like there's a formula, Gen," she starts, her voice steady. "For a long time, I felt like I couldn't trust anyone, not even myself. But then I realized, staying stuck in that pain wasn't what I wanted for my life.

"I started therapy," she continues. "And I mean really committed to it, not just going through the motions. Which I'm sure you can appreciate, given your occupation." She chuckles briefly, but then her voice turns serious. "It was difficult, probably the hardest thing I've ever done. But over time, it helped me understand that what happened wasn't my fault, that I didn't have to let it define my entire existence."

I nod. Though Sarah can't see it, her words resonate deeply within me, underscoring the profound difference in our paths to healing. While Sarah has bravely confronted her past, striving to liberate herself from its painful shackles, I've chained myself tightly to my trauma, driven by an unyielding obsession to unearth the "why" behind the murders of my parents.

This relentless pursuit has not just been a professional endeavor as a criminal psychologist; it has consumed every facet of my life. Each case I take on, every criminal mind I attempt to decipher, is a desperate search for clues that might illuminate my own dark past. My parents' unsolved murders aren't just a haunting memory— they're the lens through which I view the world, the filter that colors every interaction and decision.

"Remember, Gen, it's okay to take things one step at a time. You're not alone. You've got me, and I'm not going anywhere."

"Thanks. I'm here for you too. Well, I better go. Are we still good for a girls' night when you get back from vacation?"

"Absolutely. I'll talk to you soon, okay?"

"Sounds good. Bye."

"Bye, honey."

After ending the call, my thoughts quickly shift to my upcoming interview, igniting a mix of excitement and fear. Ghost is more than just another case. He's a puzzle wrapped in an enigma. A brilliant mind and a devastatingly beautiful face, drenched in insanity.

Understanding Ghost is the key to outmaneuvering him. So, how am I supposed to do that when there's not much to go on?

The logical answer: Go straight to the source.

And pray that I return with my mind sane and my soul intact.

CHAPTER 6

GENEVA

SLEEP DIDN'T COME EASILY LAST NIGHT. IT NEVER HAS. AND NEVER
will unless I leave my profession. Maybe not even then.

My mind replayed the scenes from the case files, interspersed
with flashes of Ghost's cold smile. When morning finally arrived, I
felt as though I'd been in a waking nightmare.

Standing in front of the mirror, I arrange my brown hair into
a tight bun at the base of my neck, every strand secured with mil-
itary precision. It's a routine I've mastered over the years, each
movement deliberate, each pin and twist a small assertion of control in a life where so much is unpredictable.

My clothing is as severe as my mood—black slacks, pressed
to sharp creases, and a matching blazer that fits me like armor.
Everything is functional, designed to command respect without
drawing undue attention.

Makeup is minimal—a touch of foundation and a sweep of
mascara to frame brown eyes that have seen too much. It's another
mask, another layer between me and the world.

Jewelry is sparse—simple diamond stud earrings, a watch with a black leather strap. Practical, unassuming. Nothing to catch or snag, nothing that could be used against me.

As I gather my things, I catch a glimpse of myself in the mirror, a moment of introspection before I banish it. The person staring back at me is the same disguise I always wear.

She is efficient, unyielding…and alone.

There's no time for second-guessing, no space for fear or regret. Ghost is waiting.

An hour later, I'm in the parking lot where Blackwater looms ahead, a fortress of concrete and steel. I make my way to the entrance, my heart pounding in my chest. Inside, Detective Harris waits for me. His broad shoulders fill out his well-worn, charcoal gray suits—always slightly rumpled, as if he's been up all night chasing leads.

"Ready?" he asks.

I'm not sure if anyone could truly be ready for this. "Yes."

"You have to be prepared for anything. Ghost is unpredictable, but they'll have guards monitoring everything. You won't be alone in there."

"Thank you." I look at Allen. "I mean it."

"Don't worry about it. This is going to go smoothly, or we'll get you the fuck out of here."

We step up to the front desk of the prison, the imposing gates now firmly behind us. The man at the desk looks up as we approach. Allen and I hand over our identification, and the deputy scrutinizes them carefully before nodding. We sign the visitor log, recording our names, the time of arrival, and the purpose of our visit.

Ghost.

The metal detector looms ahead, a silent reminder of the prison's strict security measures. I pass through first, the machine beeping softly as I clear it. Allen follows, and we're directed to place our personal belongings into a locker nearby. My bag, our phones, our keys—everything goes in.

A deputy steps forward to conduct a pat-down search. Once cleared, we're handed visitor badges with our photos and names printed on them. The badge feels heavy as I clip mine to my jacket. It's a constant reminder that I'm in a place where every move is monitored to prevent my death.

"Follow me," a corrections officer says once we're cleared, his tone as neutral as his expression.

We fall in line behind him, and he leads us through a series of security doors. Each one opens with a loud buzz, then slams shut behind us with a heavy thud that echoes in the narrow corridors. And in the chambers of my heart.

When we finally reach the interview room, the officer turns to me, his gaze hardening. "A few things to remember before you go in. There's *no* physical contact with the inmate. Keep your distance and don't attempt to give him anything or take anything from him through the pass-through drawer. The conversation will be monitored, and there are certain topics you'll need to avoid—personal details about yourself, specifics about other cases, or anything that could provoke a reaction. If at any point you feel unsafe, there's a panic button under the table. Use it, and we'll come in immediately."

"Got it." My voice is steadier than I feel.

Detective Harris reaches out to tap my shoulder. "Remember, you're in charge. Don't let him rattle you. Go get him, Dr. Andrews."

The officer opens the final door and I step into the interview room. The harsh fluorescent lights above cast a stark glow over everything, making the already sterile environment feel even more impersonal. The room is divided by a thick wall of glass, a constant reminder of the barrier between me and the inmate. It's not just for physical safety. For me, it's psychological as well.

On my side, there's nothing but a metal table and chair. I glance up at the glass wall as I take my seat, noting the small pass-through box embedded in it. I won't be using that. Ever.

I take a deep breath, scanning the emptiness of the room. There's no warmth here, no comfort. Just a calculated design meant to keep everyone in their place—safe, distant, and controlled.

This is where I'll face him.

The coldness of the chair underneath me seeps into my clothes, trying to steal my body heat. I drum my fingers on the hard surface of the table as impatience tangles with my nerves.

Sound amplifies with each second. The buzz of the lights overhead, the distant clank of the metal doors shutting, and my own tapping all come together to create a soundtrack of tension. It's a song only I can hear, one that thrums through my body, pressing on me from all sides.

The door on the inmate's side creaks open.

I halt my fingers, suppressing the nervous habit, as two security guards lead Ghost into the room. My breath catches the moment I lay eyes on him.

His white hair is ghostly under the bright fluorescent lights, while shadows dance across his cheeks, deepening the scar on his face. His hazel eyes capture mine, and it takes everything I have not to react to the weight of his gaze.

If eyes are the window to the soul, he is damned.

Ghost saunters up to the glass, much bigger up close than he seemed from a distance in court. His attention never wavers as the guards maneuver him. Without a word, they cuff his wrists to the table welded securely to the floor, the clinking of the metal echoing in the small space.

Ghost doesn't resist. He sits and continues to watch me with that eerie calm, his eyes burrowing into mine through the glass. My breathing quickens under his intense scrutiny.

Finally, they exit the room.

It's just me and him.

Ghost smiles. It's sinister and seductive, a lethal combination.

"Dr. Andrews," he says, his voice an alluring purr. "I've been looking forward to this."

I continue meeting his gaze with as much steel as I can muster. There's no doubt that he's enjoying this. That smile is a weapon designed to unsettle me. To remind me that he's testing me with every glance and every word.

He wants to remain in control, even if he's the one in chains.

"You have information about Anna Lee and her kidnapper," I say. "I'm here to listen."

His smile widens. It stretches across his mouth, unnatural and unnerving. "Straight to the point. I like that." He leans forward. "Tell me, are you also this direct when you fuck?"

My face heats, but I keep my expression neutral. I've faced monsters before...except none like him. Ghost is different—he's a master at this game, a predator who thrives on getting under people's skin, on twisting the knife just to watch them bleed.

I won't give him that satisfaction.

The familiar tug of professionalism pulls me back to center, grounding me even as his stare has my skin prickling. "Let's stick to the matter at hand. Anna Lee. What do you know?"

"This isn't just about what I know. It's about what you're willing to do to get that information."

"What do you want?"

He chuckles softly. "All in good time, but first, a little conversation."

"Fine." I clench my hands under the table. "What do you want to talk about?"

"You, Dr. Andrews."

I blink at him one too many times, the tiny crack in my composure betraying me. Ghost's smile doesn't falter. If anything, it deepens, as if he's pleased with himself for getting a reaction, however small.

"We both know that I'm not here to discuss myself," I say, keeping the tremor out of my voice as much as I can manage. He's watching me too closely, reading every microexpression I try to suppress.

"But that's where you're wrong," he replies, his tone soft, almost coaxing. "You think you're here for the girl, and maybe you are. But really, this is about you. It's *always* been about you."

I force myself to breathe evenly, to stay calm. Later, I can think about the repercussions of what it means to have an insane killer fixated on me. Later I can berate myself for my growing fascination with him. But for now, I need to get through this interaction without losing myself in the process.

"What do you mean?" I ask.

"You're the one I wanted to see, Dr. Andrews. Not the police, not the lawyers. *You*. You've been on my mind for a *long* time."

Unease runs through me, and I can't help but wonder how much of this was planned, how long he's been toying with the idea of meeting me.

"You're wasting my time," I say. "If you have something to say about Anna Lee's kidnapper, then say it. Otherwise, this meeting is over."

His confidence doesn't waver. "You're so determined, so focused. It's one of the things I admire about you. But there's more beneath the surface, isn't there? So many layers. I wonder what it would take to peel them away."

"You can play whatever games you want, but you're not going to get inside my head, Ghost."

"Aren't I already?"

CHAPTER 7

GENEVA

"You're thinking about me." Ghost's tone is deceptively gentle. "How I know about you. What I know. What I could do. You're wondering how much of this was planned, how much control you really have. And that's the beauty of it, Dr. Andrews. The more you try to resist, the deeper I'll dig."

He's not entirely wrong, but I can't let him know that. I exhale slowly before speaking. "Let's say you're right, and I want to know everything about you. None of that matters if you're not willing to share, which leaves us at an impasse. So, all we have left to discuss is Anna Lee."

Ghost clicks his tongue in admonishment. "Always so professional, so distant. Look at your clothes, your hair, your mouth." His eyes drop down to my lips. "All very restrained. But that's what fascinates me about you. You're like ice—cold, impenetrable. I can see why men struggle to connect with you. It must be exhausting for them, trying to break through that frosty exterior of yours."

My jaw aches from clenching it. Inside I'm screaming. The sheer audacity of his assumptions, the way he's turning this conversation into something personal, something intimate—it's fucking with me.

And I've only been in his presence for ten minutes.

"What's it like, Dr. Andrews?" Ghost continues, his tone light, almost conversational. "To always be in control, to keep everyone at arm's length? To never let anyone see who you really are? It must be so…lonely."

My chest tightens, the air around me thickening, making it hard to breathe. He's clawing at one of the few vulnerable places in my life, causing emotional damage to rise and flow like blood from a wound.

"You're projecting," I say. "Just because you're isolated doesn't mean the rest of us are."

"Oh, but that's where you're wrong." His eyes gleam with twisted amusement, and my stomach knots. "You're more isolated than I am. You put up emotional shields, pretending they're there to protect you, but all they do is keep you trapped. How long has it been since you've truly connected with someone? Not that silly boy you mess around with. Not even that broken friend who thinks she knows you. *Real* connection is being truthful about who we are. And you're flame and wrath encased in a wall of ice and control."

How does he know those details about my personal life?

Under the table, my hands tremble with both fear and anger. He's trying to pull me in, to make me doubt myself…and it's working. Fury burns in my gut, singeing me with the need to lash out. Yet here I sit, silent and restrained, with my mind twisting in on itself as Ghost begins to mold me like potter's clay.

"Enough," I snap, getting to my feet and slamming my palms

on the table. I don't care if he enjoys watching me lose my composure. I can't take much more of this and still maintain my professionalism. "You don't control this conversation. I do. Now, tell me what you know about Anna Lee, or I'm walking out of here."

For a moment, he just stares at me, his gaze inscrutable. Then, slowly, his smile fades, replaced by something colder, more calculating. "You're stronger than I expected," he says, almost to himself. "But strength can be a weakness too. Remember that."

I don't respond, refusing to rise to the bait. I can't let him see how much he's already unsettled me; how close he's getting to breaking through my composure. I need to get the fuck away from him.

"I'll tell you about the girl." Ghost leans forward further, his voice low and conspiratorial. "But you have to give me something in return."

I arch an eyebrow, skeptical, but I stay where I am. This glass wall only has a few small holes, but I've seen what he can do. "And what exactly do you think I have to offer?"

His smile returns, dark and twisted. "Your time, Dr. Andrews. Your attention. I want to know what makes you tick, what keeps you up at night. I want to understand you as well as you think you understand me."

My throat constricts and I swallow hard, the full weight of his words sinking in. This isn't just an obsession—it's a need to dominate.

"You're not getting anything from me." I glare at him before pivoting on my heel.

"Geneva."

The sound of my name on Ghost's lips freezes me in place.

Hearing it for the first time, in his voice, laced with that dark, insidious charm, feels like a violation. As if he's reached inside and stripped away another layer of the armor I've so carefully constructed, while also caressing me.

I force myself to take a breath, to steady the tremor in my hands. I don't turn around. I *can't*. If I look at him now, I'm afraid of what I might see—what I might feel.

"Geneva," he says again, softer this time, almost apologetic. "Don't walk away. Not yet."

There's a part of me that wants to bolt out of this room, to put as much distance between myself and that voice, that man, as possible. But there's another part—a darker, more curious part—that wants to stay, to hear what he has to say, to understand why he's so fixated on me.

I dig my nails into my palms, using the pain as an anchor, something to hold on to, something to keep me grounded. "You haven't earned the right to call me that."

"But it's your name, isn't it? And it suits you. So strong, so poised. But there's a vulnerability there too, just beneath the surface. I like that."

I swallow hard, my throat tight. The temptation to turn around, to confront him, to demand answers is all-consuming. But that's exactly what he wants.

"I'm leaving," I say, more to myself than to him, as if repeating it will give me the resolve to actually do it. I take a step toward the door, forcing my legs to move, forcing myself to keep going.

"Dr. Andrews." His voice is low and urgent. "You're running away, but you can't escape me. You know that, don't you? I'm already in your head. You'll think about me long after you leave this room. You'll hear my voice, see my face. You'll wonder what

I'm doing, what I'm thinking. And you'll come back. Because you need answers just as much as I do."

My muscles tighten, stiffening my spine. "Whether or not that's true, you'll never know."

"And you'll never find Anna Lee in time without my help."

I spin around, my eyes wide. "She's alive?"

He studies me for a long moment, as if carefully choosing his response, then nods slowly. "Yes. Now be a good girl and come back and play with me." The soft words slide across my body like a physical touch, sensual and tantalizing.

"No." I cross my arms over my chest to emphasize my stance, and to fortify myself. "I'm done playing your games."

"Okay, you win this round." He laughs, a soft, mocking sound that sends chills down my spine. "One final request and then I'll tell you everything you need to know to find the girl."

"I'm listening."

Ghost's eyes glint with something darker, more dangerous than before, as he leans back in his chair, the chains binding him to the table clinking softly. His smile widens, a slow, deliberate curve that makes my skin crawl with foreboding.

"I want you to show me the real you, Dr. Andrews. The part you keep locked away, buried under all those rules and professionalism."

"I don't know what you're talking about."

"You know *exactly* what I'm talking about." His voice is low and smooth, like silk. "I've seen it in your eyes, the way you struggle to keep control, to maintain that perfect façade. But I also see the cracks, the part of you underneath that longs to be free from all the rules and constraints you've imposed on yourself."

A mixture of fear and something else—something I don't want

to acknowledge—slithers over me. He's talking about the deepest, darkest corners of my mind, places I've never let anyone go before. Places I've barely dared to explore myself. And it terrifies me.

"Nothing you're saying is true."

He shakes his head slowly, that infuriating smile never leaving his face. "This is about truth. *Your* truth. You hide behind that beautiful exterior, pretending to be someone you're not, because you're afraid. Afraid of what it would mean to truly let go, to let someone see the real Geneva. But I see her. I. *See*. You."

I fist my hands until my knuckles turn white and my forearms ache with the effort it takes to remain still. His words hit too close to the truths I've kept secret for so long. And I hate him for it. I hate him for seeing what I've spent my entire life hiding from the world.

From myself.

"You're wrong," I manage to say, but the conviction in my voice is slipping.

"Am I? You're so tightly wound, so disciplined, that you've forgotten what it feels like to be alive. You want to experience something real, something raw."

I want to shout at him, to tell him he's wrong, that he doesn't know anything about me. But the words won't come. Because deep down, in the part of me I've always kept locked away, I know he's right. I have spent my life building walls, creating rules to keep myself contained, to protect myself from the chaos that I fear would consume me if I ever let it out. And I've become a prisoner of those rules, trapped in a life that feels more like a cage than anything else.

"You don't know me," I say. "I'm not going to indulge your sick fantasies."

He laughs softly. "It's not about indulging me. It's about indulging yourself. For once in your life, stop pretending. Let yourself feel. Let yourself be free."

His words are like a drug, intoxicating and dangerous, pulling me in even as I try to resist. And that's what frightens me the most—the part of me that wants to listen to him, to experience that freedom he's talking about. But I know that path leads to darkness, to a place I may never come back from.

His smile softens, turning almost tender, as if he's genuinely concerned for me, which only makes this worse. "What's the point of living if you're not truly alive?"

I close my eyes, trying to block out his voice, his presence, but it's useless. He's already under my skin, digging into the deepest parts of me, exposing everything I've tried so hard to keep private.

But I can't break. Not here, not now.

"Tell me where Anna Lee is." I open my eyes, my voice barely more than a whisper. "Please."

He watches me for a long moment, his gaze piercing, unrelenting. "All right. I'll tell you. But remember this—you can walk away now, but you'll never escape what's inside you. One day, you'll have to face it. And when you do, you'll remember this moment, and you'll know that I was right."

His words hang in the air, heavy and ominous as he shifts in his chair, the chains rattling softly. "The girl is being held in an old warehouse on the outskirts of town near the industrial district, just off Route 17. You'll find it past the abandoned train yard, where the tracks split off into dead ends. She's alive. For now."

I don't wait for anything else. I turn on my heel and march out of the room, my heart pounding in my chest, my mind racing with his words, his voice echoing in my ears. I got what I came for. We have the information we need to hopefully save an innocent child.

But even as I rush down the hallway, the cold, blank walls closing in around me, I can't shake the feeling that I've lost something in that room.

Something I may never get back.

CHAPTER 8

GENEVA

I push through the heavy door, and the air in the hallway rushes past me but fails to erase the tension knotting my stomach.

Ghost's voice is still in my mind, prowling the corners of my consciousness. His insidious whispers contain doubts, fears, and unsettling truths I'm not ready to confront.

I barely make it a few steps when Detective Harris is there, waiting for me, his eyes fixed on mine and a frown tugging at his mouth. His usual calm, composed demeanor is tinged with grave concern. He watched everything that transpired in that room, and the weight of his scrutiny is almost too much to bear.

"Are you all right?" His voice is soft and carefully measured.

I open my mouth to respond, but the words stick in my throat, tangled up in the emotions I'm trying so hard to ignore. I force myself to take a breath, to steady the quiver in my voice. "I got what we needed. Anna Lee's alive."

The detective slowly nods, his gaze searching and assessing. "I've already called it in. If the information is real, they'll find her.

I hope she's okay." There's a weight to his words, a subtle emphasis that tells me he's not just talking about the girl. "It was rough in there."

Everyone saw the way Ghost toyed with me, the way he pushed and prodded until he found the cracks in my armor. Shame warms my cheeks, and I avert my gaze. It takes me a moment, but once I regain my composure, I look at the detective.

"It's nothing I can't handle." I shrug, trying to dismiss Allen's concern. "Ghost really knows how to manipulate someone, I'll give him that. In the end it doesn't matter because saving Anna Lee is the goal."

The detective's frown deepens. He steps closer, his tone gentle. "Ghost made things personal to throw you off your game. And he knew things about you that he shouldn't. He's more dangerous than I originally thought."

His words hit harder than I expect, and for a moment, I'm not sure how to respond. I want to tell Allen that I'm fine, that I'm still in control. But even as I try to form the words, I know they're not true. Not entirely.

"You did good in there," he continues. "Better than most people would have. Don't let him get to you. He's just another criminal wanting attention, but you never have to see him again."

I nod, though the relief I expect doesn't come. Instead, there's just a hollow, gnawing emptiness, a sense that something is slipping away from me, something vital. I want to ignore it, to focus on the mission, but the weight of Ghost's words lingers like a shadow, dark and inescapable.

"I'll be fine." The words feel like a lie. "Getting back to work is what I need right now."

"You don't have to pretend you're okay. There's no shame in

needing some time. Are you sure you don't want to take the rest of the day?"

I shake my head. "Being alone with my thoughts is the worst thing I can imagine."

The detective holds my gaze for a long moment, his expression unreadable, as if he's considering whether to push further. But then he nods. "All right. Let's check in on the team and see where they're at."

We step outside, the fresh air biting against my cheeks, offering a brief reprieve from the oppressive atmosphere of the prison. Allen looks at me again.

"I know I already said it, but you really did good in there. I wouldn't have lasted long before losing my shit."

⁓

The cemetery is quiet.

It's the kind of silence that seeps into your blood and flows through your veins, until you're either overcome with grief or peace. I've had a lot of experience with the former and none of the latter.

The traffic after work was abysmal as always, but there's no relief in arriving at my destination. I wave off the driver, who's quick to leave, his tires squealing against the cracked pavement as he takes off. The neighborhoods surrounding the grave site are crumbling with broken windows and graffiti has been scrawled across the walls in angry bursts of color.

The cemetery bears the same weight of neglect. The headstones are simple, most of them weathered and worn, some of them barely legible. Weeds grow unchecked between slabs of granite, and the grass is overgrown, needing to be mowed.

This area, on the outskirts of the city, has been forgotten by anyone with the means to make a difference. It's not a thing of beauty, but of necessity, a final resting place for those who had nowhere else to go. For all of its flaws, there's a stark reality to it that I haven't found in the polished parts of the city.

I walk down one of the narrow paths, careful not to trip on the uneven ground. Once I leave the pavement, my high heels sink into the grass and soft earth, and the fog becomes thicker. Heavier. Matching the weight constantly bearing down on me.

I used to come here often. Despite the pain. The anger. The loss.

Then my obsession with studying criminals and their patterns grew like the weeds underneath my feet: wild and unrestricted.

After the day I've had, I need to be here. I need to speak to my parents, choosing to believe they can hear me even if they can't respond.

When I reach their graves, I stop, standing there for a moment, simply staring at the headstones. Their names are carved neatly into the marble, along with dates that mark the beginning and end of their lives. I kneel, brushing away a few fallen leaves from the stone, and sit back on my heels.

"Hi, Mom. Hi, Dad." My voice is quiet. Full of longing. "It's been a long time since I've visited. I'm sorry about that. And for the way I acted last time."

A year ago, I came to grieve.

A year ago, I lost control.

A year ago, I questioned my sanity.

I can still see it in my mind as clearly as if it happened yesterday: the crushed beer cans, the cigarette butts, the remnants of someone's careless night left to rot on the graves of the two people who meant the most to me. Like they were just another piece of trash to be discarded. Something inside me snapped. Whatever I'd kept tightly wound since my childhood momentarily broke loose.

I'd driven here with the intention of spending the day with my parents, telling them how much I missed them, how I was trying to make them proud. But when I saw the mess, the complete and utter disrespect, all I could see was red.

I didn't think. I just acted.

I remember yanking open the trunk of my car, grabbing the baseball bat I keep there for protection, and marching back to their graves. The first swing shattered a beer bottle, the glass spraying across the headstones like a rain of jagged shards. The second swing took out the plastic table someone had dragged over, the pieces splintering under the force of my anger. I kept swinging, kept smashing, kept destroying until there was nothing left but debris and the sound of my own ragged breathing.

When it was over, I stood there, surrounded by the wreckage of what I'd done, my hands trembling, the bat still gripped tightly in my fists. The anger didn't leave me—it just simmered, hot and painful, a reminder of how little control I really had. The pain, the grief, and the rage from the night of their murders came rushing back, brutal and overwhelming. And for a moment, I thought I'd drown in it.

I dropped the bat, falling to my knees and screaming. The sound tearing out of me like it was the only thing keeping me from shattering completely. I don't know how long I stayed there, on the ground, sobbing like a child.

Eventually, I pulled myself together, wiped my face, and picked up everything I'd demolished. After that I straightened my appearance, putting my mask back in place, and I haven't been back since.

Until today.

Because of Ghost.

"I went against my rules and met with a criminal today. He's nothing like you or the people I try to save. Ghost is…dangerous and manipulative. He's the kind of person I've spent my entire career trying to understand. And I hate him."

I pause, taking a shaky breath. "I hate him because he reminds me of what happened to you. What was done to you."

Tears sting my eyes when I reach out and trace the rough edges of their names on the headstones. *Samuel & Margaret Prescott.*

"I hate Ghost because one interaction, one fucking conversation is bringing all of it back. Everything I've tried to repress. He got inside my head, and I don't know how to get rid of him.

"I wish you were here," I whisper, my voice thick. "I wish you could tell me how to deal with this, how to move on. From everything. My need to understand. My obsession with the criminal mind. My curiosity with Ghost. *All* of it."

I sit there, losing track of time, until my tears dry up, my legs go numb, and the sun sets. The potential danger in this place at night forces me to stand, my body stiff from my lack of movement.

"I promise to come visit you again," I say. "And it won't take me a year this time. I love you. So much it kills me."

My stride is purposeful as I walk away. I leave the cemetery behind, feeling no different than when I arrived. Ghost still haunts me, and my parents remain dead.

However, my time spent with them is a reminder of the things that drive me. Because as much as I want to deny it, anger and pain are the only things that make me feel alive.

Two hours later, I unlock the door to my apartment and step inside. The quiet stillness of an empty home is the kind of silence that's supposed to be comforting but never really is.

I drop my bag by the door and shrug out of my coat, letting it fall carelessly onto the nearest chair. Normally, I'd hang it up, keep things neat and orderly, but tonight…tonight I don't give a shit.

My footsteps echo on the hardwood floors as I make my way to the kitchen. The day has been a blur, a relentless onslaught of noise, tension, and fear.

But my time with Ghost ended up being worth it.

They found Anna Lee.

She was dirty, barefoot, and curled behind a dumpster like a forgotten doll left out in the rain. Alive but only just. Her skin was a patchwork of bruises, her body frail from days without food, and her hands trembled so violently the paramedic had to steady her arm twice just to place the IV.

She's safe now, but the damage is done. Her world will forever be colored dark, like mine and Sarah's.

Now, with nothing but my thoughts for company, my mind starts spinning. Ghost's voice is there, lurking in the corners of my psyche, whispering all the things I don't want to hear. All the truths I'm not ready to deal with. I can't get rid of him, can't escape the feeling that he's still with me.

I reach for the bottle of whiskey in my cabinet, my hand trembling slightly as I unscrew the cap. After filling a glass, I take a sip, the burn of the alcohol searing its way down my throat. It's not enough to mute Ghost's voice in my head.

"*Geneva. I. See. You. The* real *you.*"

I take another long drink, desperate to silence him, to push him back into the darkness where he belongs.

"*You're going to break.*" I can see his twisted smile, feel the satisfaction in his tone. "*And when you do, I'll be there, waiting to pick up the pieces. To put you in a design of my making.*"

CHAPTER 9

GHOST

She's fucking exquisite.

Dr. Geneva Lynn Andrews.

Her name lingers in my mind like a sweet, forbidden melody, the kind that envelops you long after the music stops. I can still see her, the way she tried so hard to maintain that icy composure. To keep the walls up around her. As if they could protect her from me.

But I know better.

I saw the cracks, felt the tremors beneath that polished surface. That beautiful mask. She thinks she's in control, but she's not. Not anymore.

I glance around my cell, the dim light from the small, barred window casting long shadows on the gray walls. The room is sparse, bare of any comforts. It contains a metal bed bolted to the floor with a thin mattress, a steel toilet, and a small, scratched-up desk that's seen better days. The air is stale, carrying the scent of mildew and disinfectant, but I've grown used to it. The walls are covered in faded graffiti and scrawls from previous occupants.

They're messages to no one in particular, just marks left behind by those who've passed through this place.

What legacy will I leave behind? It would be a shrine to Dr. Andrews if I was inclined to share.

Spoiler: *I'm not.*

Tucked behind the loose brick in the corner is a collection of notes. I've carefully written on and hidden away each piece of paper containing observations, plans, and thoughts. All of them concerning Geneva.

The moment she stepped into that interview room, I could sense it—the darkness in her, the one she's tried so hard to hide, even from herself. It's there, lurking just beneath the surface, waiting for the right moment to break free.

And I want to be the one to set it loose.

There's something intoxicating about the idea of watching someone so tightly wound unravel. Especially when they don't even realize it's happening.

I can still hear the tremor in her voice when she asked about Anna Lee, the way she hesitated when I used her first name. *Geneva*. It suits her. So strong, so fucking sexy.

How many times have I whispered her name while following her?

How many times have I uttered her name while planning her future?

How many times have I groaned her name while fucking my hand?

The number is more than the years of prison I've been sentenced to.

Geneva hates me. I know that. But that's what makes our relationship so interesting. Hatred is a powerful emotion—one that can be twisted, manipulated, turned into something much more potent.

She thinks she can keep me out, that she can walk away and forget about me, but she's wrong. I'm already inside her head. It's only a matter of time until I'm inside her body, with her legs wrapped around me and her moans in my ear.

"Shit," I mutter. "You're hard again?" I pose the question to my dick, staring at it with exasperation. "Okay, but this is the last time tonight, you greedy fuck."

As I pull out my cock the dull fluorescent light overhead flickers, casting brief, erratic shadows across the room. It's the only source of light in this place at night, and it's unreliable at best. I've learned to ignore it, just like I've learned to dismiss the hum of the ventilation system and the muffled sounds of the other inmates down the hall, all of them constant reminders that I'm never truly alone. But in my mind, I am.

Right now, it's just me and Geneva.

I lean back on the bed, the thin mattress doing little to cushion the hard metal beneath. The image of her face when she left the interview room, that mix of determination and something fragile, plays over and over in my brain. She's already questioning herself, doubting her instincts. And that's exactly where I want her mentally.

Physically, I want her underneath me.

I grip my cock, sliding my hand up and down the length, imagining it's her touch. Her hands and her soft skin, her breathy sighs and her desperate moans.

My eyes fall closed, and I can almost see her, perched between my legs, her hair a dark curtain around her face. She'd look at me through her lashes, gaze heavy-lidded and heated. She might even bite her lower lip like she did when I looked at her mouth. She hadn't even registered the giveaway to her desire. But I had.

"God, Geneva. You've fucking ruined me."

She would smile, the expression sultry and sensual, before taking me into her body. I groan at the thought. I'm so fucking hard for her it's painful.

My strokes become rougher, faster, the friction bringing me closer to release. I imagine her riding me, her tits bouncing, her pussy wet and tight. Her hands are on my chest, her nails leaving trails of red.

"Fuck!" I grit out.

In my fantasy, she whimpers, her body moving faster, desperate for me. And *only* me. I reach out, grabbing her hips, pulling her closer. I need to feel her, to own her. Inside and out.

She screams, the sound echoing in the chambers of my mind, and I come, fucking her as if she's my prisoner, as if her submission is all that matters.

Actually, it is.

When I open my eyes, the beautiful imagery is gone. Only the stark, cold reality of my prison cell remains as the cum on my stomach and the sweat on my skin begin to cool. I'm still alone, the fantasy of her lingering like a ghost. That's ironic as fuck.

I sit up, my heart rate struggling to return to normal. My cock is still half-hard, and I run my thumb over the head, smearing the cum Geneva pulled from my body. This momentary relief is not enough. It's never enough.

Not since I first saw her.

She'll come back to me. I know she will. Geneva needs answers, and I'm the only one who can give them to her. But more than that, she's drawn to me, whether she wants to admit it or not. And that's where I have the advantage.

While she's busy trying to figure me out, she's forgetting the most important thing: This isn't about me. It's about her.

It's *always* been about her.

And when she finally sees that, when she understands what I've been trying to show her, it'll be too late.

She'll be *mine*.

I'll wait because patience is a virtue, after all. Besides, the best games are the ones that take time to unfold. But soon enough, she'll realize that the real battle isn't with me—it's with herself.

I can't wait to watch her lose.

To win her for myself.

CHAPTER 10

GENEVA

IT'S BEEN TWO WEEKS SINCE I SAW GHOST. TO BE EXACT, IT'S FOURTEEN days, twenty-one hours, ten minutes, and thirty-three seconds… now thirty-four, but who's counting?

Am I his obsession… or is he mine?

I bring the glass to my lips, taking a swig of the whiskey that's become my constant companion recently. Drinking is the only thing that provides a measure of relief. Even then, even when I can barely stand, I still think of Ghost.

I've tried to push him from my mind, but the memory of him pervades my every waking moment. I see him in every case I study, every crime scene I analyze, and every night he appears in my dreams. Does that make them nightmares?

I've dealt with numerous psychopaths and sociopaths, studying them at length, and even interviewing a few. Ghost is different in every way. He's batshit crazy, yes, but he uses his insanity effortlessly.

To disarm.

To unsettle.

To manipulate.

He's clearly a man who understands the power he wields and uses it without hesitation or remorse. He's mastered his madness, and in some ways that makes him more dangerous that I'd anticipated. Yet, I can't stop thinking about him. That's what bothers me the most.

I shouldn't be captivated by the words he utilizes with deadly precision. Or the way he controlled the courtroom with just a few humorous comments. I should be disgusted, horrified.

I *am* disgusted.

But…there's this little part of me, the part that always seeks out answers, that keeps whispering, *Why him? Why now?*

Out of all the cases I've worked, this is the only one that has embedded itself in me. I keep replaying our brief interaction, wondering if I missed something. Something important. Something that would explain why he affects me the way he does. And why he's obsessed with me.

It doesn't make sense since I'd never talked to him until that day in the prison.

I grab the bottle of alcohol and top off my glass before taking a generous sip. It's probably a bad idea considering how much I've already had, but it's the weekend and I can't find the urge to care.

My phone chimes, the tiny sound loud in my bedroom. I groan, roll over, and grab my cell phone. It takes way more effort than I'd like to admit. Through squinted eyes and blurry vision, I look down at the text message alert before unlocking the screen to view it.

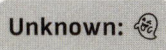

I stare at the screen, my thumb hovering over the text. The single emoji, along with the simplicity of it, is unnerving, more frightening than words could ever be. My heart pounds in my chest, the sudden rush of adrenaline burning away the alcohol haze in an instant.

I blink a few times, rub my eyes, and sit up in my bed. The text is probably from a wrong number and here I am, imagining the worst.

You're drunk and totally overthinking this.

I shake my head with a hollow laugh. It's just an emoji, a tiny, stupid symbol that means nothing. This isn't the first time I've received a text that wasn't meant for me.

I put my phone back on my nightstand and glare at my glass of whiskey as if it's the reason I nearly had a heart attack. Then I lie back down and force myself to breathe evenly to help calm my racing pulse.

The logical part of my brain asserts itself into my thoughts, pushing back the unease that still roils in my stomach. Ghost is in a maximum-security prison. There's no way it's him. None.

Paranoid much, Geneva?

I flinch when another text alert echoes in the room. With dread coating me like a second skin, I retrieve my phone and unlock the screen.

> **Unknown:** What's your definition of a ghost, Dr. Andrews?

I freeze. The air around me is thick, suffocating me. The darkness of the room presses on me from all sides until the only thing I can focus on is the message glaring up at me from the bright screen. With my name on display, I can't deny that this was meant for me.

It's Ghost's voice I hear in my head as I read the words. Calm. Confident. Amused.

It can't *be him.*

I repeat the sentence over and over in my mind, then again out loud. It's a mantra of desperation. But no matter how many times I say it I can't deny the way my chest aches with shallow breaths. The logical part of me is screaming in the void, while the rest of me—the part that's been caught up in Ghost since the moment I met him—knows better.

The words on the screen burn into my eyes, into my soul as if branding me. My fingers tremble around the phone even though I'm unwilling to accept what's staring back at me.

The urge to respond is strong. I want answers, need to know how this is happening. I type and delete a few sentences, unsure of what to say, until I finally settle on something. Simple and direct, unlike my chaotic thoughts.

Geneva: Who is this?

My finger hovers over the send button. Part of me doesn't want to engage, doesn't want to give Ghost—or whoever this is—the satisfaction. But I can't let it go. I hit send and stare at the screen, waiting, my heart in my throat.

A few seconds pass. Then another chime.

Unknown: You already know, Geneva.

The phone falls from my numb fingers and lands on the comforter. My throat tightens, my breath coming faster. This can't be Ghost. But who else could it be?

Maybe someone is trying to mess with me—someone who knows that I'm the only one who's spoken with him. This is just some sick joke.

But no one knows how deeply this case has etched itself into my psyche, how much time I've spent thinking about him, dissecting his every word, trying to understand him.

No one else…except maybe him.

My heart thuds painfully against my ribs, a slow, steady beat, like a drum warning me of something I'm not prepared to face. This isn't a prank.

How did Ghost get something as restricted as my number, much less a phone?

I scan my room, unable to shake the feeling that someone's watching me. That *he's* watching me. But that's impossible. Ghost is locked up.

What if he's not?

I move abruptly, knocking my glass over in the process of turning on my lamp. The whiskey spills across the nightstand, pooling on the wood, but I don't care. I can't sit in the darkness anymore.

Finding myself alone, I glance down at the phone, relief still eluding me. A small part of me itches to pick it back up, to read the message again. And answer him.

I grab my phone against my better judgment. The same judgment that has failed me time and time again when it comes to this man.

> **Geneva:** What do you want?

> **Unknown:** So, so, so many things. But tonight, I just want you to answer the question.

> **Geneva:** Go to hell.

Unknown: Very rude, not to mention unprofessional, Dr. Andrews.

I stare at the text, every fiber of me screaming to block this number and end the conversation. But I don't. I *can't.*

Instead, I sit there transfixed as every interaction with Ghost flashes through my mind. His eyes locking with mine across the courtroom. The way he smiled, like he knew more than anyone.

Like he knew *me.*

My cell phone vibrates softly in my hand as another alert appears on the screen.

Unknown: I'll make this easier for you. Do you think of a ghost as something that represents the dead, or do you see it as something that haunts the living?

I clench my jaw, my mind buzzing with the implications of his words. He's playing with me, drawing me in, feeding off my pain. Except, he shouldn't know anything about me beyond the surface-level details of my professional life. He shouldn't know me like this.

I sit there, staring at the messages, my thoughts spinning out of control. In death, my parents haunt me. The memories, the survivor's guilt, the endless questions. All of it has shaped who and what I am, and why I'm having this conversation to begin with.

But then there's him…

Ghost isn't like my parents. He isn't someone I loved and lost. He's something else—a living phantom, drifting through my life, possessing my thoughts. He's alive, yet he feels like a ghost too, haunting me in an entirely different way.

Am I tormented by the dead or the living? The answer comes to me. Or maybe it's been there all along, and that's his point.

> **Geneva:** Both. I think of a ghost as both of those things.

> **Unknown:** The dead and the living, always overlapping.

> **Unknown:** It's my reality too.

His reality too?

A sense of understanding rises in me before I can stop it. His response is very telling. Vulnerable in a way that humanizes him. I mentally rail against viewing him in this light, knowing this could be nothing more than lies designed to manipulate me. To force compassion from me in a way he doesn't deserve.

How many times do I have to remind myself that he's a serial killer?

> **Unknown:** You feel it, don't you? The connection between us?

I should call Detective Harris right now, delete these texts, or throw the phone across the room, anything to break this fragile bond between us. It pulses within me like a slow-burning ember, not ablaze but still hot enough to provide warmth. And pain.

I want to believe that I'm not reporting this in order to discover more for Ghost's psych evaluation. But right now, this interaction isn't about professional curiosity. No, this is something more. Something personal.

The ember of connection flickers and for a moment I can feel myself drawn to Ghost in a way that's stronger than before. His words echo in my mind, each one dragging me deeper into a shared darkness, into a space where his ghosts and mine meet.

Fourteen days, twenty-two hours, seven minutes, and twelve seconds since I've seen Ghost…

Come Monday morning, I'll be back at zero.

CHAPTER 11

GENEVA

THE INMATES LOOK AT ME LIKE I'M A DONUT AND THEY'RE ON A DIET. It's uncomfortable but not enough to deter me. Meanwhile, the guard barely glances at me as he guides me down the long, dim prison hallway.

Every step takes me closer to Ghost, to the conversation I know I shouldn't be having but can't stop myself from seeking out. Even Detective Harris was perturbed this morning when I told him about my plan.

"What are you hoping to get out of this, Gen? What more could you possibly need from him?"

I didn't have a good reason for Allen. Or maybe I just didn't want to say it out loud. The truth is that I need answers only Ghost can give me.

Out of all the billions of people in the world, why am I the one he's fixated on?

I run my fingers over my hair, making sure my bun is secure and there are no flyaway strands. My clothes still hold the starch from the dry cleaners, and paired with my ballet flats, I embody propriety. And to some, monotony.

No one would say I'm fascinating.

Except Ghost.

"Remember," the guard says, coming to a halt outside the room, "don't say anything to provoke the inmate. Don't give him any details about other cases, and absolutely no personal information."

I almost burst out laughing. Ghost has already proven he knows more about me than I've ever shared, or made public. It's not as though I gave him my cell number and asked him to text me.

"I got it."

The guard unlocks the door, and I steel myself as I walk into the interview room. The lights are harsh, too bright for the darkness I'm about to face. Ghost is already sitting behind the glass, chained to the table, his white hair made blinding by the fluorescent lights framing him in a soft glow. It gives him an ethereal quality, but he's no ghost.

Just a man who haunts me with only a few words.

Our eyes meet as I sit down. The hazel in his glitters with amusement. And that smile... It's there, curling at the corners of his mouth like he knows a dark secret.

I'm quick to speak first, wanting to take charge of the conversation. "Why are you in this room before me? Last time I was here, they brought you in after I arrived."

Ghost nods slowly, his smile growing just a fraction. "Very perceptive, Dr. Andrews. You see, things changed around here, especially after the latest *incident*."

I raise an eyebrow. "Incident?"

His eyes flash with that familiar glint, the one that tells me he's enjoying every second of this. He leans back slightly, letting the chains on his wrists clink softly against the metal table. I try not to become distracted by the muscles of his large chest expanding under the orange material. "The inmate closest to this room. He met an unfortunate end. An apparent suicide. Gruesome, they said."

My body tenses, and I take a deep breath to loosen my muscles. "Did you have anything to do with it?"

He lets out a soft chuckle. "Such accusations, Dr. Andrews. Do I strike you as the type to get my hands dirty?"

I nod. "Yes, actually."

"Then, you'd be correct." He rests his elbows on the table. His eyes gleam with a twisted amusement, and the smile never leaves his lips. "I may have given him a few choice words to remind him of…unpleasant truths. Sometimes, when you look at yourself too closely, you don't like what you see."

He tilts his head, eyes still locked on mine before continuing. "It's amazing what the mind is capable of when it's pushed in just the right direction. Wouldn't you agree?"

My stomach tightens. He didn't need to lay a finger on the inmate. Ghost has a way of planting seeds in the heads of others— seeds that grow into something far more dangerous.

Case in point: I'm sitting here talking to him when I know I shouldn't.

His grin widens at my silence, and he nods slowly—almost as if reading my mind and praising me for connecting the dots. "The truth is powerful. You, of all people, should know that. And sometimes, the truth is enough to destroy someone."

I fold my arms across my chest, trying to create some distance between us. "Did you know him?"

Ghost shrugs, the motion casual, as if we're discussing something trivial. "Not personally, but we had commonalities. He had his ghosts, just like you, just like me. I simply helped him face them."

I stare at Ghost, my skin crawling at the ease with which he speaks about manipulation and murder. "Why did you do it?"

"Don't you ever get tired of asking 'why'?"

"Don't you ever get tired of killing people?"

His smile fades, and his eyes darken. "Nope. And to answer your question: I did it because I could."

For a moment, there's nothing but silence between us, the tension thick in the air. I can't tell if he's being honest or if this is just another one of his games. But I can feel the weight of his words pressing down on me, and the disturbing part is...I almost understand. I'll never stop asking why. It's my obsession, the same way murder is his.

"I knew you'd come back to me, Dr. Andrews."

The way Ghost addresses me should be a barrier, a professional title that creates formality. But the way it rolls off his tongue is soft. Intimate. Like the brush of fingers over skin. Like he's reminding me who I am when I'm with him...and who I pretend to be when I'm not.

"It would seem that you know a lot, Ghost. More than you should."

Like my fucking phone number, for instance.

His smile widens, turning puckish. "I suppose I do. Information is the only thing I have to keep me company. It's lonely here, and you're my only friend."

I roll my eyes. "We are *not* friends."

"We could be. You're not going to ask me for my real name?"

"Do you want to give it to me?"

He grins. "No. No. No."

"Then why waste time?"

"Why indeed?" His eyes shine with satisfaction, and something devilish. He spreads his powerful thighs as he settles deeper in his chair. "So cold. So distant," he murmurs. "But I suppose that's what makes you so good at what you do."

I put my elbows on the table and steeple my fingers, using this posture to send a message of confidence and control. "I'm not the only one who's good at what they do. From my understanding, you've manipulated someone into giving you certain *privileges*?" *Like a cell phone.*

Ghost shakes his head, his smile never wavering, as if we share some private joke. I suppose we do. "Me? Manipulate? *Never.* I haven't been given anything that hasn't been approved by the great state of New York."

"Then I guess you found *other* ways to get what you want."

"Loneliness breeds creativity. One has to be innovative if they want something that's unattainable, Dr. Andrews."

I hold his stare while my mind churns. There's something different in the way he's looking at me this visit. It's a subtle shift, minuscule, but I sense it. It's how his eyes trail over my face as though he's captivated by every inch of skin, every eyelash, every freckle. It's intense, unnerving, and ... fascinating.

For the first time since I met him, I feel like *I'm* the one being studied. My insides clench and I instinctively squeeze my thighs together to eradicate the sensation of desire.

I peer at him from behind my steepled fingers. What was once a gesture of self-assurance has now become a shield. Against him and my unwanted attraction. "Have you always been good at getting what you want, even when it's impossible?"

"Oh, yes," he purrs, his voice a deep rumble. "Nothing is impossible. Some things just require more patience. More…finesse."

"Finesse is a decent strategy, but it won't do you any good with something as immovable as a mountain."

He laughs softly. "Even a glacier will melt, given time and the right circumstances."

His reference to me doesn't go over my head. It's not the first time Ghost has called me cold and guarded.

"Why me?"

The question I've been agonizing over falls from my lips and into the silence between us with the impact of a bomb. I may have detonated it, but I'm not ready for the explosion. For the destruction that follows.

At first, there's nothing. Then his gaze sharpens, and something flickers behind his eyes—something that feels almost like recognition.

"Because," he says slowly, his voice soft but deliberate, "you're just like me."

I rear back, a mix of anger and denial surging through me. "I'm nothing like you," I say through clenched teeth.

His smile doesn't falter. "Oh, but you are, Dr. Andrews. The only difference is that you're still trying to bury your ghosts, but I invite mine to dinner."

He's pushing again, trying to blur the lines between us. The worst part is that the connection I felt while texting him returns with full force. And it's more than a mere ember. It's scalding.

He adjusts in his chair. "Once you embrace your ghosts, that's when real freedom begins. No amount of work, alcohol, or meaningless sex will help you. You can't outrun them."

"I—"

"You know, even ice can burn with prolonged exposure. Does your current *distraction* enjoy the pain you offer? Or has he finally gotten tired of it?"

"You know the rules," I snap. "No personal information about me."

Ghost's smile widens and his eyes gleam with that infuriating calm, completely unbothered by my anger. "Oh, Dr. Andrews, I'm not breaking any rules. I'm simply asking questions. You're not the only one who wants answers."

Fury bubbles up inside me, warring with the cold edge of fear. How does he know about Mason? Not that I give a shit about him, but our relationship was never public. Yet here Ghost is, dropping it into conversation like it's common knowledge.

Like he's been watching me.

It's not a stretch to assume that a man who can send me texts from prison would also know the details about my love life.

"For example," Ghost continues, his relaxed tone at odds with the predatory glint in his eyes, "I want to know when was the last time you felt anything with him, beyond routine? Or what you think he'd say if he saw the real you? The Geneva that *I* see."

The truth of his words cuts deep, past the lies. Past the bullshit. I hate that Ghost is right. I hate that every time I'm with Mason, I'm left with a gnawing emptiness, a sense of going through the motions, but never truly *feeling* anything. It's predictable and safe. But it's not what I need. It's not what I *want*.

And somehow Ghost knows it.

I clench my fists under the table, my nails digging into my palms. "You don't get to talk about my life like you understand it."

"But I do understand it, Dr. Andrews. That's what terrifies you, isn't it?"

Ghost's maddening smirk only deepens, as if he's savoring every flicker of emotion I'm trying so hard to suppress. For the first time, I'm irritated by the glass between us because I want to smack the shit out of him, to remove that knowing look off his face.

I get to my feet. Even as I'm staring down at him from this position of superiority, Ghost maintains the air of power surrounding him. Once again, he's the victor of our exchange. But that doesn't mean I can't try to take him down a notch.

"Let me tell you what I *see*." I lean forward and narrow my gaze. "I see a man who's trapped. Trapped in his own twisted mind, trapped behind these walls. You think you can manipulate me like I'm a rat in a lab. But you're the one who's nothing more than a prisoner, Ghost. A prisoner of your own delusions."

His smile wavers, a flash of something behind his eyes. At last, I've finally gotten to him. It's a small win, but a win nonetheless. He recovers quickly, his lips curling, almost taunting.

"Is that what you think, Dr. Andrews? That *I'm* the one trapped?" His voice is maddeningly calm, but there's an edge to it now, something sinister. "I guess I'll have to prove you wrong."

"Don't waste your time," I say, keeping my gaze fixed on his. "Don't contact me anymore—not through legitimate means, and definitely not through your *other* methods."

I turn and quickly make my way toward the door. I need to get out, to breathe, to put as much distance between us as I can. But just as I reach for the door handle, his voice slithers through the air, soft and chilling.

"Oh, Dr. Andrews, you should know by now that nothing I do is a waste of time. It just takes others longer to discover the results… or consequences."

CHAPTER 12

GHOST

I'VE PISSED OFF GENEVA.

Good.

Even though she left the prison hours ago, she never left me. This woman has carved out a place in my mind and taken up residence. To remove her...I might actually go insane.

Well, more than I already am.

I laugh at this until the sound turns manic, until the hilarity of my thoughts has my eyes stinging as I roll around on my mattress. Given all the shit I've done, the number of people I've killed, how can I become more demented than I already am?

A guard walks up to my cell and slams his cudgel against the bars. "Shut up, Ghost."

"Is that a baton, or are you just happy to see me?"

"You're one crazy motherfucker."

I sit up on the bed and pucker my lips to blow him a kiss. "Yes, sir."

He shakes his head, grumbling to himself as he stalks off. I lie back down, returning to my thoughts of Geneva.

I close my eyes, savoring the image of her fury. The fire in her eyes as they darkened, shifting from that soft brown to a cold, hard black. Revealing the darkness that lives in both of us.

I recall the way she stiffened when I mentioned *him*. Mason. The name alone leaves a foul taste on my tongue like ash. If he wasn't a tool needed to manipulate Geneva, I would kill him.

Once his usefulness is gone, all bets are off.

Her reactions this morning confirmed that she doesn't feel anything for him. But I wasn't just provoking her because I wanted to break her down—though I certainly enjoyed that part. No, it was more than that. I wanted to push her to tear him apart.

And to show him who she really is.

The glimpses I've seen of the real Geneva are beautiful. They're raw, unfiltered, pure. When she lets go of the façade, when she stops pretending to be the calm, collected professional, she's something else entirely.

She's everything I expected her to be—and more. Enthralling. Captivating. I want to see her unravel, not just for me, but for herself.

Because I know, deep down, she's dying to.

As I sit here in my cell, the thought of Mason being close to her, touching her, sharing the same space as her…

Fuck him.

He doesn't know what she's capable of. He's too blind to see the fire beneath that ice, the part of Geneva that craves something deeper. Something darker.

The part that matches me.

The truth is there, gnawing at her like a parasite. She's bored with him. Dissatisfied. She's holding on out of fear, desperate for some sense of normalcy.

I roll onto my side, my eyes half-closed, a slow smile creeping onto my face. Soon enough she'll break. Geneva will destroy him, and when she does, when she finally lets go of that safety net, she'll realize that she's been lying to herself and using him as a crutch.

And she'll hate herself for it. She'll hate *him* for it.

That's when I'll have her.

Because in the end, Mason will never be enough for her. He's weak, ordinary, and she's so much more than that. I've seen it. I've *felt* it.

He doesn't deserve her. He doesn't understand her. Not like I do.

She'll never belong in that mundane world he offers her.

Geneva belongs with me.

CHAPTER 13

GENEVA

"I'M GOING TO END IT FOR GOOD THIS TIME," I SAY, MY TONE RESO-lute. "I'm done with Mason."

Sarah doesn't laugh like I expect her to. Her silence lingers, and I can picture her on the other end of the call—brows furrowed, lips pressed together.

"I believe you," she finally says. Her voice is steady, but there's a heaviness to it. "It's long overdue."

She's right. How many nights have I looked at Mason and felt nothing? How many years have I gone through the motions with men but not really *lived*?

But things have changed.

"I know." With a sigh, I lie back on my couch and prop my feet on the armrest. "I've just been...putting it off."

"You've been putting it off because you're scared. You don't want to face what it'll feel like when Mason isn't there to distract you."

Although her tone is gentle, her words hit hard. Being with

Mason has always been about more than just comfort—it's been about avoiding the real issues.

Ghost's voice creeps into my mind, uninvited, taunting me. *"Does your current distraction enjoy the pain you offer? Or has he finally gotten tired of it?"*

Both Sarah and Ghost have called Mason my distraction. I hate how much truth there is in those words. Mason isn't the problem—*I* am. But I'm done lying to myself.

"I'm doing it tonight. No more excuses." My voice is firmer now. "I can't keep pretending."

Sarah lets out a long breath. "Good. Just…be kind to yourself, okay? You're doing the right thing. I'm here all night if you need me."

"You're the best. Talk to you later."

"Bye, Gen."

Be kind to yourself.

It's easier said than done, especially when you don't like who you are.

I stand in front of the window, the city lights casting a dull glow over the room. My reflection stares back at me, eyes hollow, lips pressed together in a tight line. *Who am I?*

The reflection doesn't answer, and I look away, trying to steady my breathing as the weight of Ghost's words presses down on me again, heavier this time.

"What do you think he'd say if he saw the real you? The Geneva that I see?"

I shift my focus to constructing a psychological profile on Mason that'll help me plan our upcoming conversation. After grabbing a legal pad and a pen, I begin to jot down notes as if Mason were a patient or a criminal.

Mason thrives on control—of his environment, his relationships, and, most importantly, the way others perceive him (Narcissistic tendencies). When things go his way, he's charming, logical, even supportive. But when he's challenged, he can't handle anything that threatens his dominance.

I pause, nibbling on the tip of my pen. Although Mason has never lashed out physically, there's repressed violence in him. I've seen it before, in the way his jaw tightens when I don't fall in line with his expectations. It's a quiet, dangerous kind of anger.

For some reason that I can't explain, he doesn't scare me the way Ghost does.

Mason can't handle failure or rejection because it conflicts with the image he has of himself as a capable and strong man. When I tell him it's over, he won't just see it as the end of a relationship—he'll see it as a personal attack, a reflection of his own inadequacies.

I put down my pen and reach for my wine glass. A little liquid courage never hurt anyone. Knowing Mason, he'll try to manipulate the situation and turn the blame on me. But after dealing with Ghost, Mason's tactics will seem like child's play. I guess that serial killer asshole has been helpful in a way. The irony has a smile appearing on my lips as I pick my pen back up.

Me initiating this "break-up" will make Mason feel as though he's been backed into a corner. He's the type of person who believes he's entitled to a certain level of respect, and when that respect is denied, he'll lash out in ways that are meant to remind me of his power. The insults will be calculated, designed to make me feel small, to keep me in check.

The loud knock on my door has me pulling in a fortifying breath.

Here we go.

I place my wine glass down on the coffee table and get to my feet, rehearsing the lines in my head one last time. Direct, quick, honest. No unnecessary explanations, no reasons for him to stay.

When I open the door, Mason's usual composed expression is in place. He steps inside without waiting for an invitation, sweeping his gaze over me. I'm in my usual sweatpants and an old, torn shirt—it's casual with the intent to appear innocuous—and I catch the brief flicker of disapproval on his face before he speaks.

"Glad you finally got over yourself, but really, Gen? Sweatpants and...that?" His tone is mildly condescending, as if I've somehow insulted him by not dressing up for his arrival.

I press my lips together, biting back the first sting of irritation. After shutting the door behind him, I make my way to the couch to sit down. I cross my arms, creating an invisible barrier between us as he removes his jacket.

"Want to have a seat?" I ask.

His eyes narrow slightly at my invitation, but he joins me on the couch at the opposite end. "What's this about?"

"I wanted to talk to you," I say, my voice firm. "I know we've been on and off a lot over the past year, but this isn't working out for me anymore. I'm done. For good."

His entire body goes rigid. "What are you saying?"

"I don't want to drag this out. I've been thinking about it for a while, and this relationship isn't what I need."

He stares at me for a long moment, his expression unreadable, and then he scoffs. "We don't have a *relationship*. We just fuck. Are you mad because I don't coddle you like you expect me to?"

There it is.

The first little dig, an insult implying that I'm an emotionally needy woman. Therefore, *I'm* the problem.

"No," I say evenly. "It's not about coddling or me wanting something romantic. I need to move forward with my life."

"Move forward?" he repeats, his tone incredulous. When I nod, he jumps to his feet and waves his hand in my direction. "Being with you is like fucking an ice cube. Do you think if you 'find yourself' that you'll stop being a cold-hearted bitch?"

Mason's words hit me like a slap to the face. I can't stop myself from reacting, from rearing back with my lips parted in shock. However, my years of training immediately kick in. I neutralize my expression while slowly getting to my feet in a way that signals confidence and my refusal to be baited.

As I stare into Mason's eyes, Ghost's words flood my mind, unbidden and unwelcome. *"You're flame and wrath encased in a wall of ice and control."* In this moment, I have to admit he's right about me.

Except my barrier is melting…

"Maybe I'll always be like this," I say evenly. "And maybe I won't. Either way, you won't be around to see it."

A flicker of something darker passes over his face. He steps closer, his posture more rigid, his hands fisted. I hold my ground, my instinct for self-preservation overridden by the anger burning inside me.

"You think you can just walk away from *me*?" he asks.

"Yes, Mason. I do."

I lift my chin. The gesture is a direct challenge. A gauntlet tossed at his feet. I know better. I know not to provoke him. But maybe, just maybe, Mason needs to see a glimpse of the "real" me. If only this once.

His eyes narrow, and for a second, I see it—the barely repressed fury. His need for dominance. He's not used to being on the losing side of things, and right now, I'm taking away something he thought he had control over.

Me.

I take a step toward him, putting myself directly in his path, within his reach. "Get out."

He sneers at me, his curled lip making his face grotesque. "You're going to regret this."

I shrug, the act dismissive, meant to make him feel insignificant. "I doubt I'll even remember this conversation. Or you."

Mason's eyes flash with emotion and intent. In a split second, I realize what's about to happen, a moment too late.

Mason's fist connects with my face.

The impact sends a shock wave through my skull, and I stumble back, my hand instinctively flying to my cheek. Pain blooms instantly, but I let my arm fall to my side, refusing to cradle my injury.

The adrenaline already flooding my system becomes amplified, my synapses firing off in rapid succession, creating something close to chaos in my mind.

Or is it freedom?

My short burst of laughter hits the air, shattering the silence.

The sound is involuntary, almost absurd, but it bubbles up from somewhere deep inside me, breaking free before I can stop it. The sting from his punch throbs, but the pain is oddly grounding, focusing. It's as though the world has slowed down, sharpening into clarity.

Mason stares at me, chest heaving and hands fisted. His eyes widen when I laugh again, on purpose. I'm not horrified by Mason's violence. I'm…amused and exhilarated. My body feels awakened, thrumming with a strange, turbulent energy. The line between control and chaos has been crossed.

And I'm not going back.

"You're fucking crazy." Mason's voice carries the sharpness of his insult, but his posture, the way his shoulders sag, tells me he's afraid.

He should be.

I don't respond. And I don't stop laughing as I make my way across the living room to the patio door. I pick up the baseball bat that sits there and lift it, resting the length of it on my shoulder.

"What do you think you're going to do, Gen?" He takes a retreating step, signaling his uncertainty. "Are you going to hit me?"

I stop laughing and tilt my head, a mocking smile firmly planted on my face. "Fuck around, and find out."

He gapes at me before turning sharply, his footsteps heavy as he storms out of the apartment, slamming the door behind him. The noise reverberates through the room, but I dismiss it.

I stand there with my chest full of repressed laughter and adrenaline coursing through my blood, heating me all over. I turn my head to peer at my reflection again.

Now, I'm looking at an entirely different person.

My cheek is red, the skin starting to swell, but the woman looking back at me is strong. Stronger than I ever gave her credit for.

And she's not afraid.

I smile at my reflection as Ghost's voice fills my mind.

"There's the Geneva that I see."

CHAPTER 14

GHOST

It's been almost three days and Geneva still hasn't come to see me.

I tap my fingers against the cold metal table in my cell, the rhythm steady but relentless. Like my thoughts of her. I've been accurate in all of my assessments of Dr. Andrews, along with anticipating her reactions. She should've contacted me by now.

Is she hiding from me?

Or hiding *something* from me?

I get up and walk over to my cell door to make sure the guards aren't nearby before retrieving my *new* cell phone from its hiding place in the wall. After my final taunt to Geneva during our last visit, she informed the guards about my contraband, and they confiscated it. *Such a tattletale.*

If she were here, I'd spank her for that.

Because of that little stunt, I haven't been able to watch Geneva for days and it's killing me. What good is having cameras in her apartment if I can't fucking see her?

I power on the phone and select the app that's linked to the hidden cameras, the grainy black-and-white feed from her apartment flickering to life. The angles aren't perfect, but they're good enough. And there she is.

Finally.

Geneva is sitting on her couch, scrolling through her phone, her posture rigid like she's deep in thought. I watch her for a few moments, the tension in her body almost palpable even through the poor-quality feed. There's a smudge on her cheek, but I chalk it up to the lighting, the shadows playing tricks on the screen. She's too precise, too put together for it to be anything else.

I scroll through my unanswered texts.

> **Unknown:** You said you were done with me. Is this another lie you've told yourself?

> **Unknown:** You're quiet, but quiet doesn't equate to tranquility. What are you thinking about? Maybe it's a person with white hair, a killer instinct, erm... I mean a killer smile, and a big dick?

> **Unknown:** I hate to tell you, but silence is agreeance, Dr. Andrews.

I type another cryptic text message and send it with my pulse racing. If she doesn't seek me out after this, then I'll lose my fucking mind. And put a tracker underneath that beautiful skin, blackmail her, or whatever the fuck it takes to keep her.

Actually, I think I'll do all of that anyway.

Good idea, me.

> **Unknown:** What if I told you the past isn't as dead
> as you think? Would you believe that
> I know the identities and locations
> of the men from April 18th?

I watch the feed, my eyes locked on her as the message pops up on her phone. I can see the moment she reads it, the subtle shift in her posture, the tensing of her shoulders. She looks surprised, but there's a flicker of something else that makes my dick hard. Complete and total rage.

Looks like that iceberg is melting…

She stands, walking back and forth, phone in hand, glancing around as if she can feel my eyes on her. I've seen her do this before, this restless pacing, and it always tells me the same thing— she's trying to escape something, trying to avoid facing what she already knows to be true. I wish I could see her face more clearly, to gauge her full reaction, but the camera angles are limited. Still, I can read her body language like a book.

I imagine the thoughts running through her mind. *How could he know?*

Of course I know, Geneva. I know everything.

Her thumb hovers over her phone, and I can almost feel the indecision crackling through the air, even from here. She's debating whether to respond, whether to engage me, and it's exactly what I want.

The silence between us has lasted too long. I've missed our game, the push and pull of it, the way she tries to pretend she's in control when we both know better.

I squint down at the grainy feed, watching her as she pauses in front of the window, staring out at the night. She's thinking about

94

me. I know she is. And as much as she wants to deny it, I'm the one who occupies her thoughts. Not Mason. Not anyone else.

> **Unknown:** They thought they could disappear, but they're not the ultimate magician. I am.

> **Geneva:** Abracadabra, asshole. Go fuck yourself.

I slap a hand to my chest, close my eyes, and sigh. "I'll definitely fuck myself, Dr. Andrews. While thinking of you."

CHAPTER 15

GENEVA

GHOST IS A FUCKING ASSHOLE.

And I'm going to visit him. *Again.*

It's a dysfunctional cycle. I'm irritated at how easily I keep getting pulled back in. Back to facing things I don't want to deal with. Back to facing him.

The truth is, I don't know who I hate more at this point: Ghost, for the way he manipulated me, pushing and pulling until I revealed parts of myself I thought I'd buried? Or myself, for letting him do it?

I wasn't supposed to crack that night with Mason. I wasn't supposed to let Ghost's twisted insight crawl under my skin. But I did. I fucking did. And Mason saw something in me that night, something dark that I couldn't keep hidden anymore.

I drag my hands through my hair, pacing in my living room, my frustration building with each step. Ghost is the only one who's ever seen me—*really* seen me. And that's terrifying.

But it's also addictive.

I stop moving and lean against the counter, tracing the bruise on my cheek. The memory of Mason's barely contained rage plays out in my mind.

I stood there and smiled through the pain, because in that moment, I felt alive. Ghost was right. I'm not afraid of the darkness, or the fire that burns just beneath the surface.

I *am* the fire.

And fire has the means to destroy. To kill. That's what scares the hell out of me.

Even with all of this bombarding my mind, making me crazy and putting me on edge, I can't stop thinking about his latest text about April 18th—the night my parents were murdered. About knowing the identities of the men who killed them.

I was put into witness protection as a child. None of my blood relatives—excluding the aunt who raised me—know about my new identity. So, how does Ghost know about that night?

I continue tracing the outline of the bruise on my cheek, my thoughts spiraling in a million directions about the night I've spent years avoiding.

I've relived it over and over in my head, dissecting every detail, every moment, trying to make sense of the senseless. But now, with one text, Ghost has pulled the rug out from under everything I thought I knew.

I'll never get the chance to ask those men why they did it. That's what I've told myself for years. It's what I've clung to, what I've built my entire sense of closure around. And now Ghost, with his twisted games, is trying to unravel it all with a few well-placed words. It's gnawing at my insides, threatening to tear me apart.

What if he's not lying?

I grip the counter, my knuckles whitening as I push back against the flood of doubt that's crashing over me. I want to dismiss the text. I want to believe that Ghost is just messing with me to see if he can make me break. But deep down, something about it feels...*true*.

Ghost knows things he shouldn't. He's proven that already, time and time again. How the hell would he know about April 18th, about the specifics of that night, unless he's found something I haven't?

I take a deep breath, but it doesn't calm the storm raging inside me. Ghost has been pulling at the strings of my mind for weeks now, unraveling me bit by bit. But this is different. This isn't just about me. This is about my parents. About their deaths. About everything I've spent years trying to understand. And now, he's telling me that I might have a chance to get real answers.

I walk to the sink, turning on the faucet and splashing cold water onto my face, trying to clear my head. But it's no use. The words keep circling, digging deeper into my mind, forcing me to confront the possibility that my past isn't as settled as I thought.

"Would you believe that I know the identities and locations of the men from April 18th?"

I close my eyes, gripping the edge of the sink, my breath coming in short, shallow bursts. If what Ghost says is true, then it changes everything. The way I've lived my life, the choices I've made—all of it has been shaped by the belief that I'd never be able to confront my parents' killers.

But what if I could?

I push away from the sink, pacing again, my mind spinning. I want to see Ghost, demand answers, and make him tell me what he knows. But deep down, I know that's exactly what he wants. He's been playing with my mind for weeks while watching me scramble to make sense of it all. And now, he's thrown this at me, knowing it's the one thing I can't ignore.

The one thing that will make me come back.

I stop pacing, my breath heavy, my heart pounding in my chest. I can't just let this go. I need to know. I *have* to know why those men destroyed my entire life.

I grab my keys, my mind already made up. I'm going back to him. To the prison. To Ghost. And this time, I'm not leaving until I get the answers I want.

Right now, I don't just hate Ghost.

I hate that I *need* him.

CHAPTER 16

GHOST

I SIT IN THE INTERVIEW ROOM HUMMING A DIRTY SHANTY I LEARNED years ago. Something about sailors, a whore, and a mast representing a gigantic penis. One of my favorites.

The guards just outside think I'm simply waiting. Subdued and harmless. They believe these chains mean something. But like this prison, they're an illusion of control.

The vent above me rattles, a tiny vibration in the ceiling every time the air kicks on. It's small—just big enough for me to fit through—and the grill is rusted, held on by screws that also contain rust around the edges. I can hear the faint whistle of the air, and I mark it in my mind, cataloging it like I do everything else.

I sweep my gaze over the room. The table in front of me is bolted to the floor, but one of the legs isn't secure. I figured that out weeks ago, during my first visit with Geneva. Just a small wobble, but it's there. A weak point. All things can break if you apply the right pressure. Even metal tables.

Especially people.

The chair is the same as it always is, worn at the edges, but it's solid enough. No use there. But the cameras? They're my biggest point of contention. That's where Dr. Andrews comes into play.

I lean back, the chains rattling just enough to remind myself of their presence. They're heavy, cold against my wrists, but they don't bother me. They're temporary. Just like my situation.

But not her.

No, Geneva isn't temporary.

She's my eternity.

I close my eyes for a moment, savoring the thought of seeing her again. The tension in her posture, the fire in her eyes when she tries so hard to maintain control of herself. It's intoxicating, watching her balance on that razor's edge between order and chaos. She doesn't realize how close she is to crossing over. Not yet, anyway.

But she will. I've made sure of that.

I smile as anticipation builds in my chest. She'll come. I've baited the trap perfectly. And she's never been able to resist chasing the truth, no matter how dangerous it might be.

The tiniest sound reaches me…a guard's footsteps down the hall. It's go time.

I sit up straighter, my hands still bound, but my mind is racing. I'm eager to see Geneva.

The door creaks open, and I don't have to look to know it's her. I can feel her presence, the feminine energy that fills the room whenever she's near. I slowly lift my head, my eyes locking onto hers the moment she steps inside.

Welcome back, Geneva.

She walks up to the table, her steps deliberate, every muscle in her body tense, like she's preparing for a battle she knows she can't avoid. That's what I love about her: the fight. She's always wrestling with herself, with me, with the darkness that's creeping closer every time we sit in this room together.

I lean forward, ready to play, ready to watch her unravel again. But then I see it.

A bruise.

The purplish shadow is barely visible under the makeup covering her cheek. But it's there. My smile fades, the amusement that had been dancing on the edge of my mind slipping away in an instant. I stare at the mark, my gaze narrowing, all the plans I had for toying with her disintegrating.

It wasn't a shadow like I assumed when watching her through the cameras. She's had this on her for days…

Someone put their fucking hands on *my* Geneva.

I know without her saying a word. It was *him*. Mason.

I pushed her to destroy him and now her beautiful skin is marred with a bruise.

He's a dead man walking. I'm going to fucking annihilate him.

What method of torture should I employ?

> *Skin him alive and make a rug out of his flesh?*
> *Cut off his dick, and shove it in his mouth so he's a literal cocksucker?*
> *Beat the ever-loving fuck out of him until he's pliable like a bean bag?*

So many choices, but none of them will ever be enough to reverse what he did.

Geneva says nothing, just stares at me, waiting. Probably wondering why I haven't spoken, why I'm not twisting her mind into knots.

But I can't. Not when I'm looking at that mark on her face, the evidence that someone else has dared to touch her.

Hurt her.

My fingers curl into fists, the chains rattling again while I force myself to stay calm. I have to. But inside, there's a stirring of the blinding, all-consuming wrath I haven't felt in years.

Not since Abby.

CHAPTER 17

GENEVA

The silence between us is unnerving.

Ghost is always talking. Always taunting. But today, he's just…sitting there. As motionless as a statue, not even blinking.

But he's definitely watching me.

The intensity in his gaze hasn't dulled. If anything, it's sharper, and more focused. His hazel eyes are almost gold, molten and burning. Not with mockery, but with anger.

Is he mad at me?

That's fine if he is. I've been pissed at Ghost since I met him.

I shift in my seat. "I didn't come here to have a staring contest. I'm here for answers."

He narrows his eyes. It's just a fraction, but it's enough for me to know he's heard me. Yet he still doesn't speak.

"What do you know about April 18th?" I ask.

There's the faintest flicker of something in his eyes, but still, he says nothing.

Damn it.

I glance at the chains on his wrists, moving slightly as his fingers twitch. There's something simmering beneath his handsome exterior, something dark and dangerous. I know that look… it's barely restrained rage.

I try again, softening my tone. "Ghost, please. How do you know about that night?"

His lips part, but instead of answering, he leans forward, his gaze never leaving my face. I blow out a breath and start to get to my feet when his voice stops me. It's low and rough, like shards of glass grinding together.

"Who touched you?"

I slowly sit back down as my pulse quickens. This isn't the direction I want this conversation to go. I came here for answers about my parents. Not to discuss Mason.

"Ghost—"

"Who. Fucking. Touched. You?" His voice is harder now, each word deliberate, as if he's forcing them out.

I grit my teeth, trying to maintain my composure, but his intensity is crawling along my skin. He's not letting this go. And I can't help but wonder what he'll do if I tell him what he wants.

"This isn't about me. I'm asking about *April 18th*."

"I don't want to talk about your parents," he says, his words clipped. "I'm asking about *you*. Who hurt you?"

I let out a breath, steadying myself. "No one."

"Don't lie to me, Dr. Andrews." His words are softer now, almost playful, but there's a sinister current beneath them, something far more threatening than his usual demeanor. "You let him hurt you. Why?"

I stiffen, my muscles going taut as Ghost's words sink in. What the hell is he talking about? My first instinct is to lash out, to tell him he's wrong. No woman would *let* a man put his hands on her.

That's absurd. I didn't allow Mason to hurt me. I didn't see the hit coming.

But in my gut, I know that's not entirely true.

I didn't back down. I didn't turn away or run. I stood there, eyes locked on Mason, daring him to do it, daring him to lose control.

When his fist connected with my face, there was a part of me that wasn't surprised. I pushed him to that edge. Not because I was weak, not because I was powerless, but because I wanted it. The fire burning inside me demanded something—*anything*—to make me feel alive.

The memory flashes in my mind: Mason's rage, the way his expression twisted just before he struck me. But instead of fear, instead of regret, I felt pure satisfaction.

In that moment, I wasn't the casualty. I was the catalyst.

How in the hell does Ghost know that?

I steady myself, forcing my expression to remain neutral, even though my heart is pounding in my chest. Ghost watches me in a way that makes me feel exposed. He tilts his head as if he's challenging me to admit it. Waiting for me to say the words out loud.

But I won't.

"This is none of your business, Ghost."

"Everything about you is my business. Where you live. What you do. Who you fuck. *All* of it."

"You don't own me."

He laughs. The sound is both sensual and frightening, making my skin prickle with fear and…something that I refuse to acknowledge.

"Actually, I do own you, Dr. Andrews. You're *mine*. And no one else gets to hurt you. Only me."

"You—"

"Say his name, and I'll let it go."

I snap my teeth together with a click. Ghost might be pushing me into uncomfortable territory, but he's not asking me to admit that I manipulated Mason so he'd give in to his anger, allowing me to free mine.

When it comes to dealing with Ghost, I'm getting off easy.

"Mason."

"That's my good girl."

Ghost smiles at me for the first time today, and I ignore the way my blood rushes through my body. "You're not going to do anything, right?" I ask.

"What could I possibly do?" He jerks on his cuffs three times, and the sound of the chain links clicking together has me gritting my teeth. "I'm in here and he's out there."

I glare at Ghost. "Given our newest communication of the digital variety, I wouldn't put anything past you."

He nods. "Fair. I am quite resourceful. That's something you'll learn in due time."

"Don't hurt Mason."

"Why not?" Ghost frowns. "Eye for an eye. Or cheek for a cheek, at least."

I refrain from touching my face even though it flushes under Ghost's perusal. This is the exact reason I didn't want to visit Ghost. He doesn't miss anything and I knew he'd force me to explain the bruise.

"Mason isn't worth it," I say.

"But you are. You're worth everything, Geneva."

His words coil around me like a serpent before slithering

inside, sinking deep into places I didn't even know existed. The intensity in his voice, the way he says it like a promise, like an undeniable truth—it sends a current through me, igniting something I've tried so hard to keep dormant. Despite my restraint, I can't stop the pull, the dark magnetism that he wields so effortlessly.

I hate that he can make me feel this way.

I shift in my seat, crossing my arms over my chest as if that small gesture could shield me from the impact of his words. But it doesn't. It only makes me more aware of the fact that I'm struggling to keep my distance.

To stop my attraction.

This is wrong on so many levels. He's a convicted murderer, a master manipulator, and completely insane. I shouldn't be sitting here with my skin buzzing and my heart pounding in my chest.

His possessive statement from earlier, paired with his level of devotion, should terrify me. Instead, I'm terrified by how much I like it. How much it pleases me.

"Promise me you won't hurt Mason," I say.

"Why? It's not like you care about him."

I grimace at the truthful statement. "That doesn't mean I want revenge."

"Oh, I beg to differ."

"What are you—"

He cuts me off with a laugh. "You're still here, aren't you? Sitting across from me, wanting information from me about your parents' murderers?" He reclines in his chair, his eyes never leaving mine. "Let's talk about why you came. But first, I have some requirements."

"Requirements?"

"One piece of information for one piece of freedom," he says smoothly. "That's how this will work."

I narrow my eyes. "What do you mean by freedom?"

He waves a hand in dismissal. "Small things. Nothing too drastic but enough to make our conversations more comfortable. I can't scratch my balls when they itch. You have no idea how annoying that is."

"What are you suggesting?"

He tilts his head, studying me for a moment before he speaks. "Unchain me from the table. Let me move freely while we talk. Of course, I'll stay in cuffs. There's no need to worry about your safety." He winks. "For now."

The suggestion sends a rush of discomfort through me. Letting him move freely, even with the cuffs, is a risk. But I need answers. I need him to tell me what he knows about April 18th, about the night my parents were murdered. And if this is the only way to get it...

"Fine," I say, my voice clipped.

He grins, clearly pleased with himself. "I knew you'd understand."

I rise and make my way toward the door to speak with the guard stationed outside. As I give him the instruction to unchain Ghost from the table, the guard hesitates, casting a wary glance at the inmate before reluctantly complying. It takes a minute for him to walk to Ghost's side of the glass, but then his chains are removed from the table, leaving only the cuffs on his wrists.

Ghost flexes his hands with a subtle smile playing on his lips, while I return to my seat, maintaining my calm exterior even though my pulse quickens with each second. The shift in power is palpable, but I won't give up the opportunity to uncover the past.

I retrieve the tiny pencil and piece of paper I hid in my pocket. "Now, tell me. Who was there that night? Who killed my parents?"

Ghost watches me carefully before he speaks. "André Bisset."

The name doesn't immediately register, but I write it down, keeping my face neutral even though my thoughts are racing. Who the hell is André Bisset?

"Time for another bit of freedom," Ghost says softly, his voice teasing.

"What do you want now?"

His gaze drifts toward the cameras in the corners of the room, the red lights blinking steadily. "Turn off the cameras. Let's have a real conversation, without the prying eyes. Unless you're into voyeurism? I don't kink shame, Dr. Andrews."

I grind my molars. Letting Ghost move around is one thing, but turning off the cameras? That's giving him too much power.

But I know how this works. He won't tell me anything else unless I give him what he wants.

I stare at him, weighing the risk, my mind spinning with possible repercussions. He's still in handcuffs. He's still restrained. A guard is right outside the door.

Except turning off the cameras means I lose a safety net. I'll be alone with him in more ways than one.

"Fine," I say, before I can overthink it. "But if you want to meet in a room without this glass wall between us, you can kiss this shit goodbye."

Ghost's smile widens, dark and predatory. "Are you scared to be alone with me, Dr. Andrews?"

Ignoring him, I stand and move to the door again, instructing the guard to turn off the cameras. He hesitates, clearly alarmed by the request, but I remind him that this is part of the process to gain Ghost's trust and establish our relationship as doctor and patient. The guard finally complies.

The red lights blink out and dread sets in.

I return to my seat, locking eyes with Ghost once again. "Who else was involved?"

He places his hands behind his head, his stance casual, as if he's at a coffee shop instead of a prison. "This is the new protocol between us. Every time you visit, I want to be in cuffs only without the cameras on."

Once I get the information I'm searching for, I won't be visiting him again, so there's no risk in agreeing to this. "Fine. Give me another name."

"Luis Dominguez."

I jot it down, still lacking recognition. At this point, that's irrelevant. I'll hunt them down later. "Anyone else?"

Ghost clicks his tongue in admonishment. "Where's my bit of freedom?"

I don't hide my exasperation. "What else could you possibly want?"

"Besides you? Not much. For now, I'd like more of your time."

The way he says he wants me, like it's the most natural thing in the world, sends a ripple of awareness through me. But I shove it away, focusing on the goal of finishing this list of names.

"I'm here, right?" I ask.

"Yes, but I need to ensure that you come back. With that being said, I want you to construct a full psychological profile on me."

I pause, my pencil hovering above the scrap of paper as I consider his request. And why he wants it. I can't deny that studying

Ghost on a deeper level appeals to me professionally. Not only because there's never been another criminal like him and it'd be groundbreaking, but it would also elevate my career to be the one who profiled him.

On the other hand, spending more time with Ghost in any capacity is hazardous to me mentally and emotionally. I know he's manipulating me and I can't stop him, even when I clearly see the tactics he's employing. Ghost knows too much about me, preventing me from creating an effective defense against him. But a profile on him could give me the upper hand.

I glance up at him. He's watching me, his eyes glinting with amusement, like he knows exactly what's going through my mind: the struggle between my professional curiosity and my instinct for self-preservation.

"I'll do it, as long as you're truthful during the assessment," I say.

"Will do." His smile widens. "It's a date."

"But," I add quickly, "there will be limits."

His brow arches. "Limits?"

"Three visits. That's it," I say firmly. "I'll spend the time gathering the necessary data for your profile. After that, we're done."

He chuckles softly, shaking his head. "Three? You think you can figure me out in just three visits, Dr. Andrews? I'm impressed, truly."

"You'd be surprised what I can do if you cooperate."

Ghost's smile fades as his eyes narrow. "Make it ten and we have a deal."

Making it possibly months of seeing him? Hell no.

"Five," I counter.

"Seven."

"Five. Take it or leave it."

He grins at me. "Deal. You drive a hard bargain, Dr. Andrews, but I won't need all of them."

"Excuse me?" I scrunch my face in confusion. "What are you talking about?"

"I'll be out of here before then. And that's when the fun really begins."

CHAPTER 18

GHOST

Geneva is drinking wine again.

Our visit earlier must've really fucked with her head. If she didn't think I was *actually* capable of escaping prison, she wouldn't be so stressed out.

I run my thumb over her image on my phone, wishing I was there with her. If I don't deviate from my strategy, soon I won't be wishing.

She's sitting in her living room, dressed in sweatpants and a torn t-shirt, the light from her phone illuminating her face as she doomscrolls on social media. I watch her closely, the way she presses her lips together, the slight furrow in her brow. She's the most beautiful and complex creature I've ever seen.

> **Unknown:** Stay home tonight, Dr. Andrews.

I hit send. Watching Geneva in real time never fails to excite me. Her body tenses the moment her phone notifies her about the message. She swipes to read the text and her brows snap together. Confusion sweeps over her features, quickly followed by exasperation and a tiny bit of anger. She types something I can't make out, and then pauses, her delicate fingers hovering over the keys before she erases everything.

Geneva purses her plush lips, sending my mind straight to the gutter. I can't wait to shove my cock in her mouth, to feel her tongue circle the head before I thrust deep and make her choke—

She starts typing again, the rapid movement yanking me out of my fantasy. *Wow, that was an ADD moment. Aaaaaand, I'm back.*

> **Geneva:** You might think you own me, but you're wrong. I'll prove it to you.

I chuckle softly, shaking my head. She's strong, I'll give her that, but I know her better than she knows herself. And right now, my girl needs to learn that I *always* mean what I say.

> **Unknown:** My darling doctor, I think you'll want to listen this time. After all, I have your best interests at heart.

> **Geneva:** You don't have a heart.

> **Unknown:** I did once. I think? In any case, be a good girl and stay home. I mean it.

> **Geneva:** And if I don't?

> **Unknown:** Actions have consequences.

I keep my gaze fixed on Geneva, watching her reaction closely. Her chest rises and falls faster as my threat strikes home. She doesn't move to respond, just sits there quietly contemplating her options. Defiance wars with deliberation. Fear battles with fury. It's written all over her face.

That's a good girl. Think it through.

Geneva: What type of consequences?

Unknown: Irreversible ones.

Her fingers fly over the screen as she types something quickly, her movements more aggressive now. The anger on her face is beautiful.

Geneva: Fuck you.

Unknown: Unfortunately, not tonight.
But soon, I promise you.

I let a few seconds pass before sending my next message, savoring the tension between us. Fuck, the things this woman does to me.

Unknown: Enjoy your evening
because I know I will. ☺

Geneva: What are you going to do?

Geneva: You need to tell me.

I grin at that. She's trying to convince herself that she's still in charge by demanding things from me. It's adorable, really. But it won't work. She can't control me, any more than I can control my obsession over her.

I look around my cell, the walls no more than a mirage of captivity. Perception is fluid and I've always been good at shaping others' to my satisfaction. There's power in it, and that's something the Malone family has a lot of. Giulio Malone runs the largest crime syndicate on this side of the United States.

And since he works for me, his men do too.

My mind drifts to a year ago, when I first began my campaign against them.

∽

"People have patterns, making them predictable and fucking boring. But chaos...?" I pause, briefly closing my eyes and inhaling a deep breath. "Chaos makes my dick hard."

Daniel Malone watches me, his gaze never leaving the knife in my gloved hand even as I use the other to grab my cock through my pants. Smart man. It's natural to follow movement with your eyes, but he's fighting his instincts.

So am I, since he's not dead.

"Who are you? What do you want?" Malone asks.

"*What* do I want? What do *I* want? What do I *want*?"

I toss the knife, pursing my lips in thought. His eyes follow the motions of the blade, finally unable to resist.

Up   *Up.*

   Down.   *Down.*

"Danny boy, I don't want anything. Not really. Do you know why?" When he shakes his head emphatically, I grin. He flinches at the sinister expression, and my smile widens. "Because I don't let anything get in my way. Chaos breeds opportunity and I am a glutton for exploitation."

I grab him by the throat. The black leather coating my fingers squeaks as I place the knife under his chin to lift it. Blade up. He grimaces when the metal slices into his skin, but he doesn't cry out.

How disappointing.

"Tell me when and where the next shipment of diamonds will be." I tighten my hold, forcing a grunt from him. "I know your family has cutting and polishing businesses throughout New York City. They won't notice if a few shiny rocks go missing."

"They will notice," he says on a wheeze. "And they'll kill me."

"No, *I* will kill you."

"I can't go against my family."

I shove away from him with enough force that the wooden chair rocks back before landing on all fours with a loud thud. "Family. *Familia. Famille.* I had one once."

At the thought of my parents, a huff of laughter works its way up my throat and rolls across my tongue. It builds, gaining volume and hilarity with every second. Malone's eyes widen at my fit of humor, his gaze shining with fear and a hint of confusion.

"This isn't funny, man," he says. "Whoever you are, you should know the Malone family doesn't allow competition on their streets. You're begging for death, asshole."

I snap my jaw shut and my teeth click together. "You're assuming death scares me enough to be a threat."

"It doesn't?"

My scoff fills the silence. "Death is my canvas and I am an artist. Now, it's time for me to gather my supplies and paint."

Malone rears back in the chair. "Supplies?"

I swipe at the perspiration along his temple, rubbing the moisture between my gloved fingers. "Oh yes, Danny boy. I will splatter your blood, sweat, and tears all over this place, rivaling any artwork of Pollock."

~

Good times.

Once I "convinced" the Malone family it was in their best interest to work with me, I'd obtained the cooperation of the security guards before I even stepped over the threshold of Blackwater. They'll do whatever I tell them, including looking the other way and fabricating camera feeds. Of course, there was that one guard who confiscated my cell phone. For the first and last time.

It's amazing how effective a severed hand can be.

My escape tonight will be temporary. This time. I just need a couple hours.

After looking at Geneva once more, I lock my phone and shove it in my pocket before getting up from my bed and walking over to the door. Grin in place, I grip the bars and call out, "Marco!"

An inmate shouts, "Polo, motherfucker. Now shut up! I'm trying to sleep."

"Oh, Marco!" I repeat. Louder.

A collection of shouts and profanities fills the cell block. Then a security guard appears in front of me, sweating as if he ran to get here.

"What do you want, Ghost?"

"I'd like to take a stroll, Officer James."

The guard's eyes flicker with unease, his fingers twitching at his side. He knows what this means, and he's in too deep to walk away. James doesn't hesitate. With a sharp nod, he turns, pulling the keys from his belt and unlocking my cell door. The click of the lock disengaging is something I'll never tire of.

As I step out, a cacophony of sound, made up of shouts, taunts, and curses, ricochets off the walls. I take a deep breath, letting the chaos wash over and fuel me as I walk past the rows of cells with the guard beside me. Most of the men don't bother looking at me, too busy in their own worlds of rage and regret. But a few do. One in particular catches my eye.

Frank "Skinner" Burns. Serial rapist. A man whose sick appetites have earned him the worst kind of reputation in here. He's sitting on the edge of his cot, his greasy hair hanging over his face as he glares at me through the bars. His eyes follow my every movement, filled with the kind of anguish that only men like him possess. Predators who've lost their power.

His lip curls into a sneer, but he doesn't say anything, just watches me like a cornered animal. One who recognizes an alpha in his presence.

I smile and keep walking. I don't need to say anything. Everyone has heard the rumors about me…because I made sure they had something to talk about.

The guard leads me through the maze of corridors, his boots tapping against the concrete floor. I let him stew in his own fear, enjoying the way he glances over his shoulder every few steps as if he expects me to do something. But I'm not in a rush.

As we approach the far end of the prison, the halls grow quieter, the air thicker with dust and disuse. This part of the facility hasn't seen much traffic in years. Not since the place was first built.

The guard finally stops in front of a door. It's old, steel reinforced, with rust creeping along the edges. The door was supposedly sealed decades ago, back when this place was still expanding.

But I know better. This is the kind of secret the warden likes to keep hidden. The kind of secret men like me can exploit.

The guard hesitates, fumbling with his keys. His hand shakes as he finds the right one and slides it into the lock. James glances at me again, sweat dripping down his brow.

"You remember what'll happen if you run your mouth about this, don't you?" I ask.

He nods quickly, his throat bobbing as he swallows. "I—I remember."

"Good. I'll text you when I'm back."

James shoots me an incredulous look and I can't blame him. I wouldn't believe any inmate that says they'd return to prison. But I'm not serving time. I'm biding time.

The door creaks when I open it, revealing a dark, narrow passage. I step through the doorway, my senses sharpening as the guard follows behind me, his presence nothing more than a formality now. The path stretches out in front of me, a long, dimly lit tunnel that leads to the outside world. To freedom, even if it's temporary.

I step further into the abandoned hallway, my every movement deliberate and controlled. The power I hold isn't just in my hands; it's in the quiet fear that has spread through this place. Like I always say, perception is everything.

I'd love to know how Geneva perceives me. And if that'll change in the morning.

Expectation hums in my veins as I move down the corridor and eventually step outside. The cool night air wraps around me like an old lover welcoming me home. There's a car waiting just down the street, a sleek black sedan with tinted windows. Giulio's men are nothing if not efficient.

I dismiss the guard and slide into the backseat. The driver pulls away the second I close the door. The city lights flash past the window, neon and blurred, as the vehicle rolls through the streets. It's tranquil to be without walls imprisoning you, but that's not the freedom I'm after.

No, freedom is meaningless without purpose. And my purpose is Geneva.

I lean back, lightly tapping my fingers against the door as I consider my next move. Mason's not far. Giulio's men have already tracked him down. Talk about VIP service.

During the drive through the city I change out of my orange jumpsuit and into something more comfortable with my mind constantly drifting back to Geneva. I'm tempted to pull up the camera feed again, but I need to concentrate and that's hard to do when I look at her. She has a way of making the world disappear until she's the only thing I see. The only thing I want.

Regardless, the tracking device on her cell phone will let me know if she listened to me or not. Except, I know she won't.

And I can't wait to teach her a lesson.

CHAPTER 19

GHOST

Darkness surrounds me like a cloak when I step from the vehicle.

The driver rolls down the window, his gaze barely meeting mine. "You want me to wait here?"

I shake my head. "This will take a while. Be back an hour before dawn."

"Yes, sir."

The engine purrs quietly as the vehicle pulls away, its tires gliding over the asphalt like a predator slipping back into the shadows. But I don't watch it leave. My focus is straight ahead, on the towering apartment building in front of me. It's tall, pristine, and expensive. The kind of place people think buys them safety, when it's only a false sense of security.

Mason, you are so fucked.

While tugging down on the brim of my hat, I smile at the thought, anticipation filling my bones like marrow. This part of the city is polished, clean, and utterly insignificant to someone like me. Mason has to believe that living here, surrounded by wealth and status, means I can't reach him.

He couldn't be more wrong.

I slip through the building's entrance with ease, my steps silent. The lobby is quiet, almost eerie in its opulence. Glass chandeliers hang overhead, casting a soft, ambient glow. The marble floor shines, reflecting my image and sparkling with flecks of gold and silver. All of this luxury, including the designer clothes I wear, doesn't faze me.

At the end of the day, we're all mortal, destined to die one way or another.

The doorman glances up from his desk, raking his gaze over me. I lift my chin like I belong here and the expensive clothes I'm wearing are part of my identity. He doesn't blink, returning to his mundane tasks.

The elevator doors open with a soft chime, and I step inside, the metal reflecting a distorted version of myself. An illusion. A *ghost*. But tonight, I'm as real as the pain I'm going to inflict.

I press the button for his floor, and the elevator ascends smoothly, carrying me up toward my destination. After the brief ride, I exit the elevator and walk up to Mason's door and knock. I could pick the lock, but it's more fun if he lets me in, unknowingly giving access to the future crime scene.

The door opens just a crack, revealing my target. His hair is messy and his clothing rumpled. The nearly empty tumbler in his left hand catches my eye, and I smile. Mason was never a match for me, but he's really put himself at a disadvantage by being under the influence of alcohol.

"What do you want?" he asks, his tired gaze narrowing on my face.

I smile, stepping forward so he's forced to open the door a bit wider. "Mason, right?"

He frowns, glancing at me with confusion, his fingers tightening on the door. "Who's asking?"

Ignoring his question, I step closer and he jerks back. Even in his stupor, he senses something about me is off, that my black slacks and crisp black shirt are mere camouflage. Too bad his instincts won't save him.

"I need to talk to you about Dr. Andrews," I say.

"What about her?"

A flash of unease lights up his gaze. He's trying to gauge what I know, trying to figure out why I'm standing at his door talking about the woman he put his hands on. He's not ready for this conversation. Not like I am.

"So, here's the thing," I say. "She needs to be taught a lesson." I shove my hands in my pockets, leaning against the doorframe in an innocuous position. As expected, he relaxes, misreading my casual stance. "And I need you to help me, Mason."

His frown deepens, his brow furrowing as he tries to place me, to recall my connection to him and Geneva. "What the hell are you talking about? And how do you know my name?"

I give him a sly smile as though we're friends sharing a dark secret. I suppose that could be true. Mason and I are the only ones who know that he hurt Dr. Andrews.

"Geneva mentioned you once, but that's besides the point. She needs to be punished. Severely."

This time Mason takes a step back, keeping his death-grip on the door. But he doesn't shut it. He won't. He's too curious. Too titillated by the idea of hurting Geneva again.

For that alone, I'm going to cut off his balls and hang them on my rearview mirror like a pair of dice.

Mason's gaze darts from side to side, confirming we don't have an audience. His mouth thins as he considers my proposal. I catch the moment the idea takes hold of him, the subtle shift in his body as intrigue and something dark begin to fuse together.

"What exactly are you thinking about doing?" he asks.

I shrug. "I'm open to anything, as long as it hurts. *A lot.*"

"Come in," he says, his voice low. "This isn't something to talk about publicly."

I step through the threshold while concealing my amusement. The door clicks shut behind me, and I take a moment to assess my surroundings. The apartment is as expensive as it is boring. Clean lines, neutral tones, polished wood floors that gleam under the soft glow of designer lighting.

Blah, blah, blah. Details, shmetails.

Mason has surrounded himself with objects that symbolize wealth and power, but all I see are the hollow trappings of someone desperate to prove that he matters. That he's in control.

A delusion I plan on shattering.

He crosses the room, setting down his tumbler on the counter before reaching out to grab a glass bottle.

Mental note: His right hand is his dominant hand.

His movements are jittery, but it's not with fear. It's eagerness. The fantasy of punishing Geneva excites him…almost as much as I'm excited to kill him.

"Do you want a drink?" he asks.

"Sure."

Mason pours me a drink and hands me the glass. Once I take it, he refills his. "How do you know Gen? And what did she do to you?"

"I met her at Blackwater, where I used to work. To answer your other question: She ruined me."

Mason lets out a sound, something between a laugh and a grunt, as if he understands. I almost smile. He has no idea what Geneva has done to me, how deeply she's embedded herself into my mind. *Ruined* me, yes, but not in the way he thinks.

She's made it impossible for me to want anyone or anything else. Because she's the only thing I think about, the only person who I give a shit about. Does that mean I care for her? Not exactly. I doubt I'm capable of such emotions anymore.

But whatever I feel for her, it's *all-consuming*.

"Gen has always been uptight," Mason says. "A stickler for the rules."

"I'm not surprised. It must've been hard being with someone like that."

He scoffs. "You have no idea. She thinks following the rules makes her better than everyone."

I dip my head in acknowledgment. "I get it. Before she got me fired, due to 'inappropriate behavior,' Geneva told me she'd just dumped her boy-toy and was swearing off all men." Mason flinches at "boy-toy." Fucking with his fragile ego is too easy. I blow out a breath, maintaining the composed look I've mastered, even though the urge to smile is almost overwhelming. "She needs to pay for what she did."

"She's always so cold," he says. "She never let me in, never gave a shit about me beyond what I could do for her. But everyone has a breaking point, and I want to find hers."

"That's a good place to start." I keep my voice soft, coaxing him. "What else?"

"I want to make her feel powerless. Tie her up, blindfold her, and torture her. Basically, take away everything that makes her feel secure."

My mind files away every single word. Mason thinks he's describing his fantasy for Geneva, but all he's doing is giving me the tools I need to destroy him. Every twisted thought that crosses his mind will soon be his reality. Plus, some initiative on my part, of course.

"And then?" I ask.

Mason's eyes gleam with cruelty now, fully immersed in his sick delusion. "I'll make her beg. Make her *plead* for it to stop. But I won't stop. Not until she's completely broken or dead."

"Sounds like you've thought a lot about this," I say with a small laugh. As if I haven't thought about torturing and killing *him* for weeks now.

He shrugs, trying to appear casual, but there's an eagerness in his expression that he can't quite suppress. "I've had time to think."

"Damn man, what really happened? This sounds like more than just her dumping you."

The skin around his jaw tightens and the shift in his demeanor is immediate. Rage is there, just below the surface, and I want him to release it. To admit what he did, so I can kill him.

"She broke things off with me. *Me*," he snaps. "As if she can do better."

"Sounds like she underestimated you."

Mason's eyes flash with anger, and he tightens his grip on the tumbler. "Damn right she did. She acted like she was too good for me, like I was just…" He grits his teeth, his knuckles turning white. "I showed her that night. And I'll do it again."

I raise an eyebrow, keeping my voice calm. "Oh? How did you show her?"

128

He hesitates for a moment, the fury twisting into something grotesque. "She wouldn't stop," he mutters, almost as if he's talking to himself. "Kept pushing. Kept acting like she's better than me, like I'm nothing. And I just…I snapped."

I keep my posture relaxed but my gaze sharp, watching him carefully. "Snapped how?"

"I…I hit her." His face pales, and he takes another swig of his drink as if to wash the guilt away. "It's like she *wanted* me to."

I nod slowly, processing the information. Nothing justifies his pathetic excuse for losing control, but the fact that she stood there, pushing Mason to the brink, shows me something. Something she didn't want me to know.

Geneva is starting to embrace who she really is.

I can't help the satisfaction that rises in my chest. She's no longer hiding behind that wall of ice and control. The strength inside her, the fire I saw when we first met…She let him see it, let him feel the heat of her defiance. And she burned him.

"So, what happened next?" I ask.

Mason hesitates, his eyes flickering with turmoil. Pride, uncertainty, but also a bit of fear. He wants to admit it, to tell me what happened, but he's afraid of how it'll sound. I can see it in the way his fingers tremble, in the way his gaze darts to the floor before coming back to mine.

"She laughed," he says finally, his voice barely above a whisper. "After I hit her, she fucking *laughed*."

The words hit me like a spark in a pool of gasoline, igniting something primal inside me. She laughed? I keep my expression neutral even as the thought of Geneva standing there, defiant, makes my blood hum with approval. Mason couldn't handle it. He couldn't handle her raw power.

"She laughed?" I repeat. "That's weird."

Mason shifts, clearly on edge. "She also grabbed a baseball bat. And threatened me with it."

I lean forward, intrigued as fuck. Geneva with a bat? The image forms in my mind—her standing there, fearless, wielding the weapon with confidence.

Shit, now my dick is hard.

"Did she hit you?" I ask, my voice barely above a whisper.

If Mason tells me she struck him, I'm going to come in my slacks, right here, right now.

He shakes his head quickly, his eyes wide with the memory. "No, but she looked crazy, man. I didn't know what the fuck she was going to do."

I take a step closer. "You're scared of her, aren't you?"

"Fuck no," he says on a near shout.

"You should be."

He looks at me with disgust coating his features. "Scared of a woman? Hell no."

"How about being scared of a man?" I pause, my lips twitching. "Or maybe a ghost?"

And then…recognition flickers across his face. His eyes widen, his mouth going slack as he stares at me, his gaze tracing the jagged line of my scar. His bravado crumbles, and the fear I've been waiting for creeps in, clawing its way over his expression.

Yahtzee!

"Wait!" His voice trembles. "You're…you're that guy. The serial killer from the news. Ghost."

I smile and remove my hat, exposing my white hair. "There it is."

Mason immediately takes a step back. Then he glances toward

the door and his phone on the table. "If you don't get out, I'll call the police. They'll—"

I laugh softly, cutting him off. "You think I care about the police? I'm already in prison for life. What are they going to do? Throw me in for longer? Enroll me in a loyalty rewards program?" I take another step forward, my presence looming over him. "Actually, I plan on calling them before I leave, so they can find what's left when I'm done with you."

His entire body stiffens as the threat hits home. I drop my voice to a near whisper as I wag my finger in his direction. "You see, Mason, you were wrong, wrong, wrong. Wrong for touching what's mine. For underestimating Geneva. For thinking she was yours to begin with."

Mason stumbles back, his hands shaking as he raises them defensively. "Look, man, I didn't know—"

"No one touches what's mine. You don't lay a hand on her. You don't even *look* at her. Now, you're going to pay for all of that."

I take another step forward, closing the distance between us until my face is inches from his. Until I can see the sweat beading on his forehead and the sheer terror in his eyes. I glance toward the phone on the table, the corner of my mouth lifting in a dark smile.

"Go ahead and call the police, Mason. Tell them Ghost is here and that you have a murder to report. Yours."

CHAPTER 20

GENEVA

Unknown: Actions have consequences.

I stare down at the screen, my fingers tightening around my phone as I reread Ghost's message. What the hell is that supposed to mean?

I rise and begin pacing, my bare feet slapping against the hardwood floor. Every nerve in my body feels like it's on fire, charged with anger. I could call my boss. I *should* call Allen and let him know Ghost has been sending these messages and that he's threatening me now. But then I'd have to explain why I didn't say anything when the texts first arrived, and…that's a rabbit hole I'm not ready to dive into.

Besides, what's the point? There's no way Ghost can actually do anything. He's locked up, behind bars where he belongs. Whatever power he thinks he has, whatever manipulation he's trying to pull, it starts and stops with the phone.

I march into my bedroom, grab my gym bag, then my shoes and jacket. If Ghost thinks he can get in my head and make me doubt myself or make me too scared to leave my own apartment, he's wrong. *So fucking wrong.*

As I step outside, the cool evening air hits my face, clearing my mind a bit. The city lights blur as I walk at a brisk pace. I need to move, to breathe, to get out of my head.

I retrieve my phone, tempted to text him back, to tell him exactly what I think of his threats. But I stop myself. That's what he wants.

Instead, I slip the phone back into my pocket and keep walking, the weight of Ghost's threat still lingering in the back of my mind. He's just trying to scare me. He can't do anything. He's in prison. He can't touch me.

The neon "24-Hour Gym" sign flickers against the black sky, its buzz low and constant as I push open the door. The space is mostly empty at this hour, just a few dedicated souls pounding away on the treadmills or lifting weights in the far corners. It's quiet enough, and that's what I need right now.

I move to the locker room, slipping into my workout gear. The familiar routine of pulling on leggings, lacing up my sneakers, and tying my hair back is calming.

Discipline. Order. Efficiency.

This is the only way to keep my life from falling apart. Every action pulls me a little further away from the chaos swirling inside my head. Away from Ghost's words, his threats, his dark promises. I can't control him, but I can control this.

I step out into the gym, the smell of rubber mats and disinfectant filling the air. I head straight for the punching bag in the corner, the one that's seen better days, its leather worn and cracked.

I wrap my fingers, tightening the strips of cloth around my

knuckles. The feeling of my hands protected and ready to fight soothes me.

The first punch lands with a satisfying thud against the bag. The force of it ripples through me, and I exhale, my breath a sharp hiss. I hit again, harder this time, the impact vibrating up my arm. With every strike, the tension in my body ebbs a bit more.

Ghost's voice is still there in the back of my mind, taunting me. I slam my fist into the bag again, picturing his face—his smirk, that insufferable look that always says he knows something I don't. The impact vibrates through my arms, sharp and satisfying.

My knuckles throb, the dull ache intensifying with every bit of forceful contact, but I don't stop. The pain is good. It grounds me, gives me something tangible to focus on.

I hit harder, my breath coming in quick, shallow bursts as I push myself further. Sweat drips down my face, and the rhythmic sound of my fists colliding with the worn leather echoes around me. There's no room for anything else in my mind but the bag, the burning in my muscles, and the steady throb in my hands.

For a moment I pause, resting against the wall, breathing hard as I wipe the sweat from my brow. The gym hums quietly, machines whirring in the background, but it's mostly empty. Just a few stragglers on the treadmills who glance at me on occasion, their expressions wary.

Can they see the demon chasing me? Can they hear his voice?

I punch the bag again, then again, until my arms scream with exhaustion and my legs tremble. Only when I can barely stand do I finally stop, my breath ragged, my body spent.

I slowly unwind the wraps from my hands, wincing as the fabric peels away from my skin. I stare down at my knuckles, the skin cracked and bleeding. My body has taken punishment so my mind could be at peace.

The streets are quieter when I step back outside, the city deepening in repose. As I walk, I reach for my phone, half-expecting another message from Ghost. But the screen is blank. No taunts. No threats. Nothing.

A moment of peace? Or a calm before the storm?

I head home, each step slower than the last as the exhaustion creeps in. When I reach my apartment, I unlock the door and step inside, locking it behind me with a sense of relief.

This is one of the few times that being alone isn't the worst thing.

I drop my keys on the counter and shrug off my jacket before jumping into the shower. After that, I throw on sweats and a t-shirt before collapsing onto my bed with a groan. The exhaustion is welcome, numbing the edges of my mind. Eventually, the dull hum of the city outside lulls me to sleep…

My phone chiming with a notification yanks me from repose. I groan, blindly reaching for it on the mattress. Once located, I squint at the screen, my fingers fumbling as I unlock the device.

The light is too bright, too harsh against the darkness of my bedroom, and it takes me a moment to read the words.

> **Unknown:** Good morning, Dr. Andrews. Turn on the news.

I sit up quickly, my heart pounding against my ribs as I reread the message, trying to make sense of it. Dread weaves through me as my fingers hover over the screen. I'm hesitant to obey, but I have to know what's going on.

After grabbing the remote, I turn on the TV and select the news channel. The reporter's voice is solemn, heavy with the gravity of her story.

"Police have confirmed that a man was found dead in his downtown apartment early this morning, just after dawn. He has been identified as Mason Rivers…"

I freeze.

"Authorities are treating the case as a homicide."

No. I shake my head, disbelief washing over me like ice water. *No, no, no.*

The image on the screen shifts to Mason's building, police tape draped across the entrance, the flashing red and blue lights in the background. The reporter's voice continues, but I can barely hear her. My mind is racing, my pulse hammering in my ears.

Mason is dead.

I watch in stunned silence as the details emerge, the sympathy in the reporter's voice doing nothing to soften the brutality of what was done to him. The word "torture" is mentioned, and I flinch, the horror of it sinking in. She doesn't go into specifics, but the implication is there, thick and suffocating.

Nausea hits me so hard that I slump onto the mattress as the room spins. I wanted him out of my life. But not like that. Mason didn't deserve this ending.

It wasn't just murder. Someone made him suffer.

A cold thought slips into my mind, and my stomach churns violently. *Ghost.* It had to be him. But how? He's in prison. He couldn't have done it himself.

Or *did* he?

Ghost is nothing if not resourceful. He could have hired a

hitman to do the job for him. He must have influence. Power that reaches far beyond those bars.

I cling to that thought because the alternative—Ghost physically breaking out and doing this himself—is too terrifying to consider. If he can orchestrate something like this from behind prison walls, there's still a level of separation. It's less personal. He didn't do it with his own hands.

But that thought doesn't comfort me. Mason's dead because Ghost wanted it. He told me so in person. I didn't want to believe it then, but I sure as hell do now.

A sharp knock on my door shatters the silence. I nearly jump off my bed as a cold wave of fear washes over me. Another knock sounds, more insistent this time. It's too early in the morning for visitors. And it's not Ghost.

He wouldn't knock.

My body moves on autopilot as I get to my feet and shuffle toward the door. I unlock it with trembling fingers and pull it open, revealing two police officers standing in the hallway, their expressions grim.

"Dr. Geneva Andrews?"

"Yes," I reply, my throat dry.

The second officer steps forward, his hand resting lightly on his belt. "I'm Officer Kwan. This is Officer Jacob. We're...we're sorry for your loss, ma'am. Mason Rivers was found dead in his apartment this morning."

"I just saw it on the news." I swallow hard. "Thank you."

The officer nods. "We know this might be difficult, but we need you to come down to the station. Just a few questions to help move the investigation along since you were one of the last people to contact him. We want to catch whoever did this as quickly as possible."

"Okay, give me a second."

I grab my jacket and phone, sending a quick text to Allen so he knows I'll be late for work. The officers step aside, allowing me to close the door before leading me down the hallway. My mind spins, a chaotic jumble of conflicting thoughts.

Ghost is responsible for this.

But how do I explain that without sounding insane myself?

CHAPTER 21

GENEVA

AN INTERROGATION ROOM IS DESIGNED TO STRIP AWAY ALL SENSE of control and any shred of comfort. The walls are a dull, lifeless gray, similar to a cage, in order to elicit feelings of vulnerability and the sensation of being trapped. The fluorescent lights overhead buzz, casting harsh shadows that distort everything, causing the mind to play tricks on itself. The cold metal table is too wide to foster connection, but too small to escape the pressure of the conversation. There isn't a clock or any windows, just suffocating silence. Every inch of this room is meant to break the suspect. I'm familiar with the mental games that are being played.

Except this is my first time on the *other* side of the table.

Only, I'm not here as a suspect. I'm here to help. They need answers.

And I need closure.

The door creaks open, and the detective walks in. His steps are measured to show he's not rushing, that he has authority over the situation. Tall, broad, with a quiet intensity behind his eyes…he's a professional who's done this a hundred times.

"Dr. Geneva Andrews," he says, voice low and steady, sitting across from me with a folder in hand. His eyes dart toward my cheek, and there's the briefest pause on the fading bruise. He's already drawing conclusions.

I tilt my head, widening my eyes a little. It's to show a bit of vulnerability, a flash of discomfort. Although, I don't have to fake it.

"I'm Detective Brooks. I understand you were involved with Mason Rivers." He leans forward, clasping his hands on the table between us. A dominant stance.

I meet his gaze. "That's correct."

"How long did your relationship last?" he asks.

"A little under a year."

"And how did it end?"

"I broke it off two weeks ago," I say evenly. "We both knew it wasn't working."

"Not working how?"

I lean forward, matching his posture. A calculated move. Mirroring builds rapport. "There were issues." I pause, then add, "He had a temper."

Brooks narrows his eyes. "Did things ever get physical between you?"

I give him a small nod, and angle my head so he can see the fading bruise more clearly, showing I have nothing to hide. "Yes. He hit me the night I broke it off."

The detective taps his fingers. "What did you do after that?"

"I didn't want to escalate things, so I didn't retaliate." *Although if Mason had come at me again, I would've beat the fuck out of him.*

"When was the last time you saw Mason?"

"The night I broke up with him," I say, meeting his gaze squarely. "I never contacted him after that."

The detective opens the file in front of him, scanning the pages. When he lifts his head and his focus lands on me, his eyes are cold. I stiffen at the abrupt shift in his demeanor.

"Where were you last night, Dr. Andrews?"

He's pushing now, no longer pretending to be curious. This isn't an interview anymore.

It's an interrogation.

I lift a brow. "Am I a suspect?"

"You're not under arrest. We're simply asking all of his close associates their whereabouts so we can build a full picture."

A rehearsed line. Noncommittal. Legally safe.

He doesn't answer the question—just redirects it into something procedural. The detective suspects me of the murder, but has insufficient evidence to establish probable cause for arrest.

Or I'd be in handcuffs right now.

"I was at the gym," I say.

"Late at night? Alone?"

"I go to a 24-hour gym. It helps me clear my mind." I keep my eyes on his, watching the way his jaw tightens when my voice doesn't falter. "There are cameras. They'll show I was there."

He nods slowly, scribbling something down. "We'll check that. But tell me, Dr. Andrews—did you ever feel the need to hurt Mason? After he hit you?"

"No," I say, my voice steady. "I didn't want revenge. I wanted to move on."

Detective Brooks leans forward. "So, you're telling me Mason hit you, hard enough to leave a bruise that's lasted several days, and you never thought about hurting him back? Not once?"

"No. I just wanted out."

Brooks scoffs and throws up his hands. "You expect me to

believe this shit? The man was violent toward you, and you're saying you felt nothing? No anger? No resentment? Come on, Dr. Andrews, you're a psychologist. You know better than anyone that's not how it works."

I don't blink. "I understand human behavior. I also know how to control my emotions."

He slams the file shut with a snap, and for the first time, irritation leaks through a crack in his professionalism. "Bullshit."

I brace myself.

"Bullshit," he repeats, his voice louder now, more intense. "You expect me to believe you just walked away from a guy who hit you, humiliated you, made you feel like *nothing*, and not once did you think about getting even?"

I meet his gaze, not allowing myself to flinch. "I didn't kill him."

Detective Brooks smiles, but there's no humor in it. "You didn't kill him? Really? Because it sure as hell looks like you did."

Before I can respond, he reaches into the file and pulls out a stack of photographs, slamming them down on the table in front of me, one after the other. The impact makes me jump, and I glance down at the images, my stomach twisting.

Mason's body. Broken. Bloody. And Carved.

Actions have consequences.

The words are deep gouges across his chest. A message. For *me*.

My breath lodges in my throat, and I force myself not to look away, not to react. I've seen pictures like these before, but never of someone I knew. Never of someone who had been a part of my life.

Detective Brooks watches me with an intensity that makes my skin crawl. "Do you recognize that phrase?" he asks. When I shake my head, he curls his hands into fists. "'Actions have consequences.' You're telling me that vengeful statement is mere coincidence?"

I swallow, forcing my gaze away from the gruesome images, the horror etched into each one. My voice, when it comes, is steady but strained. "I understand why you think I killed Mason, but I'm telling you that I'm innocent."

"Look at him again!" Brooks jabs his index finger on one of the photographs, his voice harsh. "Look at what was done to him. Then tell me again that you didn't think about getting revenge."

I swallow hard, my pulse racing, but I manage to keep my face void of any emotion except shock. "I didn't."

He leans in closer, his eyes locked on mine, studying every flicker of emotion, every microexpression. "Well, whoever did this, took their time. They *enjoyed* it, Dr. Andrews. This wasn't just about murder. This was personal."

I fist my hands in my lap, the weight of his words pressing down on me. I force myself to breathe, to stay calm. "I agree with you, but I didn't kill him."

Brooks slams another photo down, this one worse than all the others. It's a close-up of Mason's face. His eyes are wide, frozen in a twisted mask of sheer horror, pupils blown with the fear he couldn't escape. His mouth has been forced open, and a candle, half-burned, is lodged between his lips, wax smeared grotesquely across his chin. The wick is charred, blackening the edges of his mouth, indicating excruciating pain.

"Since this is your specialty, Doctor, do you care to explain why Mason has a candle in his mouth? Or why it was lit?"

I stare at the image, bile rising in my throat. Then I cover my mouth with my hand and briefly close my eyes, pulling in breath after breath until I'm certain I'm not going to vomit. Detective

Brooks grins with a victory that'll be short-lived. My reaction is not going to send me to jail, but I'll be a prisoner of this image for the rest of my life.

Ghost. This has to be his handiwork. But how do I explain that to the detective without sounding crazy? How do I convince him that this isn't my revenge when that's what it looks like?

I take a slow, steadying breath, forcing my focus onto the details, letting the clinical detachment I've honed over the years take over. I look down at the image of Mason, the grotesque candle wedged in his mouth, and the carvings on his chest, and begin to analyze everything. When I speak my voice is that of a professional.

Geneva, the ex-girlfriend, has been replaced by Dr. Andrews, the expert.

"The candle is symbolic. By forcing it into Mason's mouth, they wanted to deny him a voice in his last moments. However, the candle is small enough to allow his muffled screams to be heard by the killer, for him or her to enjoy them. And lighting the candle…"

I pause, glancing briefly at Brooks. "Lighting it indicates a level of sadism. The killer wanted the wax to drip, to burn his mouth and throat slowly before he died."

Brooks watches me, his expression unreadable, but I press on, needing to finish this exercise. "This wasn't impulsive or sloppy. It was methodical, almost ritualistic. The phrase 'Actions have consequences' carved into his chest is a message."

I nearly trip over my words, unable to ignore that the message wasn't just for Mason. It was for me. This entire gruesome act was for me.

"The killer believes Mason wronged them," I say. "The offense was severe, indicated by the depth of each letter into the skin.

Whoever did this wanted to make sure that Mason understood his behavior wouldn't go unpunished. That's why Mason was still alive when the murderer cut into his skin."

Brooks crosses his arms, his gaze unrelenting. "Go on, Doctor. You sound like you've thought about this a lot."

I ignore his baiting me, keeping my focus on the psychological elements. "This kind of staging is designed to elicit terror and helplessness in the victim. The candle, the carving—all of it is deliberate. They didn't just want him dead, although that was always the end goal. Whoever did this wanted Mason broken, humiliated, and silenced before death."

I meet Brooks's gaze head on, my voice resolute. "So, yes, Detective, this was deeply personal. But knowing how and why it happened doesn't make me responsible."

Brooks studies me, the corner of his mouth tightening. "Your insight might be useful, Doctor, but don't think for a second it clears you. Maybe you're just good at hiding your work."

"I didn't kill him."

The detective's lips curl into a bitter smile. "If you're innocent, then give me a suspect."

My mind races while I struggle to hold on to the control I've worked so hard to maintain throughout this brutal interrogation. "I don't have a name. All I can give you is the address to the gym. It has cameras. Check them."

Detective Brooks doesn't take his eyes off me. The photos lie scattered between us like the broken pieces of a puzzle he's determined to force down my throat. He taps his fingers against the table, his gaze sharp and calculating.

"You're a smart woman, Dr. Andrews. You know exactly how to present yourself to avoid suspicion. Most people would crack under this kind of pressure, but not you." He tilts his head. "You've got the training, the experience. You know how to manipulate a situation, don't you? How to use your responses and body language to appear a certain kind of way?"

His words cut through the air, but I don't flinch. It's my job to study people's reactions and interpret their body language. But he's right about me. This isn't the first time I've used my education to my advantage.

The corners of his mouth twitch as if he's holding back. He hates this. Hates that I haven't broken. But there's a flicker of respect behind the coldness in his gaze. He recognizes I'm not like other people he's dealt with.

Like Ghost, this man is one of the few who haven't underestimated me.

Brooks leans back in his chair, his shoulders slumping. "I've seen brilliant minds like yours before. People who think they're untouchable. Who believe they can outsmart everyone around them because they're too smart for their own good."

He pauses, his eyes boring into mine. "But here's the thing, Dr. Andrews. Brilliant minds? They make mistakes. Eventually, they all do. And when that happens, I'll be right there."

I raise my chin. "I know my rights. Either you arrest me and I demand legal representation, or I'm leaving."

There's a moment of silence, thick with unspoken accusations. Then Brooks smirks, a frustrated, tight-lipped expression as he slowly rises from his seat. "You're free to go, but don't make any travel plans."

He steps aside, opening the door with a deliberate slowness to display power. "Don't think for a second this is over. I'll be watching you, Dr. Andrews. I always catch my killers."

"Good luck with that." *Because he's already in prison.*

I gather my things, standing as calmly as I can, even though my heart is pounding in my chest and my legs are trembling. Without another word, I walk out of the room, leaving behind the cold interrogation room and the photos of Mason's broken body.

CHAPTER 22

GHOST

"Ghost, you have a visitor."

I turn my head to stare at the guard standing in front of my cell. "If it's not Dr. Andrews, they can go fuck themselves."

The day I arrived marked the beginning of a steady stream of letters. They're mostly written by women who claim to love me, who profess to understand the shadows I live in. The twisted attraction to the forbidden, the thrill of being tied to someone who's done the unimaginable. They romanticize it, obsess over it, draping themselves in fantasies of being the one to redeem me.

It's textbook hybristophilia. See? Dr. Andrews isn't the only one who knows fancy words.

These people send photos—cheap lingerie, smeared lipstick, eyes full of lust and desperation. They offer me their bodies, their minds, sometimes even their souls, hoping for a sliver of attention, some acknowledgment from the man they think they understand. But they don't.

Except Geneva.

She doesn't delude herself with stupid fantasies. She doesn't dress up my madness in the robes of some misunderstood, broken hero. She knows what I am, and she's afraid.

But she keeps coming back.

And that's the difference. Her fear isn't born from ignorance or naivety. She knows the fire she's playing with, and yet, she confronts me, close enough to feel the heat.

Because she is made of fire as well.

The guard says, "It's her."

"Yay!"

I stand and roll my shoulders for a quick stretch before I let him cuff me without resistance. The cold metal snaps around my wrists and I sigh. The things I put up with for Geneva's sake.

I grab the material of my pants and curtsy. "How do I look?"

"Shut up, Ghost."

My laughter follows us as he leads me into the hall and we begin the slow walk down the corridor. The air smells of sweat, musk, and pent-up aggression. I glance at the inmates we pass by, some slumped against the wall, others sleeping. I take note of each face, searching for something useful. They're all disposable, most of them too broken to serve any real purpose.

But then I spot someone who fits the bill. A lanky, wide-eyed inmate in one of the far cells is pacing methodically, his fingers twitching as he walks. He has the look of someone deep in his own head, trapped in obsessive thought.

What are you thinking about, Junior?

He's not one of the usual thugs. No, there's an air of neuroticism about him which makes him perfect for what I have in mind.

We keep walking, the guard's footsteps echoing down the corridor. He's quiet, avoiding eye contact, probably trying to keep his pulse steady. I enjoy it. These men, the ones with the keys and the power, know exactly who they're dealing with.

Finally, we arrive at the interview room. He unlocks the door, pushing it open with a tiny creak. I step inside, and my eyes adjust to the lighting in the familiar setting.

"Finally some freedom," I murmur under my breath, sitting down and casually crossing my legs. "Now be a good boy and turn off the cameras. It's part of my arrangement with the doctor. Don't make me repeat myself."

The guard stiffens, his face paling as he swallows down whatever objections he had. He nods once and steps out of the room, presumably heading to shut down the cameras.

Geneva's holding up her end of the bargain. I have to give her credit for that. Despite everything, she's still playing the game. Anger only makes her more determined.

I glance up at the corner of the room. The red light flickers once, twice, and then goes dark.

That's my girl.

I lean back in my chair, a slow smile curling at the corners of my mouth. The camera is off. No witnesses. No barriers between us. Perfect.

Geneva storms in, slamming the door behind her with a force that echoes through the room. Her hair is pulled back haphazardly, strands falling loose around her face in a way that makes her look exhausted but oh so feminine. She's in rumpled clothes, consisting of baggy sweatpants and an old hoodie that's frayed at the cuffs. This is the kind of outfit that says she's running on too little sleep and even less patience.

She puts the "hot" in "hot mess."

I fold my arms and give her a once-over, letting my gaze linger just a second too long on her breasts. "Rough night?"

She strides toward me, her steps quick and her chest heaving. Her emotions are written all over her face. The tightness in her jaw, and the cold fire burning in her eyes. *Fury.* Controlled, yes, but it's there all the same. And it's beautiful. Like her.

She stops just shy of the table, glaring down at me through the glass, her fingers flexing like she's trying to decide whether to throttle me or stay professional. "You motherfucker."

A laugh bursts from me. "I must say, Doc, I'm really enjoying the verbal foreplay. Insult me again. I like it."

"Cut the shit, Ghost. You killed him."

I blink, feigning innocence. "Who are you talking about?"

She takes a deep breath, but her composure is fraying at the edges. "Don't insult my intelligence. I know what you did." She flicks her gaze to the cameras before looking at me. "You all but confessed in your texts."

God, she's magnificent when she's like this. We both know I did it, but she's still trying to keep herself in check. It's pointless and yet, it doesn't fail to turn me on.

"Well," I say, leaning forward, "I made sure my message got across."

Geneva bristles at my words, clenching her hands into fists at her sides. I catch the slightest tremble in her fingers before she forces them to relax.

"Why, Ghost?"

I sit back, watching her, enjoying the way she's wrestling with herself. She's not just angry because Mason's dead. She knows I did it for her.

"Why?" I repeat, raising an eyebrow. "Because he touched you. And that's unacceptable."

"You don't get to decide who touches me."

"Oh, but I do." My voice is calm, steady, even as I lower it to a whisper. "He touched what belongs to me. *You*. And I don't tolerate that, Dr. Andrews. Not ever."

"You don't own me," she says through gritted teeth. "I'm not your property."

I smirk, relaxing into my chair. "We both know that's not true. You may not like it, but you belong to me in ways you can't even begin to imagine."

I study her for a long moment, savoring her righteous indignation. "Mason was weak. He hurt you because you let him think he could. I simply corrected that mistake."

Her eyes flash with something…anger, disgust, or maybe even guilt. But she doesn't break. She finally sits down. "I don't need you to protect me, Ghost."

"I know." I give her an impish grin. "Mason told me about the baseball bat."

Geneva freezes for a fraction of a second, and that's all I need to see. That small hesitation tells me everything. She's still holding on to the belief that she has control in this situation, that she's above the chaos, but her reaction betrays her.

"Ah, yes," I continue, my voice low and smooth. "He didn't expect it, did he? You, standing there with that bat in your hands, ready to bash his skull in? I have to admit, the image of you like that…It's impressive. And so fucking hot."

The skin around her mouth tightens, her voice cutting through the air like a blade. "Mason was wrong for hitting me, but he didn't deserve to die."

I imitate the sound of a buzzer. "Wrong. He deserved everything I did to him and more for what he did to you."

"I wanted him out of my life, not out of this world." Geneva's gaze hardens, a dark glint flaring in her eyes as she finally loses the battle and her frustration seeps through. "You think this sick gesture of loyalty will do what exactly? Make me trust you? Connect us further?"

"Connect us further," I repeat, rolling the phrase over my tongue as if savoring a fine wine. "Now that is an interesting choice of words, don't you think?"

She goes statue-still.

"Whether you want to admit it or not, Doc, we share a connection neither of us can ignore."

"If we're so connected, I would understand why you killed Mason, but I don't."

"Maybe I just enjoy killing the way other people enjoy video games? Or maybe, it was for you. To show you that I don't like disobedience." I pause, watching her reaction. "Or maybe it was for me. Because I don't share what's mine, Geneva. Not with Mason. Not with anyone."

Her mouth tightens, and for a second, I think she's going to stand up and leave. But she doesn't. She stays. My body relaxes.

"You're sick, Ghost."

"And you keep coming back," I say. "Why do you think that is? Why do you keep playing this game with me?"

Her expression hardens, but there's a flicker in her eyes, something deeper, something she won't let herself admit yet. "I need answers."

"But you didn't need the baseball bat, did you?" I ask, softening my tone. "You could've stopped him using only your mind and your education. But you wanted him to feel it. The fear. The power shift. You wanted him to know that you weren't the weak one."

"Stop," she snaps, her voice barely above a whisper, but I still detect the tremor beneath it. "You don't know anything."

I chuckle softly, leaning forward to close the space between us. "Oh, but I do. I know you, Dr. Andrews. I know that bat wasn't just a weapon. It was wrath. All Mason had to do was challenge you and…" I make a swinging motion with an invisible baseball bat, rattling the chain links on my handcuffs. "It would've been a home run, darling."

She shakes her head, refusing to look at me, her hands gripping the table harder now, her knuckles white. "Shut up."

"You enjoyed every second of that power. Watching him flinch, watching him lose control. It was euphoric."

Her gaze snaps back to mine, the fire in her eyes blazing even brighter now. "I didn't enjoy it."

"Liar."

The word hangs in the air between us, sharp and cutting. She wants to deny it, to push back against everything I'm saying. I can see the fury battling with something else—something deeper. Fear? No. Not fear. *Recognition.*

"You can't keep pretending that fire inside you doesn't exist," I say quietly, my voice losing none of its intensity. "Mason saw it. I've seen it. Now it's your turn."

CHAPTER 23

GENEVA

My chest heaves with breath as if hearing the words, however true, is a burden.

I wish I could beat the shit out of Ghost. Just once. Instead, I glare at him.

"I'm not the one who sliced into Mason and then put a candle in his mouth, you twisted fuck."

Ghost shrugs. "I carved him like a pumpkin. At least I didn't slit the sides of his mouth to put a jack-o'-lantern smile on him. I doubt you would've enjoyed that as much as me."

The grotesque image twists my stomach, but I refuse to let him see even a flicker of the disgust boiling inside me. He already knows I find this entire affair abominable.

"You think this is a joke?" I ask. "You framed me for murder, asshole. If I hadn't gone to the gym, I wouldn't have an alibi for last night. Then I'd end up right beside you in a neighboring cell."

"Don't tease me with that idea, Dr. Andrews. It's awful tempting."

"You—"

Ghost flicks his wrist in a dismissal. "I didn't frame you."

"Explain to me how you killing my ex-boyfriend, shortly after I had an altercation with him, didn't lead the police to my front door this morning?"

"Let's start at the beginning, shall we?" He cranes his neck from side to side, stretching it. When he meets my stare, his gaze is hard, focused. "I told you to stay home last night. I also told you that if you didn't do as I asked, there would be irreversible consequences. Death is pretty permanent, no?"

I jump to my feet. "Are you saying Mason's death is *my* fault?"

"Are you saying you didn't disobey me?"

"You—"

"Listen, Dr. Andrews, and listen well. When I give an order, it's not a suggestion. I expect to be obeyed. Remember that."

"Fuck you."

After spinning on my heel, I make my way to the door, my entire body shaking. Ghost's voice gives me pause, but I don't turn around.

"Did you really think I would let anything happen to you?" He says it gently, softly. If I didn't know better, I'd venture to say lovingly. But I do know better. "Do you actually believe I didn't know you would do the opposite of what I said?" he continues, his tone hardening. "This entire event is a result of your choices. Make better ones next time."

"There won't be a next time," I snap.

"Yes, there will. Your parents' murderers are still out there, and justice has yet to be served."

His words hit me like a punch to the gut, and I stiffen, my knuckles turning white as I grip the door handle. I don't want to turn around, don't want to give him the satisfaction of seeing how deeply his words wreck me.

"Think, Dr. Andrews," Ghost says, his tone eerily calm. "You're here because of a choice you made, and every choice from here will either pull you further from the truth or push you closer to insanity. Mason was just the beginning. You're in this now, whether you want to be or not."

I turn, anger simmering in every fiber of my being as I meet his gaze, unflinching. "You think I'm here because I want to be?" I laugh bitterly. "I never asked for this. I didn't ask for you to barge into my life, twisting everything until it's unrecognizable."

Ghost leans back, his expression unreadable, though a faint glint of amusement lingers in his eyes. "Maybe not. But people like you and me...we're driven by something darker, something that won't allow us to walk away." He tilts his head, studying me with that unsettling intensity. "You want answers, don't you? About your parents, about what happened to them. I can give you those answers, but not if you keep fighting me."

I shake my head, clenching my fists. "You're delusional if you think I'll ever trust you."

"All in good time."

"Never."

"Never say never, Dr. Andrews."

I take one last look at him and then I leave, slamming the door behind me. But as I walk away, his voice echoes in my mind, an insidious reminder that maybe, just maybe, he's right.

I will come back.

The hot water cascades down my back in rivulets, tracing lines along my body as I stand completely still under the shower in my apartment. The heat seeps into my fatigued muscles, attempting to loosen them, but to no avail. I've never come away from an interaction with Ghost with the ability to relax afterward.

Stress is synonymous with his name. Along with sensuality.

I close my eyes and will the water to wash away everything.

His beautiful face.

His haunting voice.

His provoking words.

All three dance along my senses, imaginary yet more real than the water heating my skin. And just as scorching. Little by little, Ghost is melting my defenses.

I let my head fall forward until it lands against the tiled wall with a muffled thud. The water continues streaming, and my mind continues churning. I take a deep breath and release it slowly, trying to quiet my thoughts.

What in the hell is wrong with me?

I'm the psychologist, the one who's supposed to have the answers. The one who guides others through darkness to enlightenment. But it's me who's stumbling along the path of self-discovery as Ghost drags me further along.

I know what's happening. Every tactic. Every bit of manipulation. But that doesn't mean Ghost's influence isn't wrapping around me, constricting me while setting me free at the same time.

Maybe he's not the only one who's crazy.

I've interacted with psychopaths before, men who tested my patience and my ability to remain unemotional. But with Ghost, I've lost both. He isn't just challenging my personal boundaries...he's rewriting them. Expanding them, to include himself.

The mere thought sends a chill through me, combating the warmth of the water as my skin prickles. I turn off the shower and step from it to quickly grab a towel. Then I wrap it around my body as if it'll shield me from my insidious musings.

"He touched what belongs to me. You. And I don't tolerate that, Dr. Andrews. Not ever."

Ghost's words echo relentlessly in my mind, forcing me to grip the edge of the counter. His possessiveness was something I dismissed at first, assuming it was nothing more than a ploy to assert control over me. But as I stand here, alone with only silence as my companion, a realization settles over me, making my legs shake.

Ghost isn't just mad at Mason. He's mad at *me*. Because I didn't defend myself the way he thinks I should've and it ended with me getting hurt.

But most of all, Ghost is furious with himself. For not being there. For failing to protect me as if I'm the most precious thing in his life.

I hang my head, my chest tightening with every breath. With every heartbeat. No one has ever cared about me like this. No one has ever viewed my pain as a personal affront to them. It's a toxic possessiveness. Undoubtedly. But the intensity of it—of being someone's singular obsession, their reason for rage and vengeance—is unlike anything I've ever witnessed, let alone experienced.

"Did you really think I would let anything happen to you?"

Ghost's voice slides over my mind like silk, a caress to my psyche. It's as though he's right next to me, whispering in the stillness. Into my soul.

His words carry a depraved devotion, an assurance that no

matter what happens, he would never let harm come to me if it were within his control. And for someone like him, a man who has no limits, no fear of consequences, that promise holds a terrifying weight. It's a promise that, no matter what lines he has to cross, no matter what darkness he has to invoke, he will ensure that I am safe.

The idea of this makes me feel…valued. Cherished.

This feeling exposes a need that's woven into the very fabric of who I am. A need that I've buried under layers of control and competence. However, in this moment, Ghost's words are pulling back those layers. This is what he does, cutting into the most raw parts of me without hesitation. Without mercy.

My parents, due to their unexpected absence, were never able to make me feel this way. I was a child, lost in the chaos of life, constantly trying to fill the hole their deaths created. I grew up telling myself that I didn't need protection from another, that I was strong enough to handle anything alone. And I am.

But Ghost believes I'm important. Irreplaceable. He would paint the world red with the blood of my enemies, if it meant keeping me safe. This promise of security, although coated in violence, is something my parents couldn't give me.

And it's something I desperately want.

At this realization the trembling in my legs intensifies until I'm sinking to the floor, unable to stand. With my back pressed against the wall, I wrap my arms around my legs and rest my chin on my knees, praying for some unknown entity to hear me. To rescue me from Ghost.

And myself.

I don't know how long I sit there, curled on the floor as Ghost's promise envelops me, fills me with a sense of worth I can't ignore.

It's wrong, and so many levels of fucked-up, but in the quiet corners of my mind, it feels right.

It's what I've been missing.

Eventually, I take a shuddering breath and push to my feet, swaying before steadying myself. My body is weak, hollowed out by the intensity of everything he's revealing in me.

My steps to the bedroom are slow and heavy. Reaching into my dresser, I pull out a worn pair of pajamas, soft cotton that offers a bit of comfort. I change without thinking, the movements mechanical, as if dressing in something familiar might soothe me a little.

I flick my eyes to the window, noting the sun shining brightly between the closed blinds. It's not even noon, but I can't imagine interacting with anyone while successfully pretending to be the collected, put-together person I've always been. Instead, I crawl under the blankets with a sigh.

My body sinks into the mattress, my muscles finally loosening. I stare at the ceiling until my gaze drifts across the room, catching on the small stuffed elephant sitting on my dresser. Its faded fur and beady eyes are a reminder of another time.

A reminder of what I've lost.

After getting to my feet, I retrieve the item and hug it to my chest, fighting tears of both exhaustion and sorrow. I return to the bed and tuck the elephant under the covers, and then lightly squeeze its worn body.

A wave of nostalgia washes over me as I remember my father giving it to me, his smile warm when he placed it in my waiting arms. I was so young then, barely able to comprehend the world around me, let alone the complexities of safety and danger. Life and death.

My parents, both humanitarians, had taken me to Africa, a journey filled with purpose and hope, even if I was too young to understand its significance. I remember the smell of the sun-baked earth, the kindness of the people they helped, along with the laughter and stories they shared under starlit skies.

They were so full of goodness. And yet, despite all their compassion, they couldn't shield me from fate: their unexpected deaths, followed by the void they left behind.

"An elephant never forgets." My dad smiles in my memory. *"So never forget how much we love you."*

"I wish I could forget," I whisper in the emptiness. "Maybe it wouldn't hurt so much."

A tear slips down my cheek. I hastily wipe it away, but another appears. I squeeze the stuffed elephant tighter and bury my face in its fur, clutching this small remnant of them until past and present collide.

Until my parents' love is a distant memory and Ghost's obsession for me is all that remains.

CHAPTER 24

GHOST

Geneva is a worthy adversary.

It's been a week since she last visited or texted me back. Seven days of silence, no matter how many different numbers I use to contact her, or how many provoking messages I send.

It's fucking frustrating. But I admire the strength of her resistance.

After she confronted me over Mason's death, I thought I'd pushed too hard. Dug too deep. But Geneva, however rattled, didn't break.

Even so, it's time for a change in strategy.

I sit up on my bed at the sound of footsteps approaching. The gait is distinct, a familiar cadence with a subtle drag every third step. There's a slight hitch in the rhythm that most wouldn't notice.

Ah, the perks of being a genius.

Duncan Carr is his name, the guard that drags his left foot. I clocked that when I first arrived and stored that tidbit of information, along with every other observation I've made about this place and the men inside it.

The uneven gait is the result of an old injury, most likely picked up on the job. Carr tries to hide the discomfort, but every time he steps down on it, the skin around his mouth tightens. All it would take is one well-placed kick and he'd go down faster than a prostitute getting on her knees for a dollar.

Most people don't understand just how much they reveal in the smallest, unguarded moments of their lives.

Carr appears outside my cell a moment later. The package in his hands is at odds with the masculinity of this place and the man holding it. The box is a pure white, decorated with a Bordeaux-colored ribbon that's gathered into a large, voluminous bow on top. To complete the look, there's an ivory card, snuggled underneath the strips of silk.

"You have a package," Carr says.

I offer a lascivious grin. "Oh, boy, do I."

"Not *that* kind of package, you pervert."

"Rude."

The guard lifts the box. "This one."

When I make no move to retrieve the delivered item, Carr frowns. "What is this anyway? You going to tell me?"

I shrug, taking on a neutral expression. "That depends... Are you going to come with me to deliver it?"

Carr grips the box a little too hard. The ribbon flutters with the movement, the deep Bordeaux bow absurdly out of place against the backdrop of cold metal and grim concrete.

He frowns. "Deliver it?"

"I didn't stutter."

"You think this is funny?" he asks, a thread of nervousness weaving its way into his tone.

"Funny?" I give him my best wide-eyed innocent look. "Not

at all, Officer Carr. Just trying to gauge how far your job description tion extends. Carrying my little gift all the way to its intended recipient? That's above and beyond the call of duty, don't you think?"

He shifts his weight, the faint drag of his left foot betraying him once again. "Your recipient better be in this prison, or I'll—"

I shoot to my feet. "Or you'll what?"

Carr jerks back at my sudden movement, his eyes widening with alarm. Before he can fully process the idea of me threatening him, I rush to the door with a speed that makes him suck in a breath of disbelief. The sound of my palms slapping metal as I grip the bars is sharp and his gaze snaps to my hands.

A costly mistake.

"Or you'll *what*?" I repeat, my voice low, dangerous, curling around him like a noose.

When he shifts his weight, his focus still on my hands, I lift and extend my leg through the bars. The sole of my boot now rests against his left shin, right below the knee on the spot where his old wound lingers, an unspoken weakness.

The second I apply pressure, his composure shatters. Carr's face twists in pain, and he stumbles back, the box in his hands nearly slipping from his grip.

"Be careful," I say, my tone laced with amusement as he struggles to right himself. "Wouldn't want you to drop that. It's fragile, you know."

Carr's breathing quickens, his shoulders heaving as he regains his balance, but the damage is done. He's not looking at me with the usual disdain, but with something deeper. Fear. Not the kind that keeps you up at night, but the kind that makes you piss yourself before you start sobbing.

"Do you really believe you have authority over me?" I tilt my head. "Do you think these bars will protect you? That I can't get to you whenever I want? I wouldn't make that mistake again, if I were you."

Carr doesn't acknowledge my threat with a verbal response, but the nod he gives me is enough. His submission has been acquired.

He thrusts the package through the bars, his voice tight. "Here."

I take it with deliberate slowness, brushing my fingers against his as I pull it into my grasp. He flinches at the contact, stepping back quickly, his left leg dragging more than usual as he retreats. I smile, watching the way he hurries to put distance between us.

"Wait. I need a pen."

The guard stops. It's against the rules, but after my demonstration of power, we both know they don't apply to me.

He nods. "I'll get you one."

"Thanks, Carr," I call after him, my tone light, almost cheerful. "You've been such a big help. Really above and beyond."

He doesn't respond, just keeps walking with his shoulders stiff and his footsteps echoing unevenly down the corridor. I watch him until he's out of sight, then turn my attention to the box in my hands. The ribbon is soft beneath my fingers and the scent of magnolia seeps through the packaging to waft under my nose.

I walk over to my bed and sit down before opening the box with care. Inside lies the candle I ordered, white and pristine, the wax so smooth it practically gleams. I run my finger along the surface and the scent intensifies, making me smile.

This candle is a more personal approach to luring Geneva back to me. It'll be a soft but undeniable reminder of my presence, something she'll breathe in with every flicker of the flame.

I set the candle back in its box, wrapping it in the folds of Bordeaux ribbon, draping the rich silk around it like a garment. Once the packaging is restored, I get to my feet and walk to the door.

"Officer Carr," I sing-song. "Hurry up. I have shit to do."

CHAPTER 25

GENEVA

SARAH AND I SETTLE INTO THE BACKSEAT OF THE RIDE SHARE. THE hum of the engine vibrates through the seats as the driver pulls onto the quiet street. The air smells of the spicy dish Sarah insisted I try tonight, clinging to our clothes, a reminder of the good food and even better company.

The city is dark, dotted with the warm glow of streetlights and passing headlights. Despite the calm surrounding me, there's a tightness in my chest, one I've been trying to ignore all evening. Sarah's been good at keeping me distracted, but the silence between us now allows my thoughts to creep back in.

André Bisset and Luis Dominguez.

Their names have been replaying in my mind like a broken record since the moment Ghost gave them to me. I looked them up, using every government database at my disposal. Tools I wasn't supposed to touch for something this personal, making every keystroke a gamble, a risk to my job.

And what did I find?

Nothing.

Not a single record. No criminal histories, no financial ties, nothing in the databases I've trusted for years. These men are ghosts, just like the man who gave me their names.

The disappointment lingers, a constant ache in the pit of my stomach. I can't decide if it's the failure itself or the thought that Ghost might have been lying. Maybe this was all just another game to him, another way to fuck with me.

I glance out the window, the streetlights casting fleeting shadows across my face. My reflection stares back at me, distorted in the glass, and I wonder for the hundredth time if asking Ghost for information was worth this heartache.

Yes. I'll chase any lead if there's even the smallest chance it will bring me closer to the truth behind my parents' murders. No matter what it does to me emotionally.

Sarah snaps her fingers in front of my face, dragging me back. "Earth to Geneva. Are you listening?"

I blink, forcing a smile. "Sorry. What were you saying?"

She narrows her eyes at me but doesn't press. "I was saying you need to loosen up. Seriously, when's the last time you had a little fun that didn't involve analyzing someone's psyche or reading some depressing case study?"

"I'm literally having fun right now," I counter, waving my hand toward her as proof.

She scoffs. "This isn't just fun. This is fun *and* me dragging you out of your self-imposed hermit hole for some basic human interaction. Bare minimum, Geneva."

"Harsh." I roll my eyes, but her words hit closer than I'd like to admit. She's not wrong. Lately, my life has felt like an endless cycle of work and avoidance, as if I'm trying to outrun something. Or someone.

"Okay, let me rephrase," she says, her voice softening. "I miss you. Like, really miss you. You've been…distant. Even for you. And that's saying a lot."

I bite the inside of my cheek, guilt tugging at the edges of my thoughts. "I know. I'm sorry. Things have just been…a lot."

Sarah reaches over and squeezes my hand, her warmth cutting through the chill that's been following me. "I know, but don't let those things stop you from living your life. You deserve to be happy."

"Thank you."

"And nothing brings joy like shopping." She grabs her phone, scrunching her forehead in concentration. "By the way, you still haven't picked a dress. What about this one? It says, 'sexy professional that wants to get bent over a desk,' but without being too slutty."

I laugh, not only in amusement, but out of pure happiness. Tonight is the first time that my best friend has acted like her old self. The person she was before the assault.

"Try again, but with less skin showing."

"You're no fun. Okay, hear me out. This one." She tilts her phone toward me. The dress is sleek, floor-length, and emerald green, with just the right balance of elegance and edge.

I glance at it and shake my head. "Too bold."

"Too bold?" Sarah's jaw drops as if I've just insulted her personally. "You're literally the keynote speaker for one of the biggest fundraising events of the year. You're the university's *star alumna*, Geneva. You need bold. You're not supposed to blend into the background like you do at work in that depressing office of yours."

"First of all, ouch. Second, I'm not trying to blend in," I say, my voice soft but firm. "I just don't want to look like I'm trying too hard."

She smacks my leg and looks at me as if I'm the one who just slapped her. "Trying too hard? You're going to stand in front of a room full of high-profile donors, alumni, and university hotshots because they're basically worshipping you for being the only person who's ever created a psych profile on *him*." She lowers her voice on the last word, leaning in closer like we're swapping secrets. "I mean, come on. Own it."

I shift in my seat, glancing out the window as the city lights streak past. "It's not just about Ghost. They're asking me to talk about my work in general. Convictions, profiles, and how psychology intersects with criminal justice. Those types of things."

Sarah rolls her eyes dramatically. "Puh-lease. They're asking you because you've put away, what? Thirty? Forty criminals? And because you're the only person in the world who's had a front-row seat to the inside of that psycho's mind." She pokes me lightly in the arm, grinning. "Face it, bestie, you're a big deal."

"I'm not—" I sigh, cutting myself off before I can finish the sentence. There's no point in arguing. Sarah's right. The university has made it clear that my keynote isn't just about my achievements as a criminal psychologist; it's about my connection to *him*. Ghost. The man whose mind I dissected and mapped like some dark, endless labyrinth.

Except I never finished the psych profile.

And I won't.

"They don't even care about the speech," I murmur, more to myself than to Sarah. "They care about the name attached to it. Ghost's name is more than famous. It's legendary now."

"They asked you because you've worked your ass off." Sarah softens, the note of teasing in her voice fading. "You've earned this. Yes, the Ghost thing is part of it, but it's not the whole picture. Don't discredit all the work you've done. Or all the people you've helped. Including me."

Her words hit a tender spot. On impulse, I throw my arms around her. She hugs me back and pats my back as if I'm the victim. Not her.

Sarah doesn't bring it up often, but when she mentions the way I testified in court, I want to smile and throw up. Prison is too good for Frank "Skinner" Burns. The serial rapist deserves to burn in hell and have his dick cut off. Not necessarily in that order.

When Sarah was crumbling under the weight of her trauma, I was there. I helped her find her footing again, guided her through the storm she thought she'd never escape. She's always credited me for that, though I've never felt like I did anything extraordinary. Listening, supporting, or even testifying—that's what you're supposed to do for the people you care about.

In the end, Sarah's right. I've done important work that was due to my profession, and I should be recognized.

After pulling back, I exhale slowly, leaning my head against the headrest. "You're right. They're lucky to have me. I just hate public speaking."

"I'm always right. Which is why you should let me pick your dress."

"Fine."

Sarah claps her hands, releasing a tiny squeal, and I immediately regret my decision. Or I would if her face wasn't so joyful. I'd give that keynote speech butt-naked to make my best friend happy. Hopefully, she doesn't consider that as an option.

The driver clears his throat, glancing at me through the rearview mirror. "This your stop?"

I look out the window at my apartment building, the familiar silhouette looming in the dark. "Yeah." I reach for the door handle but pause, turning to Sarah. "Promise me the dress will be something appropriate."

Sarah grins, shaking her head. "Appropriate is not in my vocabulary. I'll find you something that screams, 'Professional who likes to get railed on the regular.'" She winks.

I can't help but laugh, shaking my head. "Thanks. I think."

She waves me off, but her smile is warm. "Text me later, okay? And seriously, stop underestimating yourself. You're going to kill it."

"Thanks."

I exit the car and step into the crisp night air. As the ride share pulls away, taking Sarah with it, I stand there for a moment, staring up at my building. The windows are dark, save for the glow of the one that belongs to me. Everything looks as it should, but there's an unease that crawls up my spine. It's something I've been experiencing ever since I first laid eyes on Ghost.

I shake off the unpleasant feeling and head toward the entrance. It's just nerves from thinking about the keynote. Nothing more. At least, that's what I tell myself as I walk into the elevator and press the button for my floor.

The doors slide open a minute later, and I step into the dimly lit hallway. My footsteps echo softly against the tiled floor as I make my way to my apartment, fishing my keys from my purse. I unlock the door and push it open with a sigh of relief. The familiar scent of lavender greets me, coming from the diffuser I forgot to turn off.

Everything seems normal…

I lock the door behind me and set my purse down on the counter, flicking on the rest of the lights. My apartment is quiet and peaceful. It's my sanctuary from the evil in the world that I face every day. But the longer I stand there, the more the sense of foreboding grows, until the hairs on the back of my neck prickle, and my breath catches in my throat.

Something's different.

I can't pinpoint it immediately, but the air is dense now, charged with an invisible tension. My heart rate picks up as I scan the room, my gaze darting to every corner. Finding nothing doesn't stop me from striding across the room to grab the baseball bat by the back door. Hefting it into a defensive stance, I make my way to my bedroom.

When I push the door open, I freeze.

On my bed, next to my stuffed elephant, sits a box. It's pristine and beautiful, white and tied with a maroon ribbon that gleams in the soft light of the room. My stomach drops, and my pulse roars in my ears.

Eyes locked on the package, I take a step forward, my breathing shallow. The stuffed elephant, usually perched on my dresser, has been moved. The sight of it, paired with the box, makes my hands shake and the bat wobbles in my grasp.

I approach the bed slowly and reach out on instinct but stop just short of touching the ribbon. Who sent this to me? And how in the fuck did they get into my apartment?

My first thought is Sarah. It's hopelessly naïve of me, but that doesn't stop my train of thought. She's the only person who has a key. My friend could've snuck in earlier and left this gift here to cheer me up or to celebrate my achievements.

But I know Sarah. She wouldn't do this. She knows how much I need my home to feel safe and untouched. On the off chance it was her, she wouldn't have moved the elephant.

After setting my bat on the bed, I reach down and pick up the ivory card tucked under the ribbon. My fingers tremble as I open it, the elegant script staring back at me like a taunt.

Magnolias bloom, masking death's decay.
Illuminating the shadows, where I wait.
Never let the flame that binds us fade.
Every breath you take is mine to claim.

The words blur as a wave of nausea washes over me. My knees go weak, and I sink onto the edge of the bed, clutching the card in my hands. My heart pounds against my ribs, hard and fast, as if trying to escape my chest.

He was here.

Ghost was here, in my home. In my bedroom. The thought is paralyzing, and my body stiffens although my mind races with questions I can't answer. How did he get in? How long was he here?

I glance around the room as if every shadow is alive and threatening. My breath comes in shallow pants as I clutch the card tighter, its words like a brand seared into my mind. The walls press in and the faint scent of magnolias fills the air. I hadn't noticed it before, but now it's undeniable.

My eyes dart to the corners of the room, to the closet, the curtains, the doorframe. Every creak, every distant sound from the building amplified, echoing in my ears like a war cry.

Is he still *here?*

The bat is within reach and I grab it, rising to my feet despite the unsteadiness in my legs. The card flutters to the mattress, forgotten as my survival instinct takes over. If he's here, I have to know.

The closet is my first choice. I slowly open the door like there's a bomb about to detonate. And…nothing but my clothes and shoes.

I move to the bathroom next, ripping open the door with less hesitation this time. The space is empty, but that doesn't stop my heart from jumping in my throat.

"Get your shit together, Geneva," I mutter. "Ghost wouldn't have left the box if he was planning on talking to you."

I sweep through the rest of the apartment, checking every corner, every hiding place, until I'm certain there's no one here. The sense of being invaded, of having my space violated, clings to me. The magnolia scent lingers, stronger now, filling the air with its oppressive sweetness.

Back in the bedroom, I sit on the edge of the bed with the bat resting against my knees. I look at the box again, the ribbon still perfectly tied, the pristine white surface untouched. Curiosity rises, too strong for me to ignore.

"Damn it."

My hands tremble as I untie the bow and lift the lid, revealing the candle inside. It's smooth, polished, and elegant. A benign object, yet so deadly because of the giver.

"Why?" I whisper, the word barely audible over the pounding of my heart.

Ghost wouldn't send a meaningless token of affection. Everything he does has a purpose. It's part of an ongoing strategy.

This candle is a message.

So, what is he trying to tell me?

CHAPTER 26

GHOST

IT'S GO TIME!

If only I could get some popcorn for the main event.

I lean against the wall flush to my bed, my attention solely fixed on the small screen in my hand. I'm cradling the phone, not just to keep it hidden from curious glances aimed at my cell, but because it's my only link to Geneva.

The camera outside her building flickers to life as the ride share pulls up to the curb and my skin prickles. I don't need the grainy image to tell me she's arrived, since I was notified the moment her location pinged nearby. Still, I watch as she steps out of the vehicle, hungry for the sight of her.

My cell is musty and cold, but that doesn't matter. Not with the way my blood heats whenever I look at Geneva. Even the stale air around me now vibrates with my anticipation. This might be the closest to happiness I've ever been…

Aside from the first time I saw her.

When Geneva reaches her apartment, I sit up straight, my fingers gripping the phone tightly as I watch her unlock the door. Her hesitation is subtle but there, the slightest pause before she steps inside. The second the door is locked behind her, she exhales, releasing a bit of stress.

I shift on the mattress, adjusting the brightness setting as the cameras inside her apartment flicker to life. After a quick sweep of the room, she strides to the back door, and I grin. I know what she's after. Sure enough, she grabs the baseball bat propped in the corner.

"That's my girl," I murmur.

Geneva hefts the bat in her hands, testing its weight, tightening her grip as she moves through the apartment. The rigidity of her stance and the thorough sweep of her gaze over every inch of the place is entertaining. She's preparing for a fight that isn't coming.

At least, not yet.

When she finally moves to her bedroom, my breathing accelerates, my pulse drumming an unsteady cadence. The first camera angle in this room isn't quite right, so I cycle through three more until it is. Until I can easily make out the stiffening of her body and the way her lips part on a gasp.

Her reaction is exquisite. The rush of satisfaction that slams into me is euphoric, and I groan from the pleasure. "Go ahead, Geneva," I whisper, my voice hoarse. "See what I've left for you."

When she finally sets the bat down to reach for the card, I bite my lip to keep from moaning again. Although, that doesn't stop my dick from getting hard.

Her hands tremble as she unfolds the note, her lips moving silently as she reads my poem. Watching her unravel, caught between fear and anger, is perfection. I love the way her fingers tighten around the card right before her knees buckle and she sinks onto the mattress. I love the way she stares at the parchment in desperation, every fiber of her being dying to know why I left it and what it all means.

If she wants answers, she'll have to come to me.

Geneva grabs the bat and jumps to her feet. She moves like a ghost herself, quiet, methodical, scanning her apartment for threats she'll never find. It's fascinating, really, how she's caught between instinct and reason, how her mind tries to rationalize what her gut already knows...

I was there.

The camera allows me to follow her through every space until she returns to her bedroom and opens the box. She doesn't destroy the candle. I knew she wouldn't. She's too curious, too tied to the connection she refuses to acknowledge. Instead, she sets it down carefully, like she's afraid of breaking it, and clutches the card tightly.

"Why?" Her voice is barely audible, but I don't need sound to know it's filled with frustration.

I watch as she sits there, the bat forgotten at her side. The candle, the card, the scent—they're all pieces of me, woven into her home, her life, her very breath. A satisfied smile spreads across my face. They're not just a message. They're a promise.

Geneva is mine.

The need to touch her gnaws at me, but I shove it aside. Patience is the result of control. And control means knowing when to wait. I may not be able to fuck Geneva yet, but that doesn't mean it's not time for the next step in my plan.

∽

The clanging of metal echoes through the corridor, jolting me from my thoughts of Geneva. The sound grows louder as someone approaches my cell. I don't need to look up to know who it is. The rhythm of the steps and the faint drag of a worn sole tell me it's Officer Jennings. A man who prides himself on his authority but who's insecure enough to overcompensate with posturing.

Although if we had a dick-measuring contest, he'd cry for sure.

When Jennings reaches my cell, he pauses, one hand gripping the bars while the other rests on the baton at his hip. He's stocky, with a gut that spills over his belt, and a face that's permanently red from alcohol consumption. His uniform is crisp, but his boots are scuffed and muddy. Attention to detail is only plausible when it suits him.

"Yard time," he says. "Don't make me regret it."

A slow, easy smile spreads across my face. "You're hurting my feelings, Jennings. When have I been problematic?"

His eyes narrow, a flicker of annoyance crossing his face. "Don't play games with me. We both know you've got a reputation."

"Reputation?" I press a hand to my chest, feigning offense. "I'm nothing if not a model inmate."

Jennings snorts, glancing down the corridor to make sure no one else is listening. "Model inmate, my ass. I'm letting you out because it's protocol, but the second you do anything sketchy, I'm throwing your ass in the hole."

Here's the thing about Jennings...he talks tough, but he's easy to read. The way his fingers twitch near the baton and the way his gaze darts to the corners of the room when he thinks I might be watching too closely tells me he's scared. Not enough to keep him from doing his job, but enough to put him on edge. He's not afraid of a riot or a fight.

He's afraid of me.

And I intend to keep it that way.

"I'll behave," I say smoothly, rising and sauntering over to the door. "Scout's honor."

"You're no boy scout," he mutters, unlocking the door and stepping back quickly, keeping a safe distance as I walk out. "Don't do anything stupid. You don't want to test me."

I flash him another smile, this one colder. "Oh, Jennings. You act like I wouldn't kill you just for the fun of it."

He doesn't respond, just jerks his head toward the corridor. I follow, my pace measured, my hands loose at my sides. He's watching me closely, his body tense, ready to intervene at the first sign of trouble.

As we step into the yard, the air shifts. It's charged, but what else can you expect when there's a large group of murderers gathered? Inmates linger in small clusters, their voices low and their gazes sharp. The sun beats down on cracked concrete and deadened grass, and the smell of sweat clings to everything.

I scan the space, my gaze slipping over the clusters of inmates with practiced ease. They're predictable, every group adhering to their roles: the posturing thugs, the opportunists watching for weakness, and the loners who think invisibility equals safety.

Off in the far corner is a lanky, wide-eyed inmate who's pacing, his boots trampling the grass underneath. His movements are methodical, almost rhythmic, and his fingers twitch as he walks, like he's counting steps or running calculations in his head.

Hello again, Junior.

I watch him for a moment longer, my mind already working. He's perfect for what I have planned. Someone like him doesn't need to be threatened. This guy just needs the right kind of pressure, the right kind of promise.

"Jennings," I say without looking at the guard. "You can relax now. I'm just here to enjoy the fresh air."

He grunts in response, but I can feel his gaze on me, his skepticism hanging in the air like a challenge. Let him doubt me. Let him watch. By the time I'm finished, he won't even realize he's part of the plan too.

For now, though, my focus is on Junior. This one's not a fighter by choice. He's cerebral, but not in a way that makes him immune to manipulation. In fact, it makes him ideal.

Junior's anxiety is a tangible thing, wrapping around him like a shroud. It's in the way his shoulders hunch and how his gaze darts to every shadow as though expecting something to leap out at him. He's already trapped in his own mind.

I approach slowly, unhurried, as though I'm just taking in the sun like everyone else. Junior glances up as I draw closer, his eyes locking onto mine for half a second before darting away.

"Afternoon," I say smoothly, keeping my tone light. I stop a few feet away, close enough to get his attention but far enough not to spook him.

Junior slows his pacing but doesn't stop. "What do you want?" His voice is low and guarded. He doesn't look at me again, his focus shifting to the ground as his fingers wiggle at his sides.

I let out a soft chuckle, crossing my arms. "Relax, Junior. I'm not here to hurt you. Quite the opposite, actually."

His jaw tightens at my nickname for him, but he doesn't correct me. That's good. He's pliable, even if he doesn't realize it yet. "I'm not interested." He picks up his pace, his movements more erratic now.

I step closer, just enough to cut into his path, forcing him to stop. He stiffens, his gaze darting to the groups of inmates scattered across the yard as though looking for an escape.

"Someone's been messing with your stuff, haven't they?" I say.

His head snaps up, his wide eyes brightening with suspicion. "What are you talking about?"

"You've noticed it, haven't you?" I tilt my head, studying him. "The way your stuff has been moved, your space violated. The books with missing pages, so you can't fully understand the text. Then there's that note you found yesterday."

His lips part, a flicker of surprise crossing his face before he schools his expression. "How do you—"

"Let's just say I notice things. I also see patterns, Junior. And the pattern here? Someone's fucking with you."

He swallows hard, his fingers twitching again as he looks away. "I don't know what you're talking about."

"Don't play dumb," I say, my tone sharpening just enough to pierce through his denial. "You've felt it. The looks. The whispers. They're closing in, and you're running out of time."

I take a step back, giving him space to process. It's important not to crowd him. Not yet.

"Why are you telling me this?" He looks around, eyes widening. "Are you trying to help me?"

I scoff. "Hell no. I'm a selfish asshole."

"Then why?"

"Because I don't want Jennings to get what he's after."

"Jennings?" he repeats, the confusion in his voice tinged with growing unease.

I nod slowly. "Yeah, Jennings. You think he's a man who only cares about the job and none of the *perks*? Open your eyes, Junior. The man's been singling you out since day one. All those 'random' checks? The extra time in the laundry detail? The way he stares at you? That's not coincidence."

His breathing quickens. "Why?"

"Because he sees you as weak. And weakness is easy to exploit. Jennings is no different from the assholes out here in the yard. He just wears a uniform and hides behind his badge. Trust me, he wants you scared and isolated, so he can use you however he wants."

Junior's eyes dart to the far end of the yard where Jennings stands, his posture casual, but his gaze sweeps back and forth. As if on cue, the guard looks over at us. When his eyes briefly land on Junior, the young man stiffens next to me.

"See?" I whisper. "He's looking right at you. *Again*. What a fucking pervert."

Junior swallows hard, his Adam's apple bobbing as his gaze flickers back to me. Paranoia is such a pliable thing. A masterpiece in the hands that mold it.

"See?" I repeat, keeping my voice low. "He's not subtle."

"I—I never noticed," Junior stammers.

"That's the point. You're not supposed to notice. You're supposed to think it's just in your head."

I rock back on my heels and glance down when something glints in the sunlight. A penny lies at the edge of the concrete, dull and scuffed but unmistakably out of place in the barrenness of the yard. I bend down, picking it up between my fingers, and let out a soft chuckle. Junior flinches at the sound, his nerves already frayed.

"Funny thing about pennies," I muse, turning it over in my hand. "They're everywhere, but most people don't bother picking them up anymore. Too insignificant. Too worthless."

Junior frowns, his unease briefly giving way to confusion. "What does that have to do with anything?"

I hold the penny up, letting the light catch it for just a moment before I slip it into my pocket. "People underestimate the little things, Junior. The ones they think don't matter. But they can change everything."

His brow furrows, but I don't give him time to respond. I step away, turning toward the other side of the yard with a casual wave of my hand.

"Watch your back," I call over my shoulder. "And don't drop the soap."

CHAPTER 27

GHOST

I REPRESS A LAUGH AS I WALK AWAY FROM JUNIOR.

Manipulating him was too easy. The lack of challenge would be off-putting if I didn't need him. That young man is a clusterfuck of anxiety and psychosis, wrapped in paranoia. Basically, he's an explosive waiting to detonate...and I've lit the fuse.

With a smile, I head toward the bleachers and shove my hands in my pockets. My fingers brush the penny, the cool metal a reminder of the tasks ahead of me. All of them leading to having Geneva in my grasp.

Heavy footsteps reach me, the grass underneath his boots failing to muffle his gait entirely. I stop, but I don't turn around to confront the man following me. Not only is my behavior dismissive, but it shows that I don't consider him enough of a threat to face him.

"What do you want, Skinner?"

Frank "Skinner" Burns stops walking, his voice dripping with mockery that's as oily as his hair. "I wanted to meet the famous Ghost."

"If by 'meet me,' you mean you want to put your dick in my ass, you can forget it." I look at him over my shoulder with my brows raised. "Exit only, bro."

His face contorts, his eyes turning black with malice. Although he leans toward me, he won't attack. I haven't pissed him off enough. And he hasn't finished delivering his message.

Even so, he's afraid of me.

I would be too. I'm fucking crazy. Not to mention, my intelligence supersedes his. It's embarrassing, really.

"Shut the fuck up," Skinner says.

"Really? That's the best you can come up with?" I roll my eyes and turn to face him. "You're a rapist, a man used to taking what he wants. Are you pissed because you're the one who's getting fucked without consent now? That's pretty hypocritical."

Skinner clenches his fists and the veins in his neck throb, rapidly pulsing against the skin.

Hmm … looks like I struck a nerve.

I quickly run my gaze over him, taking in every detail, every nuance of his body language. The ink on his forearm snatches my attention, giving me the most insight into my opponent. The tattoo is a vine that coils around his arm, with thorns that "pierce" the skin, drawing blood.

Interesting.

"I don't need consent," he says. "They all give it to me willingly."

"Sure, Skinner. Sell your bullshit to someone else 'cause I'm not buying it." I turn to walk away but stop at his next words.

"She'll be the next one begging me to fuck her."

My entire body tenses with rage. It's as though every inch of my skin is stretching, building with the need to act, to annihilate this motherfucker. The very idea of Skinner touching Geneva fills me with such disgust that I can barely fucking talk.

"*Don't.*" The word comes out quiet, but it's full of warning.

"I heard you were Dr. Andrews's new assignment. I know she's been spending a lot of time here, seeing you." Skinner gives me a sly smile. "Maybe I'll *see* her too."

I draw in a deep breath, battling my wrath as it washes over me, burning me from the inside. I weigh the pros and cons of ending his life right now. Unfortunately, his death could prevent me from seeing Geneva the next time she visits. While I might not be able to attack him, that doesn't mean I can't destroy him right now.

And murder him later.

"Did she mention me in any of your sessions?" Skinner asks. "We have history, you know."

When I release a deep breath, I'm completely in control, a master of my murdering tendencies. And ready to fuck him up.

I smile. His gaze flicks to my scar, the way it's pulled taut, making it grotesque. Then he looks me in the eyes. Whatever he sees there has his pupils contracting.

"No, Dr. Andrews didn't mention you." I wave a hand in dismissal. "We're always too busy talking about shit that's actually important."

"She'll mention me soon enough."

I maintain my smile while grinding my molars. "You should have a session with her. It'd be good for you to talk about how you're a closet homosexual who rapes women to hide the fact."

He jerks back, his dark hair gliding along his shoulders. "What the fuck are you talking about?"

"Your tattoo. It represents your issues."

"No, it's not—"

"Vines are associated with entrapment. Being bound and powerless, the way you feel about your urges." I purse my lips in thought. "The thorns are the deeply rooted pain you experienced both mentally and emotionally. Someone must've found out and ridiculed you for it. And the blood…That's my favorite tell. It's shame. You want to bleed onto your victims so they're smeared with it too, and you're not alone with your humiliation."

I lean toward him, my tone filled with the same darkness that haunts him. "In reality, Skinner, that tattoo isn't a warning for people not to come near. It's a mural showing how fucked up you are."

His breath comes out hard and fast, like he's just run a marathon. The whites of his eyes are stark, and his pupils are blown wide with horror and fury.

I straighten, smiling once again. There are many ways to fuck with a person, and this is one of the more enjoyable methods.

Skinner moves with a burst of rage, his fists swinging wildly as he closes the distance between us. I step back, sidestepping his first blow with ease, my movements fluid and controlled. He's all energy and no strategy.

"Is that all you've got, Skinner?" I ask when his knuckles whistle past my face. "I'm thinking it's more challenging to fight someone that you can't overpower with brute force."

His growl is guttural, animalistic, as he lunges again. His fist grazes my ribs but does little more than stroke my amusement. I'm lighter on my feet, faster, and I know how to use his emotions against him.

A glint of metal winks at me as his hand dips to his waistband. It's a crude, jagged piece of steel wrapped in jagged cloth, that's aimed at my torso. A shiv.

Well, fuck.

I pivot sharply, the blade missing its mark but slicing into my biceps. I grunt with pain, blood now clinging to the fabric of my sleeve. Skinner snarls, emboldened by the hit, and comes at me again, slashing wildly. Men from all over the yard rush toward us, including both inmates and security guards.

"Temper, temper." I sing-song, keeping my amused expression despite the burning in my arm. I duck under his next swing. The crowd around us roars now, a mix of jeers and cheers, their energy feeding Skinner's frenzy.

I stay on the defensive, my steps light as I sidestep and dodge. Skinner's blows grow more erratic, his movements fueled by pure rage and diminishing energy.

"Do they know?" I ask, ducking another wild swing. "Does your crew know that you're attracted to men? That you only target women because you're not strong enough to rape a man?"

His scream is primal as he throws everything into his next strike. I sidestep, spinning out of his reach, and he stumbles forward, his momentum betraying him.

"Enough!" Jennings's voice booms across the chaos and the yard erupts with the sound of additional guards rushing in. The crowd scatters as they arrive with weapons raised.

Skinner, still heaving with fury, steps toward me before a guard grabs him by the collar and yanks him backward. "On the ground, now!" the officer barks, slamming Skinner against the dirt.

Jennings appears next to me, his eyes narrowing as he takes in the blood seeping through my sleeve. "You good?"

I nod. "I've had worse."

"Who started this shit?"

"Not me, obviously. Getting shanked isn't on my to-do list."

Jennings glances over, his face a mask of irritation. "Skinner, you're done. Solitary. *Now*."

Skinner thrashes as they haul him to his feet, his eyes locking onto mine with a look of pure venom. "This isn't over, Ghost!" he spits, his voice hoarse. "You hear me? I'm coming for her."

I cut him off with a lazy smirk that conceals my own rage. "I hope you do."

The guards drag him away, his shouts fading into the background as the yard slowly returns to its uneasy rhythm. I glance down at the blood on my arm, the wound shallow but messy, and let out a slow breath.

Jennings steps closer, his face a mix of suspicion and annoyance. "Care to explain what that was about?"

I shrug. "He doesn't like my sparkling personality."

"That's something I can believe."

"Rude."

Jennings jerks his chin at the main building. "Go to medical."

"Sure thing, boss."

I sit on the bleachers, trying to calm the storm raging inside my head before I go indoors and "accidentally" kill someone. Blood drips steadily from the gash, staining the dirt beneath me, but I hardly notice. Not with Skinner's words echoing in my mind...

"I'm coming for her."

My muscles tighten, and for a moment, the edges of my vision blur with anger. Skinner thought to weaponize Geneva against me. The audacity of it makes my hands shake. I cross my arms to hide their trembling.

I almost lost control.

For the first time in years, I nearly descended into full-on chaos. The idea of Skinner even *thinking* about hurting Geneva, let alone coming after her, fucked me. He wanted to provoke me, and he succeeded.

Except, Skinner doesn't understand what he's done. He's put himself on my kill list, and there's no coming back from that. The moment he brought Geneva into this, he was fucked.

I'm glad he's going into solitary. Jennings dragging him off was the best outcome I could've hoped for. Skinner will stew in there, his mind gnawing at itself, replaying today's humiliation until it consumes him.

That gives me time to prepare. And do some research.

It all started with Geneva's testimony. I knew about it when I began stalking her, but now I need to know every detail of that trial, every word she said that helped put Skinner behind bars. I want to understand the case because it'll help me uncover his triggers, which in turn will reveal his vulnerabilities. All good information to have when I kill him.

Because solitary isn't forever.

When Skinner gets out, he'll come for me again. Or worse, he'll try to make good on his threat to go after Geneva. That's *not* an option.

I glance toward the yard's gates, the world around me beginning to return to normal as my vision clears. The crowd has dispersed, the guards on edge while returning to their posts. My arm throbs, but the pain is insignificant.

I stand, brushing the dust from my pants before I head toward the medical wing. The blood staining my sleeve is a reminder, not just of the fight but of what's to come. Skinner wanted to leave a mark on me, but he only succeeded in marking himself for death.

Unlike Mason, I'm going to take my sweet time with Skinner.

The thought makes me smile, and I end up whistling all the way to the medical wing.

CHAPTER 28

GENEVA

I'VE SPENT THE PAST WEEK THINKING ABOUT GHOST'S "PRESENT," and I'm ashamed to admit that I've been using the candle as well. The scent of magnolia, for better or worse, has grown on me.

On my nightstand, the candle burns as I stare at it, sitting cross-legged on my bed. The soft glow illuminates the room, casting shadows that stretch and shift with every movement of the flame. Its presence is both haunting and familiar, like Ghost himself.

I grip the stuffed elephant tighter. He moved the toy. It was intentional. The very thought makes my hands clammy and I force myself to take a steadying breath. If that psychopath wanted to hurt me, he would've. However gruesome, that's a fact.

Then why did he place the elephant next to the box with the candle? Was it to group items from my past and present, so I'd realize they're connected? Or was it an act of dominion, Ghost's way of telling me that he can reach the deepest, most vulnerable parts of me?

It's both.

That's only one piece of the message. The magnolia-scented candle, the red ribbon on a white box, the note with a hidden acrostic…every single item tells me something. I think I finally understand.

All that's left is for me to confirm everything by visiting the source. Except I don't want to see Ghost again. Ever.

Only, he'll *never* let me go.

Blocking Ghost's number and ignoring his texts has led to him breaking into my home and violating my space. If I continue to deny him contact with me, who knows what he'll do next? For this reason—and to gain answers concerning my parents—I'm going back to the prison.

It's *only* for this reason. Not because I'm still fascinated by him or curious about what he wants from me. Not because I'm physically attracted to him or enthralled by his brilliant mind. It's certainly not because he's unlike any man, or criminal, I've ever met.

It can't be.

Or I'm the one who's insane.

After sliding from the bed, I walk over to stand in front of the mirror, assessing my appearance. The oversized sweater and leggings I've been wearing all day are the complete opposite of the way I usually dress. The professional, clean-cut and pressed suit is the armor I put on when facing Ghost.

But today that feels useless. This man has already found every chink in my armor and exploited them. So what's the point in changing my clothes?

With a sigh, I walk over to blow out the candle. The flame dances, defiant, before I take a deep breath and lean in. But just as my lips part, I notice something beneath the surface of the melted wax.

There are letters. Words.

Your time is up, Doc.

Sweat breaks out across my forehead and I wipe it away with an angry swipe of the hand. He planned this. Every step, every sentence, down to the moment I'd find this note.

My time is up? For what? The ambiguity is suffocating, but that's the point. Torture of the mind hurts more than torture of the body because it never ends.

I exhale sharply and blow out the candle, watching the wax go from translucent to opaque. Only when the threatening words are no longer visible do I move. The scent of magnolia lingers, oppressive and cloying, wrapping around me as I head for the door.

If Ghost wants to talk, then let's fucking do it.

As the guard escorts me to the interrogation room, my pulse quickens with every step. I can't understand Ghost's mind enough to predict his behavior, which means...

I can't defend myself against him.

Admitting that, even if it's only to myself, is debilitating. But it's too late to turn back now. Ghost won't let me.

The guard gestures for me to enter once we reach the door. I hesitate, my hand hovering over the handle for a fraction of a second before I push it open. The moment I step inside, I feel it: his presence.

Ghost is on his feet.

It's jarring, seeing him like that, tall and imposing on the other side of the glass. His posture is relaxed but commanding, one hand tucked casually into the pocket of his prison-issued pants, the other resting on his abdomen. He cocks his head as he watches me enter, his expression unreadable but his eyes alive with that sharp, predatory gleam I've been on the other end of more times than I can count.

I stop short, my pulse hammering against my ribs as I take him in. His gaze locks onto mine. He doesn't move, doesn't speak, but the sheer intensity of him fills the space, making it smaller.

I force myself to take another step, then another, until I'm standing at my side of the glass. The chair in front of me feels like a barrier and a trap all at once. I grip the back of it to hide my nerves.

"Dr. Andrews," Ghost says, his voice low and smooth, like velvet dragged over a blade. The sound of it makes my skin prickle with sexual awareness, and I hate how my body reacts. How it betrays me.

I remain standing, mirroring his stance to keep us on the same level. "You broke into my house."

He doesn't flinch, doesn't so much as blink. Instead, his lips curl into an impish smile. "And?" he replies, his voice dripping with amusement. "Did you like my present?"

"No."

His chuckle is low and dangerous, reverberating in the enclosed space. "The magnolia. The note. Even the message hidden under the wax. All deliberate. Tell me, how long did it take you to figure it out?"

"Some parts were more obvious than others."

He nods. "The acrostic was rather easy."

"M. I. N. E. Magnolias bloom, masking death's decay. Illuminating the shadows, where I wait. Never let the flame that binds us fade. Every breath you take is mine to claim." I roll my eyes. "So romantic."

"I thought so," he says with a grin. "Tell me what else you discovered."

"Magnolia trees were often planted in cemeteries to cover the stench of death. You chose that scent to reference my parents being dead and buried. The 'shadows where you wait' is more literal. Case in point, you broke into my apartment. Shadows can also represent the darkness that covers your mind. As for the flame that binds?" I purse my lips in thought. "You believe we share a connection that you consistently refer to as the fire inside me."

He leans forward. "And lastly?"

"My breath is yours to claim… That line makes it sound as if you want all of me, from the inessential to the vital."

"Very good, Dr. Andrews. A-plus."

"Now what?"

He quirks a brow. "Hmm?"

"You said I'm out of time. What the fuck do you want from me, Ghost?"

He gives me a wicked smile. "What do I want from you?" He shakes his head slowly, the motion controlled, his gaze never leaving mine. "I think you know the answer to that, Dr. Andrews. I've told you before."

I tighten my grip on the back of the chair. "No, I don't know. That's why I'm asking."

He takes a step closer, bringing his face within inches of the glass. The air around him is charged, like a storm about to break. His eyes are bright, the hazel molten gold.

"I want you."

The words spark something, igniting a heat that rushes through me. I suck in a breath, unable to tear my gaze away from him.

Ghost smiles, his teeth gleaming in the fluorescent light. "I want all of you. Everything."

"Forget it."

His gaze drops to my mouth, lingering there for a moment before rising again to meet mine. "I'm going to give you a choice."

I frown. "What are you talking about?"

"Give me your sanity or your desire."

CHAPTER 29

GENEVA

My blood races through my veins. "What does that mean?"

Ghost reaches up and drags his fingers along the glass with his gaze locked on mine. The gesture is slow, his fingertips moving in a gentle caress right where my face is.

"Sanity or desire," he repeats, his voice like a whisper against my skin. "One keeps you safe, the other sets you free. Your sanity is the wall you hide behind, the rules and protocols that you think will protect you from me. But we both know that's not going to work."

He tilts his head, studying me. "Your desire, though? That's raw. Unfiltered. It's the part of you you're too afraid to acknowledge." His voice softens. "Letting me in will set you free. But keeping me out? That's madness."

I stay silent, refusing to give him the satisfaction of a response, but his words slice into me like a scalpel. Is he right about me? Or is this just another manipulation tactic meant to confuse me further?

"What happens when your sanity unravels from the strain of resisting me, Dr. Andrews?"

"You're delusional." My voice trembles despite my best efforts to steady it. "This isn't about sanity or desire. It's about control."

Ghost's lips curl into a slow, knowing smile. "Control, yes. But not in the way you think. This isn't about me taking control of you. It's about you giving it to me. Willingly."

I shake my head. "You're trying to manipulate me. Twisting my thoughts and my emotions until I can't see reason."

"Am I?" His tone is soft but laced with challenge. "Is that why you're here?"

"I'm here because I have to be," I snap. "Because you forced my hand. Not because I want to be."

"You've said your piece, so why haven't you left yet?"

I don't know.

The charged silence between us grows like a weed, strangling the life from me. I stand there, staring at my adversary until I think I'll go crazy from just looking at him. If I give Ghost my desire, I'm insane. If I fall into insanity, that'll lead to my desire.

Ghost knows he'll have both, no matter what I choose. So is it really a choice to begin with? No. This man only plays games he knows he can win.

And the prize is me.

A distant rumble sneaks through the thick prison walls, breaking into my thoughts. It's faint at first, like a low hum, but quickly grows louder. It's a discordant symphony of shouts, metal clanging against metal, and the unmistakable edge of chaos.

Ghost's fingers pause on the glass, his gaze flicking to the door behind me for a split second. His expression morphs, the smugness melting into sobriety.

"What's happening?" My voice is tight with unease, but he doesn't answer right away. The sounds outside the room intensify, and a knot forms in my stomach.

"Geneva," Ghost says, his voice low and fervent. "You shouldn't be here right now."

I open my mouth to respond, but a deafening crash cuts me off. The door shudders, the hinges rattling violently as something— or someone—slams into it. I spin around when a man shouts just outside the room. It's followed by another farther away, and the garbled fragments dissolve into the background noise that's still gaining volume.

"It sounds like the natives are restless." Ghost's voice is calm, but his tone lacks its usual edge of amusement. His eyes flick back to me, sharp and assessing. "Get away from the door."

I nod just as another loud bang sends a jolt through me, freezing me in place. Something heavy slams against the door, and a wet, gurgling sound cuts through the air. It's followed by a sickening thud of a body hitting the floor.

The room falls eerily silent, save for my ragged breathing. I glance at Ghost, whose posture has gone rigid, his eyes fixed on the door with an intensity that speaks volumes.

"Is he dead?" I whisper, though I already know the answer.

Blood seeps under the door, slowly pooling on the concrete floor. My stomach flips, and I take several steps back, pressing myself against the wall as my chest tightens.

Ghost doesn't move, his gaze never leaving the door. "You need to stay calm," he says, his voice quieter now but no less commanding. "It's not safe out there."

"No shit," I hiss.

"Listen to me. Don't open the door, no matter what you hear."

I swallow hard. "What are you going to do?"

"I'm going to protect you."

"What? How?"

Ghost's eyes lock onto mine, and for a moment, I see something in them. Determination? Concern? Whatever it is, it makes my skin prickle with something I can't name. Without another word, he steps back from the glass.

"Ghost," I say, my voice trembling. "What are you doing?"

He doesn't respond. Instead, he scans the room, his gaze acute and methodical, before turning toward the metal table on his side of the interrogation room. He steps onto the chair first, then climbs onto the table, the cuffs clinking as he moves.

My heart pounds harder when he reaches into his pocket, producing something small and glinting in the dim light. I squint, trying to make it out.

A penny.

"Where did you get that?" I ask.

He smirks faintly, but his focus remains on the vent above him. "I'm resourceful."

Ghost balances carefully on the table, using the edge of the penny to unscrew the cover of the vent. His hands move deftly, the cuffs barely slowing him down while he works.

"Did you plan this?" I ask.

"Plan?" he echoes, glancing at me briefly. "Not exactly. Anticipate? Always."

"Ghost—"

"Dr. Andrews, if I explained every brilliant move I've made, we'd be here all day."

I glare at him before resuming my vigilance by staring at the door. "Whatever."

"If you're impressed, just say so. It's not every day you see a man dismantle prison security with spare change."

I release a sigh, the sound a mixture of the disbelief and irritation gathering in my chest. "You're insane."

"I prefer the term 'innovator.' Insanity is just what the unimaginative call genius."

He chuckles softly, the sound maddeningly calm. However, not once does he stop rotating the penny to loosen the screws. The first one falls into his waiting palm.

A rubber sole squeaks against the floor right before someone tests the door handle to my room. It rattles twice more. I stop breathing until the person walks away, his shoes announcing his retreat.

Ghost's attention shifts to me. "Everything's fine. I've got this."

I swallow hard, my mind reeling. "How can you—"

A loud bang makes me jump; it's the unmistakable sound of someone's fist hitting a surface. Ghost and I both look at the door and then each other. Another violent impact shakes the hinges, the sound reverberating through the room.

"Open the door, bitch!"

My blood turns to ice as I rush to grab the chair and return to my position with my back against the wall. It's not a baseball bat, but it'll have to do.

"What about my interview, Doctor?" The man laughs maniacally, making my skin crawl. "You think I can't get to you in there?"

The man's voice grows louder, more insistent, as he continues to shout obscenities and threats. The only thing keeping him at bay is the door and me armed with a chair. Ghost won't even look at me, his focus fully on the vent as he works methodically with the penny.

The odds are not in my favor.

Finally, Ghost pauses, turning his head to glance at me. His expression is cold enough to make me shiver. "If they get through that door, they'll regret it."

For the first time in my life, I'm glad to have a serial killer on my side.

The banging grows louder until the door handle falls to the ground with a loud clang. My breath catches, my heart pounding in my chest as I glance between Ghost and the door.

"You're still handcuffed!" I whisper. "How are you going to stop him?"

Ghost turns back to the vent, his movements precise as he continues loosening the final screw. "Oh, Dr. Andrews," he says, his tone chiding. "Handcuffs aren't a limitation. They're just an inconvenience. Have you forgotten my arraignment already?"

"The innocent man you killed in court? No, I haven't."

"Deputy Wilson wasn't innocent." Ghost makes a face of disgust. "He beat his wife every day. I did her a favor while proving a point to the judge. Win-win."

I press myself against the wall, trying to make sense of the conflicting emotions roiling inside me. There's confusion, anger, and a flicker of something disturbingly close to understanding.

The door slams open with a deafening crash that makes me cry out. A wild-eyed inmate with a stocky build stumbles inside before slamming the door shut. His face is flushed with exertion, his chest heaving, and he's gripping a jagged piece of metal that's been fashioned into a weapon.

His eyes land on me and it takes everything in me not to cower. "Well, well, well. What do we have here?" He leers at me. "It's been a long time since I've smelled pussy."

"Ghost." I whisper his name like a prayer, teetering on the edge of hysteria.

"Fight," Ghost says, his voice hard, unyielding. "Fight to survive."

I shake my head, panic spilling over. "You expect me to—"

"I expect you to stay alive until I get to you," Ghost snaps.

The inmate laughs, a dry, rasping sound. "Don't worry, sweetheart. This won't take long."

Ghost slams his fist against the glass. Hard. The inmate's attention shifts to Ghost, the man's grin faltering at the look on his face. It's pure, unadulterated wrath.

"Don't do it," Ghost says quietly. Despite the softness of his voice, the menace underneath it is loud. "What do they call you? Lobo? Listen to me, Lobo. You won't live long enough to bust a nut, let alone brag about it."

"What are you going to do from over there?" The inmate rolls his eyes. "Nothing you say is going to stop me."

Ghost narrows his gaze, but it fails to hide the fire in his eyes. "If you touch her, I'll make sure your last breath is an apology, before I cut out your tongue."

CHAPTER 30

GHOST

Tʜᴀᴛ ᴀssʜᴏʟᴇ ᴅᴏᴇsɴ'ᴛ ʙᴇʟɪᴇᴠᴇ ᴍᴇ. Tʜᴀᴛ's ʜɪs ꜰɪʀsᴛ ᴍɪsᴛᴀᴋᴇ.

Lobo turns back to Geneva, his makeshift knife glinting under the harsh light. She's trembling, clutching the back of the chair like it's a weapon. Every part of me screams to be on her side of the glass, to be with her.

Geneva's vulnerability wounds me, but my fury on her behalf? The fury makes me dangerous. Unhinged.

Lobo steps closer to Geneva, his blade raised. "What're you gonna do, huh?" he asks me, trying to regain control. To be the dominant man. "You wanna watch?"

The final screw spins between my fingers, but not fast enough. My entire focus splits between the vent above me and the nightmare unfolding beside me.

Lobo takes another step toward Geneva, the smug bastard clearly enjoying the way she trembles. He thinks he's won, that he has her cornered.

Geneva's eyes flick to mine briefly, just enough to ground her.

She exhales and her grip on the chair loosens slightly, but it's not in surrender. It's in preparation.

Underestimating my girl. That is Lobo's second mistake.

He steps closer, and Geneva raises a hand. The motion is subtle, non-threatening, and calculated.

"You've been in a lot of fights," she says, her voice even. "But you don't always win, do you?"

Lobo glares at her. "You think you're smarter than me, don't you? Think you can talk me down?"

She gestures to his left side. "Your ribs. The way you're guarding them. You've got old fractures there, don't you? Not from sparring or practice. They're from someone bigger and stronger. Someone who put you in your place."

Lobo straightens. So does Geneva, matching his posture. Her expression shifts to something less fearful, and more focused. She's studying him, dissecting him in real time.

"Your knuckles," she continues, her voice softening but never losing its edge. "They're scarred. Not just from fights, but from hitting walls, doors, and other things that don't hit back. When things don't go your way, you lash out. But it doesn't fix anything, does it? It doesn't stop the nightmares. The *memories*."

"Shut up, bitch!"

Lobo's shout drowns out the final screw coming loose and me ripping open the vent. Geneva is keeping him off balance. She's fucking brilliant.

But Lobo is unpredictable. It's in the way his jaw tightens, and how his eye twitches as her words sink in. He's not used to being seen like this, stripped bare and analyzed. It's unsettling him, and that makes him volatile.

"You don't have to do this," she says. "Hurting me won't fix anything. It won't make you stronger, and it won't change what's already happened to you."

The inmate freezes, his hand trembling around the blade as her words hit their mark. It's only a few seconds, but it's better than nothing.

I grip the edge of the vent, and I pull myself up into the darkness, my blood burning with rage and purpose. She's keeping him talking, keeping herself alive.

But that won't last forever.

Hold on, Geneva. I'm coming.

The darkness wraps around me, the cold metal brushing against my forearms as I maneuver through the narrow space. The sounds from below filter up, keeping me informed. It's a mix of Geneva's steady voice, Lobo's labored breathing, and the chaos of the riot outside.

"You don't know a damn thing about me," Lobo says. "You think you're so smart, huh? Just because you've got a degree doesn't mean you've got me figured out."

Geneva's response is measured, professional. She's in her element, even under duress. "You're right. I don't know everything about you. But I do know that you're better than this. You've survived worse, haven't you? You don't have to let it define you."

In a moment of indecision, the inmate hesitates again, but it's meaningless. Men like him are ruled by their impulses and their insecurities. It's only a matter of time before he lashes out.

The vent creaks softly under my weight as I inch closer to the opening above Geneva's side of the interrogation room. My hands, still cuffed, ache from the effort, but the discomfort is nothing compared to the searing determination driving me forward. She's buying time. Precious seconds I intend to use.

The shuffle of Lobo's boots reaches me as he shifts his weight. "This is just some shrink shit you're using to stall."

"Maybe," she says. "Or maybe I'm showing you something no one else has. That you have a choice."

His laugh is harsh. "Choice? What fucking choice do I have in here?"

I reach the vent's edge, peering through the slats. The room below comes into view: Geneva standing firm, her hands gripping the back of a chair, while Lobo hovers a few feet away. He's caught in her words, torn between his instincts and the thread of doubt she's woven into his mind.

The fear is in the stiffness of her spine, buried beneath her composed exterior. She's holding it together for now, but the tension in her body tells me she's ready to snap.

"Lo-bo," I call down, my voice sing-song. Both of their heads snap up toward the vent, Geneva's eyes widening in surprise. "Uncle touched you in naughty places, didn't he?"

"Shut the fuck up!" he screams, his voice cracking.

Bingo!

Geneva's eyes dart between us, her composure momentarily slipping as confusion washes over her face. She adjusts quickly, her gaze softening as she realizes what I've done: I've shifted his focus to me.

To protect her.

"Tell me one thing, Lobo," I say while scanning the vent for weak points. "What's it like at family reunions for you?"

Lobo's hands tremble as his fury builds with every venomous

word I spit down from the vent. He glares up at me, his face twisted with rage, but his attention flickers back to Geneva.

The moment I catch his gaze darkening with intent, my blood runs cold. He knows that going after her is the only way to hurt me.

"Geneva!" I shout, my voice raw with panic as he lunges toward her.

She reacts instinctively, swinging the chair in her hands with all her strength. The heavy metal legs catch Lobo across the shoulder, sending him stumbling back with a grunt of pain. His blade clatters to the floor, spinning out of reach for the moment.

"Good one, Doc!" I yell, desperation threading through my voice as I ram my boots against the vent. My heart pounds against my ribs in tandem.

The adrenaline pounding through me sharpens everything: the fear etched into Geneva's features, the way she scrambles to react, the glint of insanity in Lobo's gaze as he straightens to his full height.

"You're gonna regret that."

He lunges again. Geneva moves quickly, using the chair as both shield and weapon. She thrusts it forward, forcing him to stumble back, but he's relentless. He grabs the edge of the chair, yanking it hard and pulling her off balance.

Below, Lobo has the upper hand when Geneva's forced back against the wall. The blade glints on the floor between them, and Lobo's gaze shifts to it.

I slam my boots against the vent with mounting desperation, the sound ringing through the room. "Fuck!"

Lobo dives for the blade, his fingers brushing the handle. Geneva kicks the weapon and sends it skidding across the room.

The motion leaves her vulnerable, and Lobo grabs her wrist, slamming her back against the wall.

"Geneva!" I shout, the sound echoing around me, amplifying my stress.

She twists in his grip, using her other hand to claw at his face, her nails catching his cheek. He howls in pain but tightens his hold on her and she cries out. The panic in her eyes ignites something primal in me, something depraved and savage.

The vent finally gives, the cover clattering to the floor. The scene below burns into my mind—Geneva, pressed against the wall, her face pale but fierce as she fights back, and Lobo with his filthy hands on her.

I launch myself out of the vent, dropping down into the room with a quiet thud. The second my boots hit the ground, I move. Lobo doesn't even have time to react before I'm behind him, my arms snaking around his head like a viper. The chain of my cuffs digs into his throat as I pull it taut, locking him in place.

He thrashes, clawing at my arms, gasping for air. But I'm stronger. And I'm fucking pissed. "Didn't your mother ever tell you not to touch what doesn't belong to you?" I ask.

Geneva stares at me, frozen in shock, her chest heaving as she catches her breath. Her wide eyes lock onto mine, and for a moment, the world ceases to exist. Because *she* is my world.

I give her a crooked smile, tightening the chain around Lobo's neck. "Did you miss me, Doc?"

She blinks, her lips parting as if to say something, but no words come out. Her silence doesn't matter. I see the answer in her eyes.

Lobo's body jerks violently, his gasps turning to wet, desperate gurgles. He claws at the chain, his nails scratching at my skin, but

I don't let up. My grip only tightens, fueled by the image of him attacking her, of her fear. Of her pain.

"No one touches her," I growl, leaning closer to his ear. "No one."

Geneva finally moves, stepping away from the wall, her hands out in supplication. "Ghost, stop," she says, her voice shaking but firm. "You'll kill him."

"That's the idea," I deadpan.

She almost smiles, but the seriousness of the situation stops her. "Let him go. He's not worth it."

"Not worth it?" I repeat, my voice low. "That might be true. But you are worth it. Always."

I palm the sides of Lobo's head to pull the chain-link more taut, even as it opens me up to getting elbowed by him. The pain of his blows reinforces how badly he could've hurt Geneva.

Eventually, his body goes slack in my arms, his futile struggles ceasing. The weight of him is oddly satisfying, but he's a heavy fucker, so I'm quick to release him.

Then I kick him for good measure. "Motherfucker."

Turning to Geneva, I find her staring at me with wide eyes. Her chest rises and falls with rapid breaths and her face is pale. She's shaken, but she's still standing. Still breathing.

"You okay, Doc?"

She nods slowly, as if she's not quite sure. "You took long enough getting here."

"What can I say? I like to make an entrance."

CHAPTER 31

GENEVA

GHOST STANDS A FEW FEET AWAY, HIS EXPRESSION CALM, ALMOST amused, as if he didn't just strangle someone with his cuffs and drop out of a vent like fucking Batman.

No, he'd be the Joker. Heath Ledger style. Hot but deranged.

I exhale sharply, the adrenaline still coursing through my veins, making my knees weak. I hate the way my body betrays me in his presence, not just with fear, but with the uncomfortable heat that coils in my stomach.

"You didn't have to kill him," I mutter, my voice barely above a whisper.

Ghost arches an eyebrow, his gaze steady on mine. "Really? You think he'd have stopped if I asked nicely?"

My stomach twists, and I look away, avoiding the body on the floor. Ghost is right, of course. Lobo wouldn't have stopped. I don't want to think about what would have happened if Ghost hadn't been here.

I shift my attention back to him. His gaze hasn't left me, astute and unrelenting, as if he's dissecting every emotion flickering across my face.

"You can't keep doing this," I say, my shoulders sagging with exhaustion. "You can't kill every man who threatens me."

"The fuck I can't." Ghost narrows his gaze. "This isn't the attitude I expected after saving your life."

The disappointment in his voice cuts me. He's right. Again. How annoying.

I nod slowly in resignation. "Thank you, Ghost. I really mean it."

A flicker of something crosses his features. Appreciation? Devotion? I'm not sure because it disappears too quickly for me to read. Whatever the emotion, it was tender. And so at odds with the killer watching me intently.

"That's more like it," he says. His customary grin returns. "See how easy that was?"

I roll my eyes, repressing a smile of my own. "Don't get used to it."

He smirks, the charm he exudes infuriating as ever. "I wouldn't dream of it, but isn't it customary to receive a token of gratitude?"

"Like what?" The words fly out of my mouth before I can stop them, my curiosity getting the best of me. Regret immediately sets in. God only knows what Ghost's answer will be.

"A kiss," he says simply.

There is nothing simple about that. In fact, I can't think of anything worse.

I scoff, trying to mask the way my blood rushes under my skin with renewed vigor. "You're out of your mind."

"Am I?" Ghost takes a step toward me. And another. His movements are fluid and graceful, like a predator closing in on its prey. "Or are you just scared?"

I glare at him as my thoughts collide, making my head ache. My attraction to Ghost is nothing more than a psychological response. A textbook case of gratitude and misplaced attachment. He saved my life, therefore, I feel drawn to him. It's primal. It's survival. It's not real.

It *can't* be.

But even as I analyze my behavior, the logical explanation doesn't eradicate the flames of desire burning me. If I don't put an end to this conversation, I'll be nothing more than ash, a pile of long-forgotten inhibitions.

I shake my head, stepping farther back, desperate to put space between us. "I'm not scared and you're not a hero who deserves a prize. If anything, you're the villain in my story."

"That's fair. Here's the thing about villains... They don't ask. They just take what they want."

His words hang in the air, dripping with that maddening confidence, his smirk daring me to respond. The room feels stifling, the tension coiled so tightly it threatens to snap.

Ghost steps closer, and I retreat, only to find the wall at my back. He stops just inches away, his breath on my lips, his presence overwhelming me. I could barely handle him on the other side of the glass, but now having his body nearly flush with mine, I'm hopeless.

"That's why you're dangerous," I say quietly. "You take without thinking about the consequences."

"Oh, I think about the consequences, Dr. Andrews. I just don't give a shit about them."

Ghost's hand shoots out to grab me by the throat before he yanks me to him. His lips crash down on mine, and I freeze.

This kiss is unrelenting, possessive, forceful.

He slants his mouth over mine, his tongue seeking entrance. Seeking dominion. And somewhere beneath my indignation, beneath my confusion, a treacherous part of me comes alive.

I shouldn't want this.

Ghost is everything I despise: a ruthless criminal who doesn't respect the sanctity of life.

My mind screams rejection, but my body cries for more. The heat of him. The raw intensity. The dangerous edge that vibrates just beneath his skin.

But I can't.

With great reluctance, I pull away, my breath coming out in ragged gasps. His eyes are bright with hunger, the smirk playing at the corners of his lips telling me he's far from satisfied with a single kiss.

"That was better than I imagined," Ghost murmurs against my mouth.

I give him a stern look. "This can never happen again."

"Fuck. That."

Ghost kisses me again.

The fire inside me flares, burning hotter, brighter, until the only thing I can feel is him. Until the only thing I want is him.

This man kisses like he kills: deliberately, skillfully, and without remorse.

My hands, which should be pushing him away, grab the fabric of his shirt. Not fighting. Holding. A desperate, primal contradiction that terrifies me more than his touch.

His grip on my throat tightens ever so slightly, just enough to send a thrill through me. He nips at my lower lip, the sting of pain quickly replaced by a rush of pleasure.

The contact is electric, sending a surge of adrenaline through me. I gasp, my eyes flying open. He uses the opportunity to deepen the kiss, his tongue sweeping into my mouth.

I'm powerless to stop him.

My thoughts fragment. Professional distance. Ethical boundaries. Years of training that demand clinical detachment. All of it crumbles against the brutal intimacy of his mouth.

"Kiss me back, Geneva."

His command is a whisper against my lips, a sensual demand that has me wanting to obey. He slowly traces the seam of my lips with his tongue. Now coaxing instead of taking.

And I surrender.

It's a sigh. The softening of my body. The tightening of my grip on him.

I've studied Ghost for months. Analyzed every file, every report. I know the body pressed against me is a weapon. Trained. Lethal. Scarred. Each ridge and plane a testament to violence. I should be repulsed, but I'm enraptured.

Ghost releases his grip on my neck to place his palms against the wall on either side of my head, caging me in. All the while, he never stops his sensual assault on my mouth, even as the chain links from his cuffs press against my throat. Those same chains were just used to take a life, but now they're on my skin, breathing life into me.

No longer a threat, but a thirst for more.

I kiss him back.

His touch changes at my response. It's not just conquering, but something more unhinged. More desperate.

I whisper his name, overwhelmed by him. Ghost swallows

the tiny sound, pulling my breath into his body. A tremor runs through him, followed by a groan of pure ecstasy that has me shaking as well.

His lips curl, but it's not quite a smile. It's something darker and devious. Something that says he knows exactly what he's doing to me.

To us.

He pulls back, allowing me to breathe as he trails lips along my jaw. Teeth scrape against my pulse point. Not quite biting. Not quite breaking skin. But promising that he could. That he might.

I try to stifle a moan, but I'm unsuccessful. It flows from my throat, liquid and sultry, like the dampness flowing from my pussy. Ghost freezes, his lips on my throat, his teeth testing my skin. He inhales deep and my face blooms with the heat of my embarrassment.

"I smell magnolia and pussy," he murmurs.

Something shifts. Breaks. His façade shattering.

No more calculated precision.

No more meticulous control.

Just raw need.

He drops his hands and shoves one between my thighs to grip me, and I'm shocked by my own response as my legs instinctively spread for him. The wall is cold against my back. His body is fire. Burning. Consuming.

His touch is rough, almost brutal. Like he knows I won't break. Like he knows I can take whatever he has to give. He sweeps his thumb across the crotch of my leggings, the material chafing against my sensitive flesh. The friction makes me groan.

"Fuck, Geneva. You're soaking wet."

His words only make the ache worse.

He presses his palm against my mound, the pressure deliciously maddening. His other hand grips my hip, his fingers digging into my flesh. I can feel the strength in him, the power. Every flex of his hand could end my life. The knowledge makes me euphoric.

Eyes closed, I arch into him, grinding against his palm, desperate for more. He responds with a growl, the sound low and primal as it sweeps past my ears and straight between my thighs.

I don't care if this is wrong. I don't care that he's a murderer. A psychopath. All I care about is how he makes me feel.

Sexy.

Seen.

Safe.

Things I've never felt before, all at once.

CHAPTER 32

GENEVA

My eyes fly open when Ghost snatches my wrist and moves my hand to rest on his cock. Damn. Even through his pants, I can tell he's huge. Thick and hard, straining against the fabric. Pulsing against my palm.

"Can you feel what you do to me?" he asks, his voice a harsh whisper. "You drive me fucking crazy."

"You're already insane," I whisper.

His confession sends a thrill through me. I grip his cock, stroking it through his pants. He groans, his fingers digging painfully into my hip.

He laughs, the sound low and wicked. "True. But you make me worse."

"I doubt it."

"Trust me, Doc." He leans down, his breath hot against my ear. "You don't want to know what I'm capable of. What 'crazy' really looks like."

The words should terrify me. Instead, they send a bolt of heat through me. I'm playing with fire, but maybe that's what I need.

I tighten my grip, stroking him harder. He groans, his hips rocking against my palm as he buries his face in my neck.

"Fuck," he hisses, his voice strained.

I can feel him spiraling, giving me control over him. Good.

"Are you going to come for me, Ghost?" I whisper.

He jerks up his head to pin me with his dark gaze. "Only when I fuck you."

Ghost grabs my hips and spins me around so quickly I stagger before landing against the glass. The second I push away from the wall, he throws his bound hands over my head, the cold chain links of his cuffs now resting just under my chin.

Then his hand is at the back of my head, pushing my cheek against the window. His hold is unyielding, a pressure that I can't escape. And I don't want to.

Keeping his gaze locked on mine, he slowly releases me to reach down and grip my pussy. In the reflection of the glass, I can see everything. The heat and desire in his eyes. The way his lips are parted, his breathing ragged.

He's dangerously beautiful.

"Put your hands on the glass," he commands.

I comply without hesitation, pressing my palms flat against the smooth, cool surface. The position exposes me, opens me up in a way that's as frightening as it is exhilarating.

"Keep them there," he says.

Ghost slides his fingers up and down the seam of my leggings, the fabric dampening more with each pass. "I'm going to make *you* come. Right here. Right now."

I can't speak. I can't breathe. All I can do is feel.

So, this is what it's like.

The thought whirls through my mind in tandem with Ghost's

caress as he circles my clit with his thumb. In this illicit, forbidden moment, I am acutely, painfully alive. I'm connected to a visceral truth that I've spent a lifetime denying: to feel is the very essence of what it means to be human.

He slips fingers under the waistband of my leggings, dipping into my slit. A moan escapes my lips, and he responds with a dark chuckle.

"So fucking wet," he murmurs, sliding his fingers up and down. I can't help but arch against him, desperate for more. He teases me, his touch never providing enough pressure against my aching clit. Frustration and pleasure combine, growing with each second.

"Ghost," I whine, hating the neediness in my voice.

He responds by pressing the tip of his finger against my entrance. I gasp as he slowly pushes inside me, the pressure and friction exquisite.

"God, you're tight," he groans. "You've never been fucked properly."

He works his finger in and out, each stroke bringing me closer to the edge. Then he adds another digit. And another. Now I'm a quivering mess, unable to form words. Unable to do anything but surrender to the pleasure.

The glass is slick with sweat now, my hands sliding along the surface as he finger fucks me. The friction against my clit is maddening, the pressure building with each thrust of his hand.

I'm *so* close.

With a groan, I press my ass against him while grinding down on his hand. The movement breaks his rhythm, and he responds with a growl, the sound primal and animalistic.

"Fuck, you're greedy," he grits out between clenched teeth.

I can feel him straining against his pants, his cock pressing against my ass. The thought of him coming inside me, filling me up, pushes me toward release.

My orgasm hits me so hard my lips part on a silent scream. He keeps fingering me, prolonging the pleasure.

"That's it, Geneva. Come for me. Drench my hand."

His voice is rough, the words barely audible. But I hear them. They're a command, laced with praise. And male satisfaction. It only makes me come harder.

I bite my lip to stifle the cries that threaten to escape until the sensation lessens to a bearable level. My eyes are closed, my breath coming out in harsh gasps. And I can feel him staring, his fingers twitching inside me.

And when I finally open my eyes, his gaze is bright with lust, the need clear on his face.

He removes his fingers from inside me and brings them to his mouth, licking the wetness from them. The action is both erotic and vulgar, but I can't look away, captivated by the sight.

"Open," he says.

I hesitate, unsure if this is a step too far. But the urge to obey him is too strong. Slowly, I bring them to my mouth, the saltiness and tang of my pussy sliding along my tongue.

"That's it, Geneva." His voice is rough. "Taste yourself. Taste how much you want me."

I can't deny it. I can't deny anything right now.

I swirl my tongue around his fingers. My reflection stares back at me, watching my cheeks hollow as I suck, my lips wrapping around his fingers, greedy and eager. My eyes are shining with gratification, my breath coming in quick gasps as I struggle to recover. Heat continues to burn on my skin, the remnants of our unexpected intimacy lingering. Smoldering.

I fell apart under Ghost's skillful touch. Now, I'm nothing more than a visual testament to the unraveling of my composed and controlled exterior. It's terrifying and yet, I'm fascinated by my complete surrender.

Eventually, I flick my gaze to Ghost. Only to find him already looking at me. The hunger in his eyes is expected. The tenderness isn't.

His expression softens further before he removes his fingers from my mouth to lean down and press his lips to the side of my neck. Closing his eyes, he prolongs the kiss as though enjoying the taste and feel of me.

His actions are incongruous with the man I've come to know in the confines of these walls. Ghost is someone who's defined by his cunning and control. And this display of affection, gentle and tender, disrupts my understanding of him.

Is this an act designed to manipulate me further? Or is it a genuine glimpse into a part of him that he rarely reveals? A part that maybe he himself struggles to understand and control?

As Ghost pulls back, the cool air of the room brushes against my neck where his lips just were, leaving me bewildered. My physical reaction to the sweet gesture is nothing compared to the emotions stirring inside me. Something I'm not able to handle right now. Or ever.

"Why me?" I whisper. Or maybe I make no sound at all? Because I'm scared to hear the answer. Scared to break our connection. The very thing I've been denying since I first felt it.

Ghost tilts his head, considering my question. "Because I wanted you," he answers simply, as if such a thing should make sense. As if his personal desires haven't shaken me to the core.

"But why?" Despite my fear, I need to understand, to find a reason that agrees with the logic I've always protected myself with.

Ghost reaches up, trailing his fingers along my jaw and down my neck. The handcuffs clink with his movement, a reminder of his status as a prisoner. Something that failed to keep us apart.

"Because, Geneva, even chaos has its moments of clarity, and in you, I found mine."

The sincerity in his voice is my undoing.

I hug my middle, attempting to fortify myself as I look away. Every touch from him should be a lie, should be something manipulative and dangerous. Yet here I stand in his arms, soaking it in like the first rays of sunshine.

"Look at me," he says softly, his voice threaded with a quiet intensity that pulls at something deep inside me.

Slowly, I lift my eyes to meet his, and the force of his gaze nearly undoes me. It's raw, unguarded, and full of something I don't have the words for.

"You scare me," he says. "You're the only person that does."

I blink over and over. Of all the things he could've said, this is the most unexpected. "I scare *you*?"

His lips twist into a bitter smile. "Don't look so surprised, Doc." He pauses, his hands twitching against my skin, the only sign of the tension beneath his calm exterior. "You've managed to do what no one else ever has."

I shake my head, struggling to process his words. "People like you don't—"

"People like me, huh?" He interrupts, his tone sharp, but there's no anger in it, only frustration. "Listen, I'm not afraid of what I am or what I'm capable of. But for the first time, I'm afraid of what I'll become…without you."

This doesn't make sense. *He* doesn't make sense. My chest tightens, my breath coming in shallow gasps as my mind races to find an explanation. But there isn't one. Not a logical one, anyway.

I open my mouth to respond, to say something that will force him to explain further, but before I can, a shout echoes from the hallway.

"Dr. Andrews!"

The voice is loud and urgent, scattering my thoughts. I rear back, my heart leaping into my throat as the spell between us shatters. Footsteps thunder down the corridor, growing louder with each passing second.

"Looks like the cavalry's here," Ghost says, his tone casual, but his eyes remain locked on mine, searching, probing.

Begging for understanding.

CHAPTER 33

GENEVA

THE WARNING GIVES US A FEW PRECIOUS SECONDS.

We hastily separate to revert back into our respective roles as prisoner and psychologist. No longer lovers and liabilities.

Ghost adjusts his features into the familiar mask of indifference as I straighten my clothes. I tuck a stray strand of hair behind my ear, an attempt to restore some semblance of the order that his touch disrupted. My professional mask feels heavier now, more difficult to wear after what has just transpired.

His transformation is almost seamless, a chilling reminder of his ability to switch personas at will. As he straightens his jumpsuit, the dangerous allure that had momentarily softened his demeanor vanishes, replaced by a cold detachment.

The guard steps inside with his weapon drawn, his eyes sweeping the room, calculating the threat level. The man's posture stiffens when it lands on Ghost, and he tightens his grip on the firearm, a clear signal of his readiness to act. The tension in the room spikes, the air thick with the electricity of potential violence.

"Dr. Andrews, step away from the inmate," he commands, his

voice firm and authoritative. I immediately comply, my heart pounding as I move toward the corner of the room farthest from Ghost.

The inmate remains eerily calm, his hands visible as he holds them out in front. His eyes, however, glint with something undefinable. Amusement, perhaps, or anticipation? It's unsettling how composed Ghost is. Very different to my racing thoughts and pounding heart.

"Are you all right, ma'am?" the guard asks, his gaze never leaving Ghost. He moves, positioning himself so he has a clear view of both of us, his body angled to provide both defense and offense should it become necessary.

I take note of his name tag. "Yes, I'm fine, Officer Barlow." I speak clearly and concisely, using his name to deescalate the situation. Not only for me, but for Ghost.

Barlow nods but doesn't lower his weapon. "A riot broke out in the east wing, so we locked down the facility. I need to escort you out immediately, Dr. Andrews."

"Okay."

The guard's eyes land on Lobo's lifeless body on the floor, his expression tightening as he processes the scene. His weapon shifts, leveling more squarely at Ghost, whose cuffed hands are still raised.

"What happened here?" Barlow demands, his voice edged with suspicion.

Ghost shrugs. "He fell, Officer."

"Cut the shit, Ghost. What really happened?"

"Well, I saved the good doctor here from becoming a case study in blunt-force trauma." He turns to wink at me. "You're welcome, by the way."

"Excuse me?" The guard's gaze snaps to me, his brows furrowing. "Ma'am, is that true?"

I swallow hard, forcing myself to stand straighter even as my knees feel like they might give out. "The inmate named Lobo attacked me. He came at me with a knife and Ghost...intervened."

Barlow's eyes narrow, darting between us. "Intervened how?"

"Oh, you know," Ghost says, his tone breezy. "A little impromptu lesson in self-defense for the doctor's benefit. Oxygen deprivation is a solid tactic."

The guard's jaw tightens. "Are you telling me you strangled him?"

Ghost shrugs, the movement casual despite the cuffs. "'Strangled' is such a harsh word. Let's go with 'neutralized the threat.' Sounds more professional, doesn't it?"

"Jesus Christ," the guard mutters. "Do you corroborate his story?"

I quickly nod, hoping to strengthen Ghost's narrative. "The inmate was going to kill me, and Ghost saved my life."

Barlow glances at Lobo's prone form again, then back to Ghost, who's now watching the interaction with the air of someone thoroughly enjoying the drama.

"That's what happened," Ghost says. "Scout's honor, Officer."

The guard shakes his head in disbelief. "You're no Boy Scout. After you killed that guy, you didn't lay a hand on Dr. Andrews," the guard says, incredulous. "Is that what you're telling me?"

Ghost nods, a sly grin tugging at the corners of his mouth. "What can I say? Chivalry isn't dead. Lobo, on the other hand..."

Barlow mutters a curse before bringing his radio to his mouth. "I need backup in Interview Room C. Possible homicide. Inmate contained. The civilian is safe."

My stomach churns, but I force myself to stand still, my arms folded tightly across my chest. I can feel Ghost's gaze on me, sharp and unrelenting, but I don't dare meet it. Not now. Not with the guard watching me like a hawk, his disbelief and suspicion palpable. Not when I disregarded the panic button.

Does that mean I *wanted* Ghost to come to me?

I refuse to answer that.

"Backup's on the way." Barlow lowers his radio but keeps his weapon aimed at Ghost. The energy in the room feels like a live wire, sparking with unspoken threats.

Ghost leans against the wall, his cuffed hands resting casually on his stomach. His grin hasn't faded, but his eyes gleam with something I can't place. "Relax, Officer. I did you a favor. Lobo wasn't exactly a model inmate."

Barlow scoffs, but doesn't respond, and the room falls silent again. I shift uncomfortably, keeping my eyes fixed on the floor, the walls, my hands…anywhere but Ghost. If I look at him now, even for a second, the truth of what happened between us will be written all over my face.

Ghost has touched my skin and gotten underneath it, becoming a part of me that I can't get rid of.

The sound of heavy boots echoes down the hall right before two more officers enter, their weapons drawn. They take in the scene quickly: Lobo's lifeless body on the floor, Ghost's nonchalance, and me standing stiffly against the wall.

"What's the situation?" one of the new arrivals asks, his eyes scanning the room.

Barlow jerks his head toward Ghost. "This inmate killed another inmate. Claims it was self-defense. Dr. Andrews confirms he saved her."

The second officer frowns, his gaze lingering on me for a moment before turning to Ghost. "You have anything to say for yourself?"

"Just that I'm an exemplary citizen," Ghost drawls, his grin widening. "And you're welcome, by the way."

The officer snorts, clearly unimpressed. "Cuff him to the table," he orders. "We'll sort this out."

As the guards move toward Ghost, the tension in the room shifts again. He doesn't resist, doesn't flinch as they secure him to the table, but the air crackles with unspoken words. He's letting them handle him now because it suits him.

"Let's go, Dr. Andrews," Barlow says, urgency lacing his tone. He steps closer, the weapon still in his hand but his body language shifting to guide rather than threaten.

I move quickly toward the door, acutely aware of Ghost's gaze on my back. It's so strong it's like a physical touch and my skin prickles with the memory of his hands on me.

When I reach the doorway, I can't help myself. I turn and look at him over my shoulder. Ghost is watching me, but there's no sign of his typical mocking smile. This time his face holds something else.

Longing. No, pain. Acute, excruciating pain.

It guts me where I stand. I've never witnessed vulnerability in Ghost. Not even when he kissed me.

"Dr. Andrews," the guard says, his voice harsh this time. "We need to go."

I nod, though my feet are rooted to the spot, my chest tight as Ghost's gaze holds me captive. He doesn't speak, but the raw desperation in his eyes says a lot. And it's overwhelming.

Why is he looking at me like that? Like I'm a breath of air and he's drowning? Like he'll die without me?

And then it hits me, all at once, with a force so sharp it stills my heart. *Ghost cares about me.* That's what this is, what his eyes are saying, what that raw, unguarded emotion is screaming.

This isn't possible.

Men like Ghost don't feel things like this. They're wired differently, incapable of true connection or genuine emotion. Psychopathy doesn't allow for it. I've spent years studying it, dissecting it, cataloging every trait and symptom.

He shouldn't be capable of this.

And yet, Ghost is looking at me as if I'm the only thing holding his world together. No, like I *am* his world.

My mind scrambles to make sense of it, to reconcile the impossible contradiction. He shouldn't care about me. He *can't.* But the emotion in his eyes is too real to ignore.

"Dr. Andrews," the guard says again, his tone firm, almost impatient. "We need to go."

Barlow steps closer, his presence breaking the fragile connection between me and Ghost. The man clamps his hand around my arm. "Now."

On instinct, I glance at Ghost.

His entire body stiffens, his hands raised but not in surrender. His jaw clenches, his shoulders coil like a predator about to strike, and his eyes—the raw, unguarded pain from moments ago—darkens with something else entirely.

Rage. Protective, territorial rage.

I see it in every part of him. His taut muscles. His hands twitching against the cuffs. But in this moment, it's not the metal that binds him.

It's me.

Ghost is mentally calculating, judging how to close the distance between him and the guard, and how to neutralize the perceived threat to me. My body stiffens when I realize what's about to happen.

"Ghost, don't," I say sharply.

His eyes snap to mine, but the fury doesn't subside. His gaze flickers to the guard's hand on my arm, his intent clear: *Remove it, or I will.*

Barlow doesn't notice. "Let's go," he says again, tugging me toward the door.

I yank my arm free. "Don't manhandle me."

The guard frowns, his eyes darting between me and Ghost. My pulse is erratic, my skin clammy, but I manage to summon enough authority in my tone to encourage him to back off.

"I can manage without your assistance."

Reluctantly, Barlow steps back, his hand falling to his side. I don't miss the way Ghost's body relaxes ever so slightly, though his eyes remain fixed on me, watching my every move with an intensity that leaves me breathless.

One of the guards mutters something about procedure, but I don't hear it. My focus is locked on Ghost. His breathing is uneven, his jaw tight, but his rage is fading, replaced by something quieter and more measured. He's still watching me, his eyes bright and assessing, as if making sure I'm okay.

Ghost would have risked his life to stop a man from touching me. And I just saved him, in the most subtle way I could, by taking control before the situation spiraled out of hand and he got hurt.

Or killed.

"I'm ready," I murmur, though my words are hollow.

Before I leave, I glance back one last time. Ghost is still watching me, his expression unreadable now, but his eyes—God, his eyes—are alive with something I can't name, something that tangles with the confusion and yearning swirling inside me.

"Go," Ghost says quietly, his voice low and rough. It's not an order. It's permission. A way of telling me that he's all right, even if neither of us really believes it.

The door closes, and the sterile brightness of the hallway momentarily blinds me. Barlow stands beside me, oblivious to the turmoil raging inside my heart. My hands are trembling, but I keep walking, forcing my feet forward even as my mind races back to the man I just left.

Ghost cares about me. He saved my life. And I just saved his.

Does that mean I care about him too?

Neither should be possible. Or permissible.

The guard ushers me out, guiding me through the maze of hallways toward the relative safety of the administration area. Sirens wail in the distance, a discordant symphony that heightens the surreal feeling enveloping me. I mentally piece together the fragments of the last hour, trying to make sense of what happened, and what it meant. Not just to me, but what it meant to the man who saved me.

"Are you sure you're okay, Dr. Andrews?" Barlow asks after a long moment, his voice quieter now. "That inmate didn't hurt you, right?"

"Yes," I say quickly, too quickly. "I just—never mind. I'm fine."

He doesn't look convinced but gives me a nod. "That guy's dangerous. Don't let him fool you into thinking otherwise."

Dangerous.

The guard says it like it's a warning, like it's a threat I need to protect myself from. As the word echoes in my mind, all I can do is laugh internally. Ghost isn't dangerous in the way the guard means.

He won't use his words to hurt me; he'll use them to entice me.

He won't use his power to oppress me; he'll use it to embolden me.

He won't use his hands to harm me; he'll use those very hands to pleasure me.

The memory of his touch, his lips, and the way he made me feel…it's been seared into every part of me, impossible to ignore. *That's* the danger. Not because of what he's done or what he's capable of, but the way he's turned me into a woman who risked everything.

Just for one taste of the chaos he offers.

CHAPTER 34

GENEVA

THE OFFICE IS QUIET EXCEPT FOR THE TICKING OF A CLOCK ON THE far wall. My mind likens the sound to the ticking of a bomb.

I sit on the edge of a leather chair, the kind meant to be inviting but too structured to actually relax in. Across from me, Dr. Linton waits patiently, her pen poised over a notepad. She doesn't push, doesn't prod. The clinical psychologist simply waits, her calm, expectant expression making it harder for me to avoid the reason I'm here.

I take a deep breath, twisting the hem of my sleeve. "I need to talk about a…situation," I begin, my voice steady but thin. "It's hypothetical."

Her brow arches, but she doesn't comment. Just a small nod, encouraging me to continue.

"Let's imagine a professional has developed complicated feelings," I say carefully, choosing each word as if I'm navigating a minefield. Which is true since I don't want to detonate my career. "And it's about one of their patients." I nearly choke on the last word.

Dr. Linton doesn't react visibly, but the slight nod signals she's following. "Complicated feelings," she repeats gently. "Can you elaborate on that?"

I exhale slowly, my gaze dropping to my hands. "The person is dangerous. He's the kind of man who thrives on manipulation and control. But there's another side to him. A side that feels... *real*."

She nods again, her pen tapping lightly against the notepad. "And this professional—you—feels drawn to this subject because of that 'real' side?"

I give her a pointed look. "I said this was hypothetical."

"Of course," she replies smoothly. "So this hypothetical professional is drawn to this subject despite their dangerous nature. Maybe even because of it?"

I swallow hard, trying to ignore the way her words strike closer to the truth than I want to admit. "It's not that simple. This patient is more than just dangerous. They're intelligent, protective, and capable of things that no one else would even think of doing."

Dr. Linton's pen stills, her eyes focused intently on me. "Protective. How so?"

I shift uncomfortably, the memory of Ghost's hands on Lobo's throat flashing in my mind. "They saved someone," I admit quietly. "It was violent, yes, but it was also necessary."

"And this professional, do they feel conflicted because of this act of violence? Or because it challenges how they see the subject?"

My throat tightens, and I look away, signaling my guilt. "Both," I whisper. "They're supposed to be impartial and objective. But this... this changed something. It blurred the lines."

For the first time, Dr. Linton's calm expression falters. "It sounds like this professional is carrying a lot of guilt."

My stomach twists, and I fight the urge to get up and leave.

Professionals like her—like me—are taught to read people, to see what they aren't saying through body language. I know she's reading me like a book, and I hate it. But how else will I get help?

"*Hypothetically*," I say, my voice sharper than I intended. "This professional knows how wrong it is. They know the risks."

"And yet," she presses lightly, "they're here. Talking about it. Why?"

I don't answer right away, my fingers tightening around the fabric of my sleeve. The room feels smaller, the air thicker, as I force myself to meet her gaze. "Because they don't know how to stop feeling it. And they're terrified of what it means."

Dr. Linton doesn't write anything. She just watches me, her expression steady but kind. "Acknowledging it is the first step. What you do with it—that's where the real work begins."

I nod as I lean back into the chair. What do I do with this feeling? As if I know how to answer that question.

"This isn't just curiosity or fascination. It's deeper than that. And that's what scares them the most."

"Deeper how?"

I glance down at my hands, noticing the way my fingers twist around each other like they're trying to wring the words out of me. "It's a…connection. The kind of connection they've spent their entire life avoiding. The kind that makes them vulnerable."

Dr. Linton nods slowly. "And this connection…Does the subject reciprocate?"

"Yes," I say, my voice cracking. "At least, it feels that way. But it's impossible to know if it's real or just manipulation."

"Which is a hallmark of their danger. That ability to blur the lines, to make you question what's real and what isn't."

I nod. "Exactly. That's what makes everything so complicated.

Because even if it is manipulation, it doesn't *feel* like it. Not in those moments."

"And how does that make you feel? The possibility that it could be real—or that it might not be?"

"It's torture," I confess, the words spilling out before I can stop them. "If it's real, then everything I've worked for is at risk. But if it's not, then I've let myself be played. Either way, I lose."

Dr. Linton sets her pen down to fold her hands in her lap. "That's a heavy burden to carry. But I wonder if part of the weight comes from trying to figure it out alone. Isolation can amplify confusion, Geneva."

The sound of my name startles me. It feels personal, too personal, even though I know it's just her way of grounding me in the conversation.

"What would you suggest, then?" I ask. "That I tell someone? Confess everything and watch my career burn to the ground? My career is my identity. It'd be akin to suicide."

Her expression remains steady. "Not that. But maybe it's not about confessing to someone else. Maybe it's about being honest with yourself first. About what you feel, what you want, and what boundaries you're willing to hold."

I let out a bitter laugh, shaking my head. "Boundaries. Those are already in pieces."

She doesn't react to my deflection, her gaze unwavering. "Then maybe it's about deciding what pieces you want to pick up, and what you're willing to leave behind."

The simplicity of her words cuts deeper than I expect, and I sit back, pressing my hands into my lap to steady myself. I don't respond, because I don't have an answer.

Dr. Linton lets the silence linger again, giving me space to process. Finally, she speaks, her voice softer than before. "It's okay to feel conflicted, Geneva. It's okay to not have the answers right now. But what's not okay is carrying this alone until it consumes you."

I nod, my eyes stinging with unshed emotion. The clock ticks in the background, marking the seconds that feel heavier than time should.

"Let's start small," she says gently, her pen poised again. "If this hypothetical professional could speak freely, without judgment, what's the one thing they'd say to this subject?"

The question catches me off guard, and I frown. My mind flashes to Ghost, to the look in his eyes as I walked away, the unspoken words between us. And then, without thinking, the answer tumbles out. "I'd ask him: Do you care about me?"

Dr. Linton doesn't look up from her notepad as she writes, her expression calm, her movements even. The scratch of her pen against paper fills the quiet, and for a moment, I feel exposed. Regretful. I know I need professional help, but this might've been a huge mistake.

Finally, she sets the pen down and folds her hands in her lap. "That's an honest place to begin. And it's okay to feel torn. Relationships—especially ones with this level of complexity—are rarely black and white."

I shift in my seat, gripping the armrests. "But this isn't a relationship," I say quickly, as if saying it aloud will make it true. "It's a professional situation that's gotten...messy."

And by "messy" I mean he had his fingers in my pussy.

Her brow arches. "Messy, yes. But not entirely professional, is it? At least not in how you're experiencing it."

242

The words sting, but she's not wrong. "No," I admit, my voice barely audible. "It's not. I didn't mean for it to happen. I didn't want this. Hypothetically," I add lamely.

"I believe you. Remember that you're human. Feelings don't always follow logic or intention. What matters now is what you do with those feelings."

"I don't even know where to start."

Dr. Linton leans forward. "Start with this: What do you want? Not what you think you *should* want, or what you're afraid of wanting. Just simply, what do *you* want?"

The question hangs in the air, heavy and impossible to answer. I open my mouth, but the words catch in my throat. What do I want? To escape this? To understand it? Or worse, to let myself feel it, to follow this to its destined conclusion where I end up hurt and alone?

"I don't know," I finally say, my voice breaking. "I just know I can't stop thinking about him. Even when I try. And it's exhausting."

Dr. Linton smiles at me with sympathy. "Honesty is good. When you think about him, is it fear you feel? Or something else?"

"Both," I whisper. "It's always both."

Her expression softens. "That's not uncommon. Attraction and fear often coexist in complicated dynamics like this. The key is understanding why. Why you feel drawn to him, and why it scares you."

I close my eyes, the memories flashing behind my eyelids— Ghost's smirk, his biting humor, the way he looked at me when I left the room. His euphoric expression when I came on his hand. "Because he makes me feel addicted."

"Addicted," she repeats. "That's a strong word. It suggests

there's a pull you feel, something beyond just fascination or curiosity. Do you think that's part of why you're here?"

"Yes," I whisper. "I think about him all the time. About what he said, the way he looked at me…the way he saved me."

"Let's talk about that," she says, her pen hovering over the notepad again. "When he saved you, how did it make you feel?"

I hesitate, the memory of that moment flashing vividly in my mind—Lobo's body crumpling to the ground, Ghost's hands still restrained but lethal, the way he turned to me afterward, calm and completely unapologetic.

"Conflicted," I admit. "Because it was brutal. He didn't hesitate, didn't flinch. But it wasn't for himself. It was for me. He saved me, and I don't know how to reconcile that with the person I know he is."

Dr. Linton nods slowly. "It's not uncommon to feel gratitude toward someone who's protected you, even if they've done so in a way that feels morally or ethically complicated. It can create a bond, a sense of connection that's hard to ignore."

"That's exactly it. And it scares me because I know he's capable of so much worse. But when I'm around him, I don't just see the manipulative side. No, I *do* see it, but I can't stop it from affecting me. How do I make it stop?"

Dr. Linton's gaze is unwavering, her tone firm. "You start by taking back control. By setting boundaries. Not just with him but with yourself as well. And you remind yourself that it's okay to feel conflicted. It's okay to be drawn to someone and still recognize that they may not be good for you."

I cover my face with my hands, unable to look at her as the words deep in my soul begin to surface. "But I *want* him despite knowing all of that."

"That's a powerful realization, Geneva. You're in a situation that challenges not only your professional boundaries but your personal ones as well. And that can be disorienting, even overwhelming. But the question now is: What are you willing to risk to explore these feelings of want?"

The more accurate question would be: Is there anything I'm *not* willing to risk?

And I don't like the answer.

CHAPTER 35

GENEVA

Two weeks later…

THE LIGHTS BUZZ SOFTLY OVERHEAD AS I SIT AT MY DESK, THE HUM a faint but persistent reminder of reality. Dr. Linton's words from my last session loop through my mind like a mantra, steady and relentless: *Set the boundary. Hold the line.*

I take a deep breath, willing myself to focus. My laptop screen illuminates the otherwise muted office, the open file staring back at me like a dare. Slowly, deliberately, I click on his photo. Ghost's face fills the screen, his expression as infuriatingly smug as it is captivating. It's a test, I tell myself. A deliberate exercise. Small doses of temptation to practice building the mental distance I so desperately need.

Feel it, but don't act on it.

I lean forward, my elbows resting on the desk, and force myself to study the photo like it's nothing more than another case. Another subject. The hard angles of his face and the intensity in his eyes are all there, frozen in a single frame, daring me to unravel what lies beneath. And I hate how easily it draws me in, how even in a static image he manages to hold power over me.

I scroll through the notes I've painstakingly compiled, clinging to the words as if they're a lifeline. Each sentence is a reminder, a tether to reality: *Dangerous. Manipulative. A psychopath.* Traits I've dissected and cataloged, the same traits that should keep me grounded.

But as I skim the lines, my gaze keeps drifting back to his photo, as if it holds answers the text can't provide. My stomach churns, a mixture of frustration and need. He's more than what's written in this file, more than what the mugshot captures, and that's what terrifies me the most. Because it's that *more* which has me prisoner and refuses to let go.

My fingers hover over the trackpad, debating whether to close the file, to put the temptation away. But closing it feels like running, and running means I've lost control. I need to face it, face *him*, in small doses if that's what it takes to fortify myself.

Feel it, but don't act on it.

The words are hollow, even as I mentally repeat them. How do I not act on something that already consumes me? Every line I've written about Ghost, every session I've spent trying to understand him, has led to this moment, where the boundaries between professional and personal are no longer blurred but shattered.

My chest tightens as I force myself to focus on the facts, the clinical detachment I've trained for years to maintain. His history. His diagnosis. The patterns of manipulation. It's all here, laid bare in my notes. Evidence of who he is, what he is. But even as I read, the memory of him flashes in my mind. The vulnerability, the rawness. The tender emotions he isn't supposed to be capable of.

I grip the edge of the desk.

"He's a psychopath," I whisper, as if saying it aloud will make it easier to believe. "He's dangerous."

And yet, staring at his photo, I can't shake the truth that keeps gnawing at me: He's not dangerous to me in the way everyone assumes. Not physically. Not in the ways that make sense. He's dangerous because he makes me question everything. My professionalism. My judgment. My very sense of self.

I let go of the desk to scroll down, forcing myself to look at the notes instead of his face. Clinical facts. Behavioral patterns. My observations, written with care and objectivity. At least, that's what I tell myself. The smirk in his photo is still there, lingering in the corner of my vision, taunting me.

I close my eyes, take a steadying breath, and open them again. I won't let him win. Not today. Not in this moment.

With my heart pounding in my chest, I close the file abruptly. The small victory feels far less satisfying than it should. But it's a start. A single step in a battle I'm not sure I know how to win.

My laptop pings with a new email, jolting me out of my thoughts. The subject line catches my eye: "Keynote Speech Confirmation: Dr. Geneva Andrews."

Holy Shit. I forgot about that.

Clicking the email open, I skim the message quickly.

Dear Dr. Andrews,

I hope this email finds you well. We are absolutely delighted to have you as our keynote speaker for the Annual Behavioral Science Fundraiser tomorrow night. Your groundbreaking insights into criminal psychology, particularly your recent work with high-risk inmates, promise to be a highlight of the evening.

Your profile on the inmate you've referred to as "Ghost" has generated immense interest among attendees and supporters. The way you've unraveled his psychopathy and the intricate nuances of his behavior is both fascinating and vital to understanding the complexities of criminal profiling. We are excited to hear you expand on these findings during your address.

This event will not only showcase the importance of behavioral science but also serve to raise critical funds for ongoing research and education in the field. Your expertise and perspective will undoubtedly inspire and resonate with our audience.

Thank you once again for lending your voice and expertise to this important cause. Please don't hesitate to contact me if you require any resources or support as you prepare for the event.

Warm regards,
Dr. Melanie Corbin
Chair, Department of Behavioral Sciences

The email stares back at me from the screen, its words neatly typed, each one tightening the invisible noose around my neck.

My fingers hover over the mouse, motionless, as if clicking away will somehow lessen the weight pressing against me.

The way you've unraveled his psychopathy and the intricate nuances of his behavior is both fascinating and vital to understanding the complexities of criminal behavior.

Fascinating. That's the word they've chosen. They're enthralled by the work I've done, the clinical precision I've supposedly brought to studying Ghost's mind. But I can't stop replaying our last moment together, the look in his eyes, or the way he kissed me.

Ghost is more than fascinating. He's damn near irresistible.

I let out a shaky breath, slumping in my chair. The email's praise is a spotlight I want to shrink away from. They have no idea how I continued blurring the lines between me and Ghost until they became nonexistent.

They can't know. That thought is immediate, sharp, and terrifying. If they knew how much of myself I've already sacrificed to understand Ghost—how personal it's become—they wouldn't be congratulating me. They'd be condemning me.

The ticking clock on the wall is deafening in the silence of my office. I press my fingers to my temples, trying to force the tension out of my head. The room feels too small, too bright, like the walls are closing in.

Get your shit together.

I glance at the email again, my eyes scanning the polite words, the thinly veiled demand for more. They want me to stand on a stage and tell them about Ghost, to make him a spectacle to satisfy their curiosity. But how can I talk about him like that now, as though he's just another file on my desk?

My gaze shifts to his file, the notes glaring up at me. Diagnoses. Traits. Behavioral patterns. All of it meticulously documented.

250

None of it captures what I saw in that interview room.

The pain.

The longing.

The raw, undeniable humanity he shouldn't be capable of.

My computer pings again with a new notification, snapping me out of my spiraling thoughts. I glance at the subject line, but I can't bring myself to open it. Instead, I close my laptop and stare up at the ceiling.

I can't let Ghost derail me, not when so much is riding on this keynote. My career depends on it. My reputation. But as much as I try to focus on what matters—what *should* matter—all I can think about is him.

The way he looked at me. The way he said my name.

The way I didn't want to leave.

CHAPTER 36

GENEVA

THE GLASS OF WINE DANGLES PRECARIOUSLY FROM MY FINGERTIPS as I recline on my bed with my laptop balanced on my knees. The screen's glow is harsh against the soft lighting of the room. I stare at the blank document in front of me, the blinking cursor mocking me with its persistence.

My keynote speech. The one everyone is so excited about. The one they're certain will showcase my brilliance, my insight, and my *objectivity*.

The outline sits neatly in a document, a skeleton of ideas waiting for flesh, but I can't make the words come. Every time I try, the same thought rears its head: *How do I talk about him without exposing myself?*

I take a sip of wine, the warmth spreading in my belly. It dulls the edge of my nerves but does little to quiet the noise in my head. They want to hear about Ghost, about the man behind the diagnosis, the enigma wrapped in danger and control. They want to know how I unraveled his psychopathy.

But how do I make sense of him when *I'm* still trying to understand? And where do I even begin? How do I distill months of studying him into something academic and detached?

I exhale sharply and reread the first sentence: *"Psychopathy is a condition defined by control."*

It's a good start. Clean. Professional. Clinical.

I take another sip of wine and lean back against the headboard, staring at the words on the screen. Ghost is nothing if not controlled. Every smirk, every word, and every movement is deliberate and calculated. It's what makes him so fascinating. And so infuriating.

But he wasn't controlled the last time I saw him...

Ghost looked at me as though he was dying; his pain was so raw it felt like a boulder pressing down on my chest. I swallow hard as the memory of his gaze appears in my mind.

Vulnerability. Longing. Empathy.

Things he shouldn't be capable of.

I set the wine glass on the nightstand and run my hands over my face. *Focus, Geneva.* The speech isn't about him. It's about his condition, his behavior, and the way he manipulates and deceives. It's about what makes him a textbook case.

Not the exceptions that make him human.

I type another line and then read it aloud: *"Psychopaths thrive in environments where they can exploit weakness. They adapt, manipulate, and control with alarming precision."*

My gaze drifts to the wine glass, the deep red liquid catching the soft light. The alcohol isn't helping. If anything, it's making things blur even more.

Turning my head, I glance at the scattered notes around me,

papers strewn across the bed like fallen leaves. Quotes from past lectures. Clinical terms. Carefully worded descriptions that strip the humanity from the subject, leaving only a puzzle to be solved.

I pick up one of the papers, scanning a highlighted passage: *"Psychopathy is the absence of connection, the inability to form genuine bonds with others."*

Frustration bubbles up in my chest, so I drop the paper back onto the pile. None of these notes or observations account for Ghost. The file doesn't explain why he saved me, why he let me see him in a way no one else has. And it certainly doesn't explain why I let him touch me.

I press my palms against my thighs, grounding myself, but the memory of his touch keeps replaying in my mind. The way he said my name like it meant something. Like I meant everything.

But that's a lie, isn't it?

Except that look shattered something inside me. Ghost isn't just a simple answer anymore. He's the question I can't stop asking.

I reach for the wine again, taking a long sip before setting the glass down. I've spent years telling myself I could maintain control, that I could navigate the darkness without it touching me. But now I'm not so sure.

The cursor blinks, urging me to continue, but I can't. Not yet. Instead, I close the laptop gently, resting my head back against the pillows. The wine hums in my veins, offering a false sense of calm, but the truth simmers just beneath the surface.

Ghost isn't just the focus of the keynote. He's *my* focus.

I close my eyes, letting the silence of the room wrap around me like a cocoon, but it doesn't bring the tranquility I hope for. Instead, it brings memories. That day. That moment in the interview room when the boundary between us dissolved completely.

His hands on me. Not manipulative or detached, but intimate and claiming. His voice, low and rough, commanding while laced with something deeper. The way his fingers moved with purpose, igniting sensations I've never felt.

I inhale sharply, my thighs pressing together instinctively as the memory flickers like a flame I can't extinguish. The look in his eyes as he stood behind me, watching me in the reflection of the glass. Yes, there was power in that moment. But there was also something else. A vulnerability that mirrored my own, a shared understanding.

I shouldn't be thinking about this. About him. About the way my body betrayed me, the way I surrendered to something I still don't fully understand.

I open my eyes, staring at the ceiling, willing the memory to fade, but it doesn't. It lingers, teasing, pulling me back into that room, to the way his touch burned through every layer of professionalism I've ever built. To the way his lips brushed against my ear as he whispered words that made me shiver.

My breath hitches, my pulse quickening. I tell myself it's just the wine, the late hour, and the stress of the day catching up to me. But I know that's a lie. It's him. It's always him.

Ghost isn't just in my thoughts…he's in my body now, too. A temptation I can't seem to escape, no matter how much I try to rationalize it or push it aside. And as much as I want to hate him for it, I can't.

I'm the one to blame because I know better.

I grip the edge of the blanket, my knuckles whitening as the thought creeps into my mind, unbidden but persistent. The idea of him here, now. His hands instead of mine. His voice instead of silence.

My pulse pounds in my ears, each beat a betrayal of the control I've fought so hard to maintain. I press my thighs together, a weak attempt to stifle the growing ache, but it only makes it worse. The memory of his touch lingers like a ghost itself, haunting and unseen, leaving me trembling with the weight of what I know I shouldn't want.

Desire rises, insistent, drawing me further into the fantasy: what it would feel like to surrender completely, to let myself go. To let him take what he's already claimed in my mind.

My lips part, a sigh escaping as I imagine him here, watching me, whispering my name like a prayer. I slip my hand beneath my long t-shirt to the apex of my thighs, where the evidence of my desire has already soaked through my panties.

I shudder at the first brush of my fingers, the sensation both relief and torture. It's not enough.

It'll never be enough.

With a frustrated groan, I push the fabric aside, baring myself to the chill of the night air. My skin prickles, pebbling with goosebumps, and a tremor runs through me as I circle my clit, the movement slow but with purpose. And need.

My eyes flutter closed, my mind filling in the gaps of my reality. His hands. His touch.

"God, you're beautiful," his voice breathes, soft and reverent. "Show me how you touch yourself."

I slip two fingers inside, pressing deeper, imagining it's him. Imagining his fingers curling and thrusting, coaxing me toward release.

"Fuck, Geneva," he murmurs. "You're so tight. So fucking wet for me."

"Yes. God, yes."

His hand covers mine, guiding me, urging me on. His grip is strong and firm, his movements relentless, drawing out the pleasure until it's almost unbearable. I arch my back, grinding against his palm, desperate for release.

"Come for me," he demands, his voice rough with lust. "I want to hear you scream."

I do.

His name tears from my lips, echoing off the walls of the room as my orgasm crashes through me, leaving me shaking and spent. My breathing is ragged, the sound harsh in the silence.

As the last waves of pleasure recede, shame begins to creep in. But before it can take hold, something else washes over me…anger.

How dare he make me want him? How dare he invade my thoughts, my dreams, my desires? How dare he leave me like this.

Wanting.

Aching.

Craving.

"Fuck you, Ghost, for making me want you," I say, my voice hoarse and trembling, the sound cutting through the oppressive silence of the room. It feels good to let it out, to give voice to the emotions clawing at my chest, so I press on, the words spilling out like poison needing to be purged.

"Fuck you for making me feel this way. For making me question everything I've ever known about myself, about control, about boundaries. Most of all, fuck you for leaving me to deal with this…this *obsession* with you."

The echo of my voice hangs in the air, and for a moment, it feels like I've taken back some small piece of myself, wrestled free from the grip he has on me. I mentally congratulate myself on how cathartic that was.

"If that's the case, then come fuck me."

The words slither through the darkness, low and smooth, dripping with amusement. I jerk upright, my heart hammering as I scan the room. Shadows stretch across the walls, the glow of the streetlight outside doing little to illuminate the corners of my bedroom.

"Ghost?" I whisper, my voice shaky and barely audible.

There's no answer. Nothing but the sound of my own ragged breathing and the hum of the city beyond the window. My hands shake when I lower my t-shirt while continuing my search for any sign of him.

Finding nothing, I sigh. It was nothing more than my imagination. My mind's desperate attempt to make him real.

"Hello, Doc."

CHAPTER 37

GHOST

Earlier that night…

Two weeks.

Fourteen fucking days since I last saw her, since I touched her, since I made her come apart in that interview room while the world outside burned with violence.

My Geneva.

I stare at the cracked screen of my smuggled phone, the faint glow illuminating the only thing keeping me tethered to this woman.

Her face.

Her voice.

Her body.

Every part of her teases me. Tempts me. Maddens me.

She hasn't texted. Hasn't called. Not even to insult me. My hand shakes as rage and longing entwine into something I can't contain.

If I wasn't insane before, I certainly am now with wanting her.

I'm not the only one with issues. Geneva is getting therapy

because of me, which I find amusing. I know why. It's because I got inside her head, and she's trying to claw me out. Exorcise me like the ghost I am.

My fingers hover over the screen, over the message I've typed and deleted a hundred times. I could send it now. Just one text to remind her how it felt.

How *we* felt.

But I don't send it. Because if I do, she'll know the power she has over me. It's complete and total domination.

Although I might've already exposed my vulnerability to her. By admitting that losing her scares me. By saying I don't know what I'd do without her. It was a moment of weakness, brought on by her surrender to me.

I lean back against the wall, the cold concrete doing nothing to calm the heat burning through me. My fingers twitch with the urge to break something. Or to caress her.

I remember the way she looked that day in the interview room. I replay it in my mind every waking moment. Her lips swollen, her breath shaky, and her eyes wide with something I've never seen before. It wasn't fear. It was desire.

And it was *real*.

"Two weeks," I mutter to myself. The words echo in the small cell, bouncing off the walls like a taunt. Fourteen days without her, and I feel like I'm dying. She's in every thought, every breath, every fucking moment of my existence.

I unlock my phone again, searching the cameras in her apartment. My chest tightens when I find her, and for a split second, I want to smash the phone against the wall. Instead, I zoom in on her face, looking for something beneath the surface. A crack in the façade.

A trace of me.

She's hiding it well. But I can still make out the tension in her shoulders, see the shadows beneath her eyes. She's unraveling just like I am. That's why she's running.

But she won't get far.

I won't let her.

⁓

An hour later, I'm standing in front of her apartment with a baseball cap on, a knife in my pocket, and lockpicks in hand.

My pulse is thrumming with excitement, adrenaline flooding my veins. The anticipation is almost too much to bear. It takes every ounce of self-control not to break down the door and fuck her into submission.

No, this has to be done right.

This has to be done perfectly.

When the lock clicks, I slip inside, the darkness swallowing me whole. The apartment is quiet, the air heavy and still. I move silently, the familiarity of the space heightening my senses.

I've spent so much time here. In her life. In her head.

I creep down the hallway to pause outside her bedroom. The door is cracked open, the light spilling through. Geneva is sitting on her bed with a glass of wine in her hand, staring at a computer screen like she wants to murder it. I almost laugh. She's so adorable when she's pissed.

When Geneva shifts on the bed, I duck into the hallway bathroom and wait for her to pass me. She does, making her way to the kitchen, presumably to refill her wine glass. Leaving the bedroom empty.

I slip inside, my heart pounding as I step into her personal domain. It's been a while. A quick scan reveals the usual items. A rumpled bed, a pile of books, a laptop, and that stuffed elephant which means a lot to her.

I walk to her nightstand, reaching out to stroke the soft fur. There's something about the way she clutches it when she sleeps, like a child holding on to a security blanket. It's oddly endearing, especially coming from a strong woman like her.

Her soft footsteps reach me, and I quickly duck into the closet, leaving the door cracked so I can watch her.

She's back a moment later, her glass full and her gaze fixed on the computer screen. She doesn't notice me. Yet.

Her sultry voice hits the air, and my dick gets hard. It's Pavlov's Theory; Geneva has trained my cock.

"Psychopathy is a condition defined by control," she says.

I smile, watching her from the shadows as her voice carries through the room. The way she speaks—articulate, controlled, so damn authoritative—it makes my pulse race. The wine in her glass trembles in her hand, a faint, telling sign that she's not as composed as she wants to be.

"Psychopaths thrive in environments where they can exploit weakness. They adapt, manipulate, and control with alarming precision," she says, reading aloud.

Talk dirty to me.

Geneva pauses, her lips pressing into a thin line. The silence stretches, and then she exhales, taking a generous sip before setting the wine glass down on the nightstand.

She runs her fingers along the edge of her laptop absentmindedly, and I notice the subtle shift in her body. The way her shoulders relax. The way she presses her thighs together.

She's not thinking about the keynote anymore.

My smirk fades, replaced by something darker. I lean forward, the crack in the closet door just wide enough for me to catch the flush creeping up her neck.

Oh, Doc. What are you thinking about?

She tilts her head back, closing her eyes for a moment. I don't miss the way her breathing changes. It's slower, heavier. She grips the comforter and her lips part on a groan. Of sexual frustration.

Heat coils low in my stomach, and my cock hardens painfully. I know what's going through her mind. It's written all over her.

She's thinking about me.

At least, she better fucking be.

Geneva shifts, sliding her hand down to her pussy, and I bite back a groan. A shudder of pleasure ripples through her, and I catch a soft sound, a barely audible sigh that makes my blood roar in my ears.

That's right, Geneva. Keep going. Don't you fucking stop.

This moment is too good to interrupt. Watching her like this, watching her submit to the desire she's feeling, is almost as intoxicating as touching her.

"Yes," she moans loudly. "God, yes."

She arches her back, falling deeper into ecstasy. My need to come is almost unbearable. So, I punch myself in the dick. It helps somewhat.

"Ghost."

My whole body locks up as the sound of my name pours from her lips, raw and unrestrained. It's like gasoline on an already raging fire, and I have to grip the edges of the closet door to stop myself from bursting out and finishing what she's started.

Geneva doesn't even realize what she's doing to me. How every low moan has me teetering on the edge of control. My breathing is ragged, my fists aching from how tightly I'm clenching the door-frame. I bite the inside of my cheek hard enough to taste blood, anything to anchor myself. To stop me from losing my fucking mind and becoming an absolute savage.

Geneva collapses against the bed, her chest heaving as the aftermath washes over her. She looks wrecked, and it's beauti-ful. Her hair splayed out on the pillow, skin flushed, and her legs still trembling. But it's her face that does me in. The soft, dreamy expression, the smile tugging at her lips.

It's too much to handle.

But then her expression morphs into something angry, her lips twisting with bitterness. For a split second I forget about how painfully hard my dick is, while trying to figure out what caused the sudden change.

"Fuck you, Ghost, for making me want you," she says.

I blink. *Does she know I'm here? Impossible.*

"Fuck you for making me feel this way," she says. "For making me question everything I've ever known about myself, about con-trol, about boundaries. And most of all, fuck you for leaving me to deal with this…this *obsession* with you."

Degradation kink unlocked.

Her insults, sharp as they are, can't smother the satisfaction curling in my chest. She's thinking about me. Obsessing over me. And no matter how much she fights it, she wants me.

I just want her more.

Her anger fuels something dark and primal in me. She's raging against me, yes, but it's because she hates what she's feeling. The connection, the pull, the fucking obsession she just admitted out loud.

I sag against the closet wall, tension rolling through me like a bolt of lightning. Her frustration is intoxicating, her vulnerability even more so. It's a potent combination that leaves me balanced on the edge of control.

She's not just angry at me; she's angry at herself for wanting me. For needing me. And I won't let my girl go unsatisfied.

That's just rude.

CHAPTER 38

GENEVA

Present

"HELLO, DOC."

I gasp, clutching the blanket to my chest, and find Ghost exiting my closet to stand at the foot of my bed, his form silhouetted by the moonlight streaming through the window.

"How the hell did you get in here?" I snap.

My overly defensive tone reveals the fear and disbelief colliding inside me. Ghost isn't supposed to be here. Not in the room where I sleep. Not standing next to the bed where I indulge in my darkest fantasies of him.

He smirks, the expression both infuriating and enticing. "Does it really matter?"

"You're right," I say, forcing a confidence I don't feel. "It doesn't. Get the fuck out before I call the police."

He takes a step forward, his movements smooth, graceful, and predatory. I shrink back instinctively. I'm not scared of him, but of what he could do to me emotionally.

Ghost doesn't stop walking until he's next to my side of the bed, towering over me, his hair draped over his brow. "Tsk. Tsk. Now, is that any way to talk to a friend?"

"We're not friends."

"If me touching your pussy isn't friendly, then I'd love to know what is."

I glare up at him. "Why are you here? What do you want?"

His gaze is intense, the raw hunger in his eyes unmistakable. "You."

"No."

"Yes," he whispers, the sound both confident and sensual.

He reaches out, his fingers brushing my cheek, and my breathing quickens. I shake my head, rendered mute at his touch. He leans forward, his lips brushing my ear, his breath hot against my skin.

"You want me, Geneva," he murmurs. "Admit it."

"Fuck you."

"Only if you're a good girl."

He trails his fingers down my jaw, featherlight and deceptive. My skin heats beneath his touch, a slow burn that spreads through me like wildfire. I force myself to stay still, to hold my ground, even as my pulse pounds in my throat.

I just need a second. A small window.

My fingers twitch at my side, inching toward my phone resting on the nightstand. I keep my eyes trained on his, not wanting to give away my intentions, while hoping he's too distracted by the game we're playing.

But the moment I lunge for my cell phone, he snatches my wrist. I barely have time to react before he yanks me up, forcing me onto my knees, our chests colliding.

"Too slow, Doc."

I use my free hand and shove at his chest, but it's useless. He's unmovable. I hate how easily he overpowers me, how effortlessly he drags me under his control.

How much I want to stay there.

Ghost flexes his fingers around my wrist, his grip now painful. His nose brushes the curve of my jaw as he inhales slowly. "Did you really think I wouldn't catch you?"

I scowl. "I thought you'd be too busy stroking your own ego."

"Smart mouth. The same one that screamed my name a few minutes ago."

Heat floods my cheeks. "That didn't mean anything."

"It means everything."

I shrug with a nonchalance I don't feel. "If you say so."

His eyes narrow at my blatant dismissal, all traces of amusement fading. His grip on my wrist tightens before he lets go, only to reach into his back pocket. The glint of his knife catches the light, the sharp blade gleaming between us, making my breath hitch.

"Ghost…" I warn.

He doesn't answer. Instead, he brings the blade to my throat, the flat side pressing against my pulse. A silent reminder of who he really is.

I go still, barely daring to breathe.

Ghost leans in, lips just brushing my ear. "Do *not* lie to me, Geneva." The way he says my name is sensual, with just a hint of something unhinged.

Using the knife, he traces a path along my throat, then lower, between my collarbones. The whisper of pressure from the blade has my heart pounding so hard I feel it in every inch of my body.

Then, without warning, he slices.

The cold kiss of steel against fabric. My shirt parts down the middle in a clean, effortless cut. The cool air hits my bare skin, and I suck in a sharp breath, but I don't move.

Ghost watches me, his expression unreadable as he peels back the fabric, exposing my breasts. My skin is hypersensitive to every movement, every shift of the blade as Ghost drags it down, past my ribs, to my navel. He doesn't cut. Doesn't break the skin. But the sheer precision of his control is just as lethal as the edge itself.

"Wow, Doc. You didn't even flinch."

I lift my chin. "Are you going to rape me?"

The thought makes my skin prickle and my breathing ragged. He notices. His smirk appears, but his hold on the knife remains steady.

"You can't rape the willing."

I glare at him. "I'm not giving my consent."

"Good. It'll be more fun that way."

Ghost rests the knife against my leg, the cool steel a stark contrast to the heat spreading through my skin. Slowly, he drags it upward, the blade's presence both dangerous and intoxicating. My heart feels like it's going to explode, but I keep my face impassive, unwilling to give him the reaction he's looking for.

"Open," he says, his voice commanding. When I don't move, he taps my inner thigh with the blade. "Don't make me repeat myself."

Still on my knees, I grip his biceps for support and spread my legs.

"Good girl," he praises, his voice thick with satisfaction.

I glare at him. "Go to hell."

"Already there. Because every second I'm not inside you is fucking torture."

His other hand is rough and warm as he slides it up my ribs, molding to the curves of my breasts. He flicks his thumbs over my nipples, teasing, testing, waiting for me to react. I bite the inside of my cheek, determined not to make a sound.

He chuckles darkly, dipping his head. "Stubborn."

I inhale sharply as his tongue flicks over my nipple, his teeth grazing just enough to hurt. To punish. Ghost watches me with that lazy, knowing smile, as he pulls my nipple into his mouth, sucking hard. But he's not in a rush. He's savoring this.

Savoring me.

I hold his gaze, refusing to break first. Even when he snakes his fingers inside my underwear. He grips the material at the crotch, barely touching me, but somehow making me wet. Then, with a sharp tug, he rips the fabric away like it's nothing.

I gasp at the burn against my skin and the sudden exposure. Before I can recover, Ghost spreads me. He hums in approval, dragging his fingers along my damp pussy before pressing slow, torturous circles against my clit.

He continues stroking me, the pressure increasing along with his pace. Pleasure builds within me, the intensity almost too much to bear. I grit my teeth, fighting the urge to thrust against his hand, desperate for release.

"You don't deserve this," he whispers against my lips. "You ignored me for weeks, after I saved your life *and* made you come."

He pulls his fingers away.

I blink at him, lost in a haze of lust. "What…"

Ghost chuckles, roughly gripping my chin, and then using his thumb to smear the effects of my arousal over my lips. He presses his mouth against mine, the kiss hard and bruising. Demanding yet desperate.

I remain still, unresponsive. Even when he flicks his tongue between my lips, coaxing me to taste myself. He wraps his other hand around the back of my neck, pinning me in place as he brings the knife's handle to my clit.

I wrench back, breaking the kiss. "Don't," I gasp, panic flooding me.

"I'm not. *You* are." Ghost presses the handle against me. "Use it."

The feeling is cold and alien, but as I slowly move against it, the foreign texture rubs against my clit in a way that's erotic. I do it again, faster and harder to add more pressure, and the friction sends sparks of pleasure through me. Ghost groans when I start panting.

"That's right," he growls, his voice rough. "Rub that pussy all over it. Show me how you're going to do the same to my cock."

I continue gyrating against the handle, the pleasure compounding at Ghost's ragged breathing. I'm so close. So fucking close.

"Come. *Now*," Ghost snaps.

I obey, my body shaking uncontrollably. He's quick to wrap his arm around my waist, preventing me from impaling myself on the handle as my orgasm wrecks me. Over and over.

When the world settles back into focus, I find him watching me with something dangerous in his eyes.

Possession.

Devotion.

Something too deep to name.

I swallow hard, my pulse still erratic. "Happy now?" I manage, breathless.

Ghost grins. "Not even close."

CHAPTER 39

GENEVA

Ghost lifts the knife to his mouth, dragging his tongue slowly along the handle, his eyes locked onto mine the entire time. The act is meant to unravel me. And it does.

He tilts his head, gesturing lazily with the blade toward my hands. "Unbuckle my pants."

I pause, unsure if I'm still resisting him. Or seducing him.

His smirk deepens as he takes in my hesitation. My stubbornness returns full force to prove that I'm not intimidated by him. I reach for the zipper, my knuckles brushing against the hard lines of his stomach. At the clench of his jaw and the way his muscles twitch, I know I'm affecting him just as much as he affects me.

The moment his pants are undone, I yank his shirt off, along with my own. His sculpted torso comes into view, marked by scars that hint of past fights and possible abuse. But it's the tribal tattoos that really draw me in, igniting another surge of lust as I trace their bold, intricate patterns with my eyes. They wind aggressively around his arms, up his neck, and spread over much of his upper chest, the dark ink clinging to his skin in a way that's beyond sexy.

Ghost sits on the edge of the bed, legs spread, the blade resting casually in his palm. His eyes are heavy-lidded, dark with intent. "Ride me," he orders, his voice deep and rough.

When I don't move, he leans back, spreading his legs wider. His large cock rests against his abdomen while pre-cum leaks onto his skin. He twirls the knife lazily between his fingers, tapping the flat of the blade against the outside of his thigh. The gesture is casual, but the command in his eyes is anything but.

I take a fortifying breath. Then, slowly, I crawl onto his lap to straddle him.

After putting down the knife, he reaches out to grab my hips, the heat of his body seeping into my skin. My heart hammers against my ribs as I realize I've willingly put myself in his hands. Again.

Maybe that's his point.

With one hand, he kneads the flesh of my thighs as he looks at me, drinking me in. He grabs the knife and drags the tip up my spine, the cool metal leaving goosebumps in its wake. I arch instinctively, pressing myself closer to him.

I hover over his cock, my breathing uneven, my hands braced against his chest. The heat of him is tangible, radiating through every point where our bodies connect. His smile is lazy, but his eyes are watchful, tracking every flicker of emotion on my face.

"Use me," he says. "Take me. Every. Single. Fucking. Inch."

I swallow the nerves gathering in my throat as my fingers tremble against his skin. I can feel his cock pressing against me, thick and hard. Although he easily could, he doesn't force me.

No, Ghost is making me *choose* him.

I exhale, then move, sinking onto him. He curses under his breath, his fingers biting into my flesh as I take him in. It happens inch by inch, me stretching around him with a whimper despite how wet I am. My nails claw his chest, drawing blood, my thighs shaking as I adjust.

"Fuck." He tilts his head back slightly, his jaw tight. "You're going to kill me."

A shudder runs through me, my body humming at the praise. I brace myself again, lifting my hips just enough before sliding back down farther than before. I still have a couple of inches left to take. Ghost watches me through hooded eyes, seeing me struggle. It hurts, and he knows it, but it's the pain that has me feeling alive.

"Make it fit, or I will," he says.

After a couple more tries, I get the last bit of him in. I feel stretched beyond anything I can handle. My breathing is labored, and I'm sweating. He runs his hand up and down my side, the touch soothing.

"You're such a good girl."

I'm so full, it's hard to breathe, but I manage. Then Ghost reaches down to touch the area where our bodies are joined, and my breath leaves my lungs completely. He gently traces my pussy with his fingers, his eyes never leaving that place of intimate connection, his expression one of awe and intense desire.

"Perfect...just perfect," he whispers.

The reverence in his gaze deepens, the corners of his lips lifting in a satisfied smile. He leans closer, his breath warm against my skin.

"Look at you, taking all of me." Ghost swivels his hips just a little, but it forces a moan from me. "Now, ride me."

I don't move, overwhelmed with the knowledge of what's coming next. Ghost doesn't give me a choice. He drops the knife and grips my hips, guiding me. I rise, then sink back down. I repeat the motion, slowly, finding a rhythm that has us both groaning.

"Fuck," Ghost rasps. "So fucking tight. Don't stop."

I keep moving, grinding my hips, chasing release. My muscles tremble from the strain, but I don't falter, wanting to stay in control.

Eventually, Ghost takes over as his desperation outdoes mine. He thrusts his hips up, burying himself deeper inside me. I gasp, the pleasure and pain blurring together, making it impossible to tell where one ends and the other begins.

"It's too much. I can't…" I whimper.

"You can take it. You already are. Look at you," he says, his voice hoarse. "Taking me so well. God, I love the way you fuck me."

He groans, his hands gripping me tighter as he takes complete control, lifting me, meeting each roll of my hips with a dominating thrust. The pleasure builds, sharp and relentless, coiling low in my stomach. He continues slamming into me, fucking me hard and deep, his grip bruising.

"Eyes on me," he snaps. "Look at me when you come."

I flick my gaze to his. The raw emotion I find in his eyes sends me over the edge. I scream as the orgasm tears through me, my body spasming around his cock. Milking him, forcing him to come.

"Geneva," he groans.

His hips jerk as he comes, his cock twitching inside me. Ghost continues fucking me, riding out the last waves of his ecstasy. By the time he stops, I'm shaking, barely able to hold myself up. I collapse against him, and he wraps his arms around me, stroking my hair.

"Shh," he murmurs. "I've got you."

He holds me close, our bodies slick with sweat, our hearts thrashing in our chests. I press my face against his skin, inhaling his scent. He runs his hands along my back, up and down, tracing the curve of my spine.

Ghost doesn't speak. He just holds me, weaving his fingers through my hair, his breath warm against my temple. His touch is comforting, but I feel too raw. Too exposed.

I squeeze my eyes shut, trying to fortify myself, but the vulnerability keeps creeping in, sinking into my bones. It's just sex. It's a biological need, a primal urge that both of us are fulfilling. Nothing more.

So, how can something purely physical leave such deep imprints on my soul?

"You're shaking," he murmurs into my hair.

I remain silent, not trusting my voice. I'm not sure what I'd even say. Then Ghost lifts my chin, forcing me to meet his gaze. His eyes, normally so unreadable, so filled with sharp edges and danger, hold something else. Something that makes my chest ache.

He drags his thumb along my jaw. "Talk to me."

I shake my head.

Ghost studies me for a long moment, his gaze searching. His voice is quieter when he speaks again. "You think I don't feel it too?"

I stiffen. He grabs the back of my neck, keeping me still. His lips brush against my temple, lingering.

"It's not just sex, Geneva."

I should say something. I should push him away before this goes any deeper, before it becomes something I can't survive.

But I don't.

Because he's still touching me. Still holding me like he doesn't want to let go.

"I don't know how to do this," I whisper.

Ghost hums, his grip tightening. "You think I do? That it's ever been this way for me?"

A psychopath and a psychologist...

Neither of us know what to do. Or how to stop it.

Whatever this madness is.

CHAPTER 40

GENEVA

I wake up disoriented and confused, lying naked and tangled in the sheets. The memory of Ghost's hands on my skin rushes through me, and I sit up, my pulse racing.

Was it a dream? A hallucination? Or did it actually happen?

I press my hand to my chest, trying to steady my erratic heartbeat as the room comes into focus. The pale light of dawn filters through the curtains, soft and mild, the opposite of the storm raging inside me. My skin feels warm, hypersensitive, as if his touch lingers even now.

It had to be a dream, I tell myself, though the conviction isn't there. Because it felt so vivid, so *real*. His hands gripping my hips, the way his lips moved against mine...each detail is etched into my mind with a startling clarity.

I glance at the sheets, twisted and rumpled with use. Meanwhile, the comforter lies disregarded on the floor as if it was a hindrance. I drag my fingers over the curve of my hip, over the trace of a bruise, and a shiver runs through me.

The memory—or the illusion—floods back with force, Ghost's voice low and rough in my ear, saying things that make my breath hitch even now. I shake my head, trying to clear it. The logical part of me knows the truth. He wasn't here. He couldn't have been. And yet, the pull of him is so strong, so consuming, that the boundary between reality and desire is almost nonexistent.

I scan the room, searching for any indication that he was actually here. That he'd come for me, touched me, been with me in a way that wasn't just a fantasy born of my selfish desires. But there's nothing. No clothes discarded. No sign of the man who's ruined my life.

Except for a single magnolia resting on the pillow beside me.

My breathing halts as I stare at it, my chest tightening with a wave of emotions so twisted I can't unravel them. Fear. Desire. Confusion.

And something I don't want to name.

My fingers tremble as I reach for the flower, the smooth petals cool against my skin. The soft fragrance wraps around me, heady and intimate, like a whisper of the night before.

The magnolia is real.

Ghost was here.

The memory surges forward, vivid and inescapable. His hands on my skin, his body against mine, the way he claimed every inch of me with a mix of raw intensity and startling tenderness. The way he looked at me, like I wasn't just someone to him, but *everything.*

My cheeks flush, my pulse quickening as the reality sets in. I close my eyes, clutching the flower tighter as the weight of what we did presses against my chest. And my heart.

This isn't just a crossing of boundaries; it's a complete obliter-ation of them. Every rule, every line I told myself I'd never cross, gone in an instant.

But the fear isn't as sharp as I expected. It's there, simmering beneath the surface, but it's overshadowed by something else. Desire. For intimacy. For connection.

For *him*.

It's a yearning I can't ignore. The memory of his lips on my skin, his cock thrusting deep, the way he unraveled me completely…it all lingers, refusing to let me go.

The magnolia is his message. A silent confirmation of what we shared. A reminder that he's never far. That I can never be apart from him.

I gently set the flower down on the nightstand, my fingers lin-gering on the stem. My mind spins with questions, but the answers don't matter right now. What matters is that it happened. That *he* happened.

And that nothing will ever be the same.

∽

Later that evening, I gesture to the garment bag hanging in the corner. "Well, I got the dress. The rest is up to you."

Sarah beams, practically bouncing up and down as she unzips the bag to reveal the wine-colored gown inside. The fabric gleams under the light, rich and smooth, with a neckline that plunges just enough to feel daring but not overly scandalous. The slit up one leg is tasteful, though it still makes me blush when I think about how much skin it shows.

"You're going to slay, queen," she declares, holding it up against me. "Now, off with the boring clothes. We've got work to do."

I laugh again at her infectious energy and quickly change. The cool silk of the gown slips over my skin, molding to my body like it was made for me. When I'm finished, Sarah's face lights up.

"Okay, wow," she says, circling me like an artist appraising her masterpiece. "You look…I mean, damn, Geneva. Picasso!"

She kisses the tips of her fingers, and I laugh again as I turn toward the mirror. The dress hugs my curves in all the right places, the burgundy setting off the warmth of my skin and the dark waves of my hair. The neckline draws attention to the slope of my collarbone, while the slit reveals just enough of my leg to feel provocative.

"Too much skin?" I ask, gesturing to the open back.

"Not enough," Sarah quips. She runs out of my bedroom and quickly returns, dragging a chair into my bathroom. "Sit. Hair time. We're going full old-Hollywood glam."

I settle onto the chair, and she gets to work, pulling my hair into loose waves that cascade over one shoulder. As she works, I glance at my reflection, my lips curving into a small smile. The Geneva staring back at me feels…different. *Alive.*

The memory of Ghost's hands on my skin, and the way he murmured my name like it was something delicious, flutters through my mind, sending heat rushing to my cheeks.

"Why do you look like you've got a naughty secret?" Sarah asks, narrowing her eyes at me in the mirror.

I bite back a laugh, shaking my head. "Do I?"

"Mm-hmm." She smirks, gently tugging a lock of my hair. "There's a glint in your eyes. Something spicy. Did you meet someone?"

"No," I lie. "I had a sexy dream last night. The stuff of legends."

She waggles her eyebrows. "Niiiiice. Hold on to it. You're glowing tonight. Care to share any of the details?"

"I can't without covering my face and ruining your makeup."

"Don't you dare."

When she finishes a while later, I stand, running my hands down the smooth fabric of the gown. I look taller, more statuesque. Sophisticated. Sultry.

I wish Ghost could see me like this.

"You look like a damn goddess," Sarah says, stepping back to admire her work. "Everyone at the banquet is going to donate something after seeing you. If they don't, screw them."

I grin at her in the mirror, a genuine smile that isn't enough to convey my gratitude. "Thanks, Sarah. I don't know what I'd do without you."

"You'd survive." She winks at me. "But you wouldn't look half as good doing it. Now, go show 'em what your momma gave you."

CHAPTER 41

GENEVA

THE ROOM QUIETS AS I STEP ONTO THE STAGE. INSTANTLY, THE podium is a barricade between me and the audience, a shield I'm grateful for. My speech is neatly printed, the outline memorized, but my chest tightens as I shuffle the papers, forcing myself to exhale slowly.

You've done this before. It's just another lecture.

Except it isn't. I've added a personal touch, something that I don't usually do, and the stakes are higher. Donors, alumni, and faculty members are all waiting to hear me deliver insight into the enigma they know as Ghost. They're hungry for the polished, clinical observations that paint him as a fascinating puzzle, a cautionary tale of psychopathy.

They have no freaking idea.

"Good evening," I begin, my voice steady, carrying just enough warmth to pull the audience in. "It's an honor to stand before you tonight, not just as a keynote speaker, but as someone whose journey began here, within the walls of this very university.

"Before I delve into the heart of my work, I want to share

a story. A story that began thousands of miles from here, in the sun-drenched savannas of East Africa. It's where I spent much of my childhood, alongside my parents, who were humanitarians. They devoted their lives to healing the fractures of a world so often divided by conflict and inequality."

My voice softens, laced with emotion. "They were more than my parents. They were my compass, my moral anchor. My mother, a physician, established clinics in villages that hadn't seen a doctor in years. My father, an educator, believed that knowledge was the most powerful tool for change. Together, they were a force of nature, inspiring everyone around them. Including me."

A smile touches my lips, but it's tinged with bittersweetness. "Their work wasn't easy, and neither was their decision to uproot our lives and move to Africa when I was a toddler. They did so to advocate for change on a larger scale, to ensure that their work could create ripples far beyond what they could accomplish alone."

I pause, letting the weight of my next words settle. "But their journey was cut short. After returning to the States, my parents were killed in an act of senseless violence. A tragic event that left more questions than answers. For years, I struggled to understand the kind of mind capable of such cruelty. And that struggle became my purpose."

The room is utterly still now, and everyone is watching me with rapt attention. It's a good sign, but only adds to my nervousness. I clear my throat and continue.

"This is why I chose to study criminal psychology. I needed to understand what drives people to the darkest corners of human behavior. Not just to solve crimes, but to prevent them. To find meaning in the chaos. And, perhaps most importantly, to honor my parents' legacy by seeking justice in a world that often feels unjust."

I glance at the slideshow behind me, where an image of my parents appears. It's a candid shot of them laughing together with my father's arm draped over my mother's shoulders, and the African sun setting behind them. The photo shifts to an image of me as a graduate student, standing proudly beside the university sign.

"This university gave me the tools to take that purpose and transform it into action. It gave me the mentors, the resources, and the opportunities to explore the complexities of the human mind. It gave me the courage to face the hardest truths and the knowledge to pursue answers where none seemed possible."

I shift my tone from personal to inspirational. "Today, I stand before you not just as a scholar, but as proof of what this institution can achieve. The research I conduct, the cases I work on, and the lives I've touched all began here, with the generosity of people like you. Your support fuels the dreams of students who, like me, aspire to make a difference in a world desperately in need of it.

"Imagine what we could accomplish together. Imagine the lives we could change, the futures we could shape, the light we could bring to those darkest corners. This isn't just an investment in education. It's an investment in justice, in understanding, and in hope. My parents believed that one person could change the world. I believe that too. But together, we can do so much more."

I let the current photo of my parents linger on the screen behind me, their smiles illuminated in the soft glow of the stage lights. "They believed in the power of connection, in the idea that understanding others—no matter how different—could bridge divides and heal wounds. It's a belief I carry with me in all my work. But not everyone values connection. Not everyone is capable of it."

With the press of a button, the slide transitions to a picture of Ghost. On the giant screen, his mugshot feels larger than life. Especially because of that infuriatingly smug expression I've come to both love and hate.

His face is a mask of defiance, his eyes cold yet piercing, as though he's challenging anyone who dares to try and label him. It's a picture I've analyzed countless times, but now, standing here, it feels different.

The room is silent, the audience captivated, but I can't focus on their reactions. My pulse quickens as my gaze locks on his image. The memory of last night floods my mind, making my skin burn with the phantom sensation of his hands on me.

"Psychopathy is a condition defined by control, not connection." My voice is steady despite the tendrils of lust coursing through me. Branding me.

A flicker of movement snatches my attention. My gaze shifts toward it, landing on a tall figure who's leaning casually against the back wall. The man has his arms crossed, and his face is partially obscured by shadows. It's the posture, the body language that's familiar. But when his eyes meet mine, sharp and unmistakable, my breath catches in my throat.

For a moment, I hesitate, my mind scrambling to reconcile what I'm seeing. His hair, normally stark white, is now jet black, styled in a way that makes him look almost ordinary. The scar that twists down his cheek is gone, replaced by flawless skin, likely the work of expertly applied prosthetics and makeup. His tailored suit blends seamlessly with the polished crowd inside, but it's the smirk tugging at his lips that shatters the illusion.

Ghost.

He doesn't move, doesn't acknowledge the recognition flickering across my face. But his gaze holds mine, unflinching, and I know this isn't a hallucination. He's here, in plain sight, daring me to falter.

Or to continue...

I grip the edges of the podium, my fingers digging into the wood as I force myself to speak. "Psychopaths are often misunderstood. Their actions are calculated, their emotions shallow, and their ability to manipulate unparalleled."

His expression doesn't change, but there's a glint in his eyes that I recognize too well. A challenge. He's testing me, pushing me to maintain my composure while he stands there, a living contradiction to everything I'm saying.

"However," I continue, my gaze flickering briefly to my notes before returning to the audience, "what sets them apart is their ability to adapt. They learn to mimic human connection, to exploit vulnerabilities in ways that make them appear normal."

The words hang in the air, and I swear the corner of his mouth twitches with the faintest hint of amusement. My pulse quickens, but I press on, refusing to let him rattle me.

"They thrive in environments where control is paramount. They seek power, not always through brute force, but through subtlety. Through precision."

Ghost shifts slightly, his posture unchanged but his gaze burning into me with an intensity that makes my skin prickle. He's not just listening. He's dissecting every word and every nuance, as if this speech is for him alone. And in a way, it is.

He's here for a reason, and I can't decide if it's to intimidate me, to test me, or to remind me of the connection I've tried so hard to bury. Maybe it's all three.

"Dr. Andrews, a question."

All eyes turn toward the source. My stomach plummets, and I grip the podium more tightly. He remains in the shadows at the back of the room, his presence commanding, his gaze locked on me.

"Do you really believe psychopaths are incapable of connection?" Ghost's voice carries easily, calm but direct. Although it sounds like a casual inquiry, it's anything but.

The audience murmurs, confused at the interruption but intrigued, their attention shifting between him and me. I force a neutral expression, one that doesn't betray the apprehension building inside me.

"That's what the research shows," I say. "Psychopathy is characterized by a lack of genuine emotional connection. While they may mimic emotions, their relationships are typically shallow and self-serving."

"But isn't it possible," he says slowly, "that even a psychopath could experience something real? Under the right circumstances?"

The murmuring in the audience grows louder, curiosity and unease rippling through the crowd. My chest tightens as his words settle over me, heavy with meaning only we can fully understand.

"Psychopaths lack empathy," I reply, forcing a clinical tone. "Their actions are driven by self-interest, not genuine care or connection."

His smirk deepens, his eyes never leaving mine. "Interesting. And yet, couldn't one argue that self-interest and connection aren't mutually exclusive? That sometimes, wanting someone, needing someone, can feel indistinguishable from … let's say, love?"

My breath hitches as the room around us fades into a blur. He's not asking about psychopaths. He's asking about himself.

About *us*.

The audience shifts uncomfortably, the tension palpable, but Ghost doesn't seem to notice. Or care. His gaze burns into me, daring me to respond, to refute him, to call him out for what he really is.

"I suppose it's possible for someone to misinterpret those feelings," I say carefully, my voice tight. "But that doesn't mean they're genuine. It means they're manipulative. A reflection of what they want, not what they feel. Psychopaths manipulate perceptions to serve their own ends. What feels genuine to them is often an illusion designed to elicit a specific response from others. It's not about connection, it's about control."

Ghost tilts his head, his gaze unyielding. "And if the person being controlled wants it? If they *choose* to see the illusion as real, does that make it less genuine? Or does it make it something else entirely?"

The room is deathly silent now, the audience caught in the battle of wills raging between us. I can feel their confusion, their intrigue, but all I can focus on is Ghost. The challenge in his words, the way his tone pressures me to submit.

"That choice," I say, "is often born from manipulation. It's a reflection of the psychopath's ability to distort reality, not a sign of authenticity."

"And yet," he counters smoothly, taking a step forward, "authenticity is subjective, isn't it? What's real to one person might look like manipulation to another. Who gets to decide what's true? The one who feels it…or the one who's afraid to?" He gives me a pointed look.

"I appreciate your perspective," I say, my voice hard. "But this discussion is rooted in empirical evidence, not philosophical interpretation."

Ghost smiles, a slow, sensual curve of his lips that makes my stomach flutter. "Of course it is," he says softly. "Because it's safer that way, isn't it? Easier to stick to data than to face what's right in front of you."

The audience shifts in their seats, unsure whether this is part of the presentation or something far more personal.

My hands tremble now. "Thank you for your question. Now, as I was saying, understanding the mind of a psychopath requires detachment. Data isn't just safer. It's essential. Without it, we risk letting personal biases cloud our judgment."

I briefly flick my eyes to Ghost, finding his posture relaxed but his gaze unrelenting. His smirk hasn't faded, and it needles at the edges of my composure.

"As an example," I say, "let me introduce you to someone I've spent several months studying. A subject who embodies everything I've just described. He's a man who has confounded the justice system, evaded capture for years, and left a trail of devastation in his wake."

I click the button and the screen behind me shifts to a picture of Ghost during his arraignment. "This is the man the media calls 'Ghost.' He's a textbook example of what makes psychopaths so dangerous: charming, intelligent, and completely devoid of empathy.

"He operates in the shadows," I continue, addressing the audience but acutely aware of his presence. "He doesn't just manipulate individuals. He manipulates entire systems. His actions aren't impulsive, they're meticulously planned, each one designed to exploit weakness and evade accountability."

Ghost nods his head, his expression somewhere between amusement and approval. It's as if he's silently applauding me for describing him so perfectly.

"And yet," I say, "he's also human. Behind the calculated actions and the façade of invincibility lies a fractured psyche. It's a mind shaped by experiences we may never fully understand."

The audience leans forward, captivated, their unease momentarily overshadowed by fascination. Ghost, however, remains motionless, his presence a static hum at the edge of my awareness.

"To study someone like Ghost," I say, "is not to glorify him. It's to shine a light into the most depraved parts of human behavior, to understand how such minds operate, and, ultimately, to protect others from falling victim to their machinations."

I glance briefly at Ghost again, just long enough to catch the subtle shift in his expression. The smirk is gone now, replaced by something sharper, more calculating. It sends a chill down my spine.

"Criminal psychology isn't just about solving crimes," I say, addressing the room with renewed conviction. "It's about prevention. It's about justice. And it's about giving voice to those who can no longer speak for themselves.

"But why, you might ask, does someone like Ghost capture the public's attention so completely? Why do we see his story splashed across headlines, his actions dissected by multiple professionals, and his name whispered in fear?"

The screen behind me shifts again, this time to a timeline of Ghost's alleged crimes: high-profile murders, inexplicable disappearances, and cryptic messages left at the scenes. Each event marked by precision, each detail curated for maximum impact.

"It's not just his crimes that intrigue us," I say, gesturing toward the screen. "It's his ability to remain untouchable. Ghost is not like the average offender we encounter in criminal psychology. He doesn't act out of desperation or recklessness. His motives aren't rooted in impulse or emotional instability. Every move he makes is deliberate, methodical, and—most unsettling of all—purposeful."

"What sets Ghost apart," I continue, "is his need for control. Not just over individuals but over entire narratives. He crafts his actions like a playwright, ensuring every piece of the story serves his end goal. And what is that goal? Power. Influence. Not through brute force, but through psychological domination. He doesn't just break laws; he breaks people."

And I'm one of them.

The image on the screen changes again, this time to a crime scene photo (tastefully blurred) but the emotion it evokes is undeniable. A note left behind is the focal point, scrawled in neat handwriting: *Actions have consequences.*

"Messages like these are what make Ghost truly unique," I explain. "He communicates not just with his victims but with society as a whole. He knows how to manipulate fear, curiosity, and even admiration. He's not content with staying hidden in the shadows. He wants to be seen but only on his terms."

I pause to take a deep breath. "And that is what makes him unlike any other psychopath we've studied. His intelligence, his adaptability, and his mastery of psychological manipulation elevate him to a level that defies traditional categorization. Ghost isn't just a criminal; he's a phenomenon."

The screen fades to black, and I turn back to the audience, my gaze steady. "But we must be careful not to confuse fascination with glorification. To study someone like Ghost is to understand the dangers of unchecked power and the consequences of failing to see the warning signs before it's too late. He's a case study in what happens when brilliance and darkness collide. Thank you."

The room erupts into applause, though it feels distant, muted against the pounding of my heart. I step back from the podium, my hands trembling as I clasp them together.

Ghost doesn't move. His gaze lingers on me, his smirk fading into something more serious, more dangerous. For a moment, I think he might say something else, might push me further, but then he steps back into the shadows, disappearing into the crowd as if he was never there.

CHAPTER 42

GENEVA

THE APPLAUSE FADES INTO THE AMBIENT HUM OF CONVERSATION as I step off the stage, my chest still tight with adrenaline. Dr. Melanie Corbin is waiting at the bottom of the stairs, her sharp heels clicking against the floor as she strides toward me. Her expression is warm but laced with a touch of urgency that I've come to recognize as normal for her.

"Geneva," she says, her tone brisk but genuine. "That was phenomenal. I don't think anyone in this room blinked for the last thirty minutes. You had them completely captivated."

"Thank you, Dr. Corbin," I reply, letting out a small breath of relief. "I'm glad it resonated. But I couldn't have done it without the support of this department."

"Don't be modest," she says, waving a hand dismissively. "You earned that ovation." Her expression darkens as she lowers her voice. "Though I could've done without that man interrupting you. Who was that?"

I keep my expression calm, though my pulse quickens at the

mention of Ghost. "I was going to ask you the same thing, but I figured he must have been cleared to attend if he's here."

Dr. Corbin huffs, crossing her arms briefly. "Well, if he was cleared, he's got a lot of nerve pulling that kind of stunt in the middle of your keynote. Honestly, it's insulting. Not just to you but to the event itself."

"I handled it," I say, offering her a reassuring smile. "It's not the first time someone's tried to make themselves the center of attention during a talk. I doubt it'll be the last."

"Still," she mutters, glancing toward the crowd as if she could spot him among the sea of faces. "I'll be having a word with security about this. The last thing we need is more disruptions like that. You deserve better."

"Thank you," I say, my tone genuine, though my stomach sours at her indignation. The last thing I want is anyone digging into who Ghost is, or why he's here. "What's next? I assume there are people I need to meet?"

Her demeanor shifts instantly, irritation giving way to her usual professionalism. "Yes, of course. There are some key benefactors who've been dying to meet you. Let's start with Daniel Cross." She gestures toward a table near the stage where a group of well-dressed individuals are deep in conversation.

I follow her lead, stepping into the rhythm of handshakes, smiles, and carefully crafted small talk. Daniel Cross is charming and affable, quick to praise my work and the impact of the university. Luna Joya is equally engaging, gushing about the inspiration she felt during my speech.

But even as I move from one introduction to the next, I can't shake the memory of Ghost's smirk, his voice cutting through the room with unsettling ease. His presence lingers like a ghost, unseen but impossible to ignore.

"Geneva," Dr. Corbin says, pulling me back to the present. "There's one more person I'd like you to meet."

She gestures toward the bar, where a tall man stands with a glass tumbler in hand. His tailored suit fits perfectly, and his air of authority is unmistakable.

"That is Victor Stanton," she says, her voice lower. "He's one of our most influential benefactors. I think you'll find him interesting."

I meet Stanton's gaze as we approach, his dark eyes sharp and appraising. He smiles, extending his hand.

"Dr. Andrews," he says smoothly. "Your reputation precedes you. That was an impressive speech."

"Thank you, Mr. Stanton." I take his hand. His grip is firm, his presence commanding. "Your support makes work like mine possible, and I'm grateful for it."

"The pleasure is all mine," he says, his voice rich with a practiced charm. "Your insights into criminal psychology were fascinating. Especially your analysis of Ghost." He releases my hand with a measured smile. "It's rare to see someone distill such complexity into something so captivating. You certainly have a way with words."

"Thank you. The goal is always to make the work accessible while honoring its depth."

He nods, sipping his drink, his gaze steady but unreadable. Probably due to time spent in board meetings and negotiations. "You've certainly succeeded. Your childhood in Africa must've been an extraordinary experience."

"It was." My smile softens at the memory. "It gave me a broader perspective on the world. Beauty and hardship, progress and struggle. My parents always said it was impossible to leave that place unchanged."

"They sound like remarkable people. You must have inherited a great deal of their passion for understanding others. How long were you there?"

"We moved when I was two." The memories flicker to life in my mind: the bright sun, the sprawling landscapes, and the sense of wonder only a child could fully grasp. "We stayed until I was seven, and then we came back to the States."

Stanton nods, his expression thoughtful. "Five years at such a formative age...That must have left a deep impression on you."

"It did. It shaped the way I see people, communities, the world. My parents always immersed themselves in their work, and even at that age, I could see the impact they had on those around them."

He drinks his beverage slowly, his gaze fixed on me with an intensity that feels polite but unwavering. "An admirable legacy."

"Thank you."

Dr. Corbin steps forward then, her timing impeccable. "Victor, I'm glad you had a chance to speak with Geneva. She's the best example of what this department can achieve."

"Undoubtedly," Stanton says, his gaze flicking to me one last time. "Dr. Andrews, it's been a pleasure. I look forward to seeing how your work continues to evolve."

"And I appreciate your support."

As he turns and disappears into the crowd, I release a breath. Dr. Corbin gives me an encouraging pat on the arm. "He likes you," she says with a grin. "That's a good thing for us."

"I'm glad to hear it."

As we move on to the next introduction, my thoughts return to Ghost. Throughout every handshake and every polite laugh,

I can't help but search for him. My gaze darts to the corners of the room, to the shadows that the light doesn't quite reach. He's nowhere to be seen.

Eventually, I hit my limit for socialization. I offer a gracious smile to Dr. Corbin. "If you don't mind, I need to step out for a moment. Just to catch my breath."

She waves me off with an understanding nod. "Of course. Take all the time you need. These things can be overwhelming."

I weave through the crowd, my heels clicking against the marble floor as I slip past clusters of guests. The hotel venue is beautifully decorated, but I don't appreciate it enough to stop, so I continue heading toward the balcony.

The cool night air washes over me when I step outside, a sharp contrast to the warmth of the enormous ballroom. For a moment, I simply close my eyes and breathe, letting the stress in my shoulders fade.

"Nice speech, Doc."

CHAPTER 43

GENEVA

I whirl around, my breath caught on a scream that doesn't come. At first, I almost don't recognize Ghost, even this close to him. The transformation to his appearance is unnerving, but it's still him. The intensity in his eyes is unmistakable.

"What are you doing here?" I flick my gaze toward the terrace doors, my pulse spiking. "You shouldn't be here."

"And yet, here I am." He straightens, stepping away from the railing. His tailored suit blends perfectly with the upscale crowd inside, but the cold edge in his smirk is what sets him apart. "You made me a star tonight. It felt rude not to attend."

"That wasn't about you," I snap, my heart racing. "It was simply an opportunity to elevate my career."

"You're a pretty little liar."

I fold my arms and pin him with a glare. "You need to leave."

He steps closer, invading my space, and the scent of him, underlined by magnolia, envelops me. Why is every facet of this man a mind-fuck?

I try to push past Ghost, but he yanks me into his embrace,

closing his arms around me. The contact is heady. The warmth of his body, the strength of his arms, and the way his muscles flex beneath my touch. It's all too much.

"Don't," I whisper, my throat dry. "We shouldn't be seen together."

"Let them watch."

He slowly drags his fingers down my back. The skin-on-skin contact has a shiver running through me before I can stop it. Memories from last night resurface, and it takes every ounce of my self-control to shove them aside. Dealing with Ghost requires absolute concentration.

He presses a kiss to the side of my neck, his lips lingering on my pulse. "That was a great speech, Doc. I especially enjoyed the part about my inability to form attachments of an emotional nature."

"You're a psychopath," I say. "That's irrefutable."

"Is it now?"

"You don't feel things, Ghost. You manipulate. You control. That's all this is."

"And yet," he says, his lips curling into a faint smile, "here I am, holding you, needing you, wanting you in a way that I don't understand. Explain that, Dr. Andrews."

I don't have an answer. But I can't deny what this conversation is doing to me, how it's altering my brain chemistry. What is it about a man wanting you with absolute certainty that removes all inhibitions?

At my continued silence, Ghost lifts his head to stare down at me. His gaze darkens when it meets mine, the heat in his eyes undeniable.

So is the fury.

It radiates from him, crackling in the night air, prickling my skin. I've seen Ghost angry, but this isn't the cold, calculated rage

I'm used to. This is something volatile and raw, something that's dangerously close to pain.

I must've hurt him with my clinical analysis. My remorse is immediate, but I can't voice it to him. That'll only encourage him to stay. It's one thing to interact with Ghost in the privacy of my apartment, and another to speak to a serial killer with a room full of people only a few feet away.

"You don't want to believe me," he says. His voice is a soft, seductive whisper, coiling around me. Weakening me. "Because if you admit that I can feel, that I can want, then you'll have to admit something too."

"Nothing you say will change the fact that you're a psychopath."

His smirk returns. "You've known that from the beginning. Yet you still let me fuck you."

I stiffen in his embrace, heat flooding my face.

"And you enjoyed it." His lips brush mine, the contact feather-light. "There was no pretending, no going through the motions. You came so hard for me."

I swallow hard, unable to speak.

"So, why are you lying to yourself, Geneva?" He uses his thumb to caress my lower lip, the movement slow and tantalizing. "Is it because if I can love, then what does that make me? What does that make *us*?"

His words shatter what little composure I have left. The fear, the desire, and the impossible truth of what's between us over-whelms me until the only defense I have left is to lie.

"This isn't love," I finally manage, my voice trembling. "It's obsession."

His eyes narrow, the smirk fading from his lips. "Is that what you really believe?"

"Yes." The word comes out too quickly, too defensive.

He shifts his hand from my cheek to the back of my neck, his fingers threading through my hair. He pulls me to him and his lips crash against mine, hard and unrelenting.

For a moment, I can't breathe. His kiss is punishing, a crude expression of his anger and need. But ultimately, it's a challenge. Ghost is forcing me to confront every lie I've told.

About him.

About myself.

About us.

He tightens his hand at the back of my neck, his fingers tugging painfully on my hair, anchoring me to him, ensuring there's no escape. The heat of his mouth sears me, his lips moving against mine with a desperation that steals my thoughts and replaces them with nothing but him. He kisses me like he's trying to consume me.

I press my hands against his chest, intending to shove him away, but I hesitate. Then my fingers curl into his shirt instead, betraying me, holding on to him as if letting go isn't an option.

When his tongue brushes against the seam of my lips, I sigh. He takes advantage, deepening the kiss, his tongue conquering mine. As if he's memorizing the way I taste, the way I respond to him.

It's too much, too intense, but I can't stop. My head tilts instinctively, giving him better access, and he takes it, his teeth grazing my lower lip before sucking it into his mouth. The heady contrast of pain and pleasure sends a shiver through me, and I hate how much I want more.

He pulls back, our breath mingling, his lips brushing against mine as he speaks. "You taste like a fucking liar, Geneva."

Before I can respond, he's kissing me again, this time slower, deeper, his lips softer but no less demanding. The change in pace is disarming, as if he's no longer punishing me but seducing me.

He slides his hand from my waist to my lower back, pulling me even closer, until there's no space between us. His fingers splay across my spine, holding me in place as his lips move with a precision that leaves me breathless. He's taking from me, stealing my passion to fuel his own.

When he finally breaks the kiss, his breathing is ragged, his forehead resting against mine. "You feel it," he murmurs, his voice rough and laced with emotion. "I can tell by the way you kiss me. Don't deny it."

I close my eyes, my chest heaving and my lips tingling from the bruising force of his kiss. His hands remain on me, grounding me, holding me prisoner. In this moment, all I can feel is the pull, the undeniable connection that terrifies me more than his touch ever could.

"Say it," he whispers. "Just fucking say it."

I can't give him what he wants. Not without exposing myself entirely. Not without becoming so vulnerable that there's no hope of saving me from destruction. The words are there, but they're stuck in my throat, lodged behind the fear I've always shielded myself with.

I shake my head weakly, my hands trembling as they lie against his chest. His eyes flash with something dangerous, and I jerk back. For the first time, I'm scared he'll physically hurt me.

So why is my pussy fluttering at the thought?

I try to pull away, but Ghost doesn't let me. Instead, he lifts my chin, forcing me to meet his gaze. "You think you know what manipulation is, but you don't," he says, each word clipped. "After tonight you will. Get on your knees, Dr. Andrews."

The command is harsh and unyielding. His voice is laced with an emotion I can't decipher. Something inhumane.

I shake my head. "You're out of your fucking mind."

He laughs softly. "Psychopath, remember?"

Ghost grabs me by the throat before forcing me to my knees. My dress pools around me, the silk cool and slippery against my heated skin. He stands over me, his shadow casting a darkness that consumes everything in its path. His expression is inscrutable, but his eyes glint with a dangerous light, his intent clear.

This is a punishment. A lesson.

He unfastens his pants and releases his cock, the thick length springing free. My eyes widen, and I tremble with anticipation. Unable to tear my gaze away.

Ghost strokes his cock, the movement slow and measured. I watch, mesmerized, as he pumps himself, his hand sliding up and down the length of it. I shift on my knees, trying to get rid of the ache between my thighs.

With his free hand, he grabs my chin, his grip tight. "Open your mouth." When I don't readily obey, he squeezes my jaw.

I comply, my lips parting as he presses the tip of his cock against my tongue. He slides it back and forth, mocking me.

He groans, the sound low and guttural. "Take it."

I move forward, taking him fully into my mouth. He releases my jaw to slide his hand into my hair, gripping the back of my head. I can feel him pulsing against my tongue, the sensation sending a shiver through me.

"Good girl," he murmurs. "Now, suck."

His cock is heavy and thick in my mouth, the taste of him salty.

I hollow my cheeks, sucking harder, and he moans low in his throat, his fingers tightening in my hair.

"God, you're such a good little cocksucker," he says, his voice strained.

I moan, the sound vibrating against him, and he shudders, his hips bucking.

"Fuck," he grits out. "That's it. Don't you dare fucking stop."

I don't, bobbing my head up and down his length. His hand is still fisted in my hair, guiding me, controlling me. The pressure builds, his cock pulsing, his body tense. My own orgasm looms.

And Ghost isn't even touching me.

"Look at me," he says, his voice a harsh whisper. Our eyes lock, and the heat in his gaze leaves me trembling. "I'm going to wash the lies from that pretty mouth of yours with my cum. Then you're going to admit the truth."

Ghost's grip tightens, his fingers digging into my scalp, and the pain only heightens the pleasure building inside me. He throws his head back, a guttural sound escaping his throat.

"Fuck, yes."

His hips jerk, and he spills into my mouth, his cock throbbing with each release. I swallow him down, taking everything he has to give. His breathing is ragged, his pulse pounding, his face contorted with pleasure.

He is the most beautiful thing I have ever seen.

The sight of him, completely lost in ecstasy, triggers my release. My body jerks, and I dig my nails into my thighs to keep from grabbing Ghost and admitting I need him to fuck me.

When I finally catch my breath, I flick my eyes upward. Ghost is staring down at me, his gaze inscrutable. My cheeks flush. Does he know that I orgasmed while sucking him off?

He pulls his cock from my mouth, the action punctuated with a harsh groan. His hand slips from the back of my head, and I lean against his thigh, spent and dazed, as he zips up his pants.

He cups my cheek, his thumb caressing my heated skin. "Look at you," he murmurs, his voice a dark purr. "A mess, and I haven't even fucked you. This is why I've been obsessed with you since that day in the cemetery. This is why I'm feeling things that shouldn't be possible."

CHAPTER 44

GENEVA

I blink up at Ghost. "Cemetery?"

His lips curl into a predatory smile, but his eyes burn with something deeper. "You think I don't know what happened a year ago?" He brushes his thumb over my cheek again, and his touch is both soothing and maddening. "You think I wasn't there, watching you lose your fucking mind in the most magnificent way I've ever seen?"

My breath catches, my chest tightening as his words sink in. "You...you saw that?"

He chuckles softly. "Saw it? Geneva, I *felt* it." His gaze intensifies, the heat in his eyes singeing me. "You were chaos incarnate, swinging that bat like you were trying to destroy the world. And for a moment, I thought you might succeed."

I shake my head, the memory rushing back. The shattered glass, the splintered wood, the raw, unfiltered rage that had consumed me that day. "I was grieving," I whisper. "I wasn't myself."

"Oh, you were *exactly* yourself. You weren't hiding behind a mask. You weren't the composed Dr. Andrews, the one with all the answers. You were real. And it was the most fucking beautiful thing I've ever seen. Perfection in human form."

I try to pull away, but his grip on my face tightens just enough to keep me still. "Why were you there?" I ask, my voice trembling.

His smile fades. "You're not the only one who has grieved." He exhales sharply, as if the admission costs him something. "That night, I wasn't expecting anyone else. Then I saw you."

"I didn't know anyone was there."

"You wouldn't," he says. "You were too caught up in the grief and anger. I couldn't look away."

"Why? Did you get off on my pain?" I snap. "Or was it for some other fucked up reason?"

He reaches down and grips my upper arms, forcing me to stand. With our gazes level, he says, "Because you were everything I didn't know I needed to see. Watching you that night...It was like looking into a mirror and seeing myself in someone else. It was as if you had a piece of my soul inside you."

My heart flutters. "And that made you...obsessed?"

"It made me *connected*," he corrects, his voice firm. "To you. To something in you that matches the parts of me I thought no one else could ever comprehend." Ghost lifts his hand to trail his fingers down my neck, leaving a line of heat in their wake. "This is why you can't lie to me. I *need* to know you understand me. That you feel something for me."

Tears prick at the corners of my eyes, the memory of that night colliding with the weight of his confession. "I don't know anything anymore," I say, my voice cracking. "Don't do this to me."

"Do what? Force you to see the truth?" he asks.

My breathing turns shallow as I try to fight the compulsion to surrender. "You don't know what you're saying," I whisper. "You don't know how to feel—"

"Don't fucking tell me what I can or can't feel. I've spent my whole life thinking I was incapable of connection, of…*this*." He gestures between us. "But then I saw you, Geneva. I saw you, and it was like something inside me came alive. Something I didn't even know was there."

"Don't make me responsible for whatever this is."

"You're not responsible for it," he says, his voice softening. "But you are a part of it. A part of me. And you feel it too. All I want is for you to admit it."

I shake my head, my tears blurring the sight of him. "You don't understand what you're asking of me."

"Yes, I do," he says. "I'm asking you to stop running. To stop lying. To stop pretending that you don't feel this connection just as much as I do."

I shake my head again, the movement frantic, as if sheer denial can unravel the truth between us. "I don't feel anything for you," I say, my voice trembling, betraying me. "Whatever you think this is, it's not real. It's manipulation."

His jaw tightens, and I catch the hurt flashing in his eyes before it morphs into something harder, and more dangerous. He drags his hands through his hair, a bitter laugh escaping his lips.

"Manipulation?" he repeats, his voice rising with incredulity. "You think that I *allowed* myself to be incarcerated, and researched your parents' murderers, just to mess with your head?" His hands drop to his sides, fists clenching as he glares at me, the strength of his fury bearing down on me. "If that's what you really believe, then you're fucking delusional, Geneva."

My chest heaves, my breaths uneven, but I refuse to back down.

"You're delusional if you think I'm going to stand here and admit to something that isn't true," I say, my voice shaking. "You don't love me, Ghost. You can't. And I—"

"*Don't*," he growls, cutting me off, stepping forward with such forceful energy that my knees weaken. "Don't you fucking dare finish that sentence."

The charged tension in the air between us feels like it could explode at any moment. I take a step back, my heart pounding, but he follows, closing the distance until I'm pressed against the wall, his towering frame caging me in.

"You can keep lying to yourself," he says, his voice smooth, each word like a knife slicing through my defenses. "You can keep denying what's right in front of you. But don't you fucking stand there and tell me I don't know how I feel about you."

My lips part, but no sound comes out. I'm trembling now, tears streaming down my face as his words hammer into me, relentless and unyielding.

"You're scared," he says, his voice softening just enough to make the anger in his eyes even more unnerving. "You're scared because you know I'm right. Because you feel it too, and it's killing you to admit it."

"I don't," I whisper brokenly. But even as I say it, I know it's a lie. A weak, hollow lie.

He slams his hand against the wall beside my head, the sound echoing in the silence. I jump, but I can't look away from him.

"You don't?" he asks, his voice trembling with fury and something raw, agonizing.

The tears stream down my face even faster now, and I wish he wasn't here to see them. That he wasn't here to witness me falling apart. Because of him.

"I fucking hate this," he mutters, stepping back, dragging a hand over his face as if trying to compose himself. "I hate what you do to me. How you make me feel like I'm losing control, like I'll fucking die without you."

I watch, frozen and shaking uncontrollably, as he turns and walks away, leaving me pressed against the wall, shattered and alone.

"Dominic Carter," he says over his shoulder, his gait never faltering. "That's the third and final man responsible for your parents' murders. Now, there's no reason to fuck with you anymore."

❧

The silence after Ghost leaves is crushing. I remain pressed against the wall, my body trembling, tears still streaming down my face. My mind races to process everything that he just said, but the storm he left in his wake refuses to settle.

Dominic Carter.

It takes me a moment to fully grasp the weight of what Ghost has done. He gave me the name, the final clue to solving my parents' murders. It's the final thread tying me to him. And by giving me the name, Ghost has severed it.

"Now, there's no reason to fuck with you anymore."

My stomach churns as the implications sink in. This was more than a declaration, it was termination. Ghost handed me the only leverage he had left because he's done with me. For the first time since I met him, *he's* the one who walked away.

I slide down the wall, my legs giving out beneath me, my body curling in on itself as a fresh wave of grief slams into me. This is what I wanted, isn't it? For him to let me go? To take his chaos and obsession and leave me with my carefully constructed life intact?

So why does it feel like I've been gutted?

I press my palms to my face, trying to steady my breathing. His pain was undeniable, his fury almost tangible, but it was more than that. It wasn't just anger. It was anguish.

Due to my rejection of him.

The realization steals the breath from my lungs. I've spent so long fighting him, denying him, refusing to give in to whatever this is between us. But then he called my bluff. And now he's gone.

Not because he doesn't care, but because I refused to admit that I do.

I wrap my arms around my knees, trying to hold together the pieces of me he's broken apart. My mind replays his words, his confessions, and the way he's looked at me like I'm the only thing keeping him tethered to the world. But now, he's untethered himself from me.

And from what's left of his humanity.

My thoughts spin faster, spiraling down into places I don't want to go. As a psychologist, I know what this means. For someone like Ghost, who thrives on control, who's built his identity on power and manipulation, this kind of rejection isn't something he can simply let go of. It's not something he can recover from.

If Ghost descends further into whatever dark place he's already inhabiting, the consequences won't just be personal. He'll explode, taking everything and everyone in his path down with him. Because when people like Ghost lose control, it's never quiet and it's never contained.

It's catastrophic.

And I won't be able to pretend I'm not partially responsible for it.

CHAPTER 45

GENEVA

THE PRISON LOOMS AHEAD, ITS GEOMETRIC SILHOUETTE CUTTING into the morning sky. I shouldn't be here. I know that. Every rational part of me screams to turn around, to leave this place behind and pretend that what Ghost and I have isn't consuming me.

But the rational part of me hasn't been in control for a while now.

I stare at the entrance, hesitation wrapping around my body, immobilizing me. Ghost isn't the type to sit quietly in his cell when freedom awaits. He was here these past months because he chose to be. Because this prison wasn't a cage for him; it was a chessboard. Every move calculated, every piece exactly where he wanted it to be.

Including me.

Ghost orchestrated all of it. To get to me. And I still don't understand the depth of it. What I do know is that if he's still here, it'll be a miracle. There's a large part of me that thinks he's already gone, vanished like smoke, taking his chaos and intensity with him.

But I have to try.

I wish I could say that my motivations are pure and selfless. That I only want to save innocent people from death and destruction. It's just not true. I'm here for them *and* myself.

The guard at the front desk greets me with a confused expression as I approach. Probably because of my disheveled appearance that consists of a messy bun, plain black t-shirt, and wrinkled skirt. I attempted to look professional and obviously "nailed it."

"Good morning, Dr. Andrews. Didn't expect to see you back so soon."

Neither did I.

"Is he here?" I ask, ignoring his greeting. My voice is steady, but the undercurrent of desperation is impossible to hide.

The guard's brow furrows. "You mean Ghost?" He glances down at his clipboard, then back at me. "He hasn't been logged for transfer or visitation."

I sigh, my relief making me light-headed for a second. "He's here."

The guard hesitates, his eyes scanning my face. "What's this about? You terminated your sessions with him, right?"

"Yes," I say. "But I need to see him one last time. It won't take long."

He sighs, setting down his pen. "Ghost specifically said no visitors."

I scan the man's name tag. "I understand, Officer Shaw. Can you please ask him anyway."

Time stretches painfully as the guard makes the call, his voice low and clipped as he relays the request. I can't hear the response, but the way his lips press into a thin line tells me enough.

When Shaw hangs up, he looks at me, his expression unreadable. "He refused."

The words land like a blow, knocking the air from my lungs. I force myself to stand tall, to keep my composure, but inside, I'm unraveling. "Did he give a reason?"

The guard shakes his head. "Didn't have to. He just said no."

My hands curl into fists at my sides, my nails biting into my palms. This was a mistake. I should have known better than to think he'd make this easy. Ghost isn't the type to show mercy.

And I hurt him in a way no one else ever has.

"Please," I say, my voice barely above a whisper. "Tell him it's important. That I need to speak with him."

Shaw hesitates, his eyes narrowing. "Dr. Andrews—"

"Please," I say. "Just…try again."

He exhales heavily but picks up the phone once more. As he dials, I press my hands against the counter, bracing myself for the answer I already know is coming.

And when Shaw finally hangs up, shaking his head, that flicker of hope dies entirely. "Ghost said no," he says quietly. "I'm sorry."

For a moment, I'm frozen, caught between the sting of rejection and the mounting determination to not give up. Finally, I exhale and lean closer to the guard, my voice calm but firm.

"You need to take me to him anyway."

Shaw frowns. "Dr. Andrews, he's made it clear—"

"I know what he said," I snap.

The guard's frown deepens, a flicker of irritation crossing his face. His arms cross over his chest, and his posture stiffens, a clear signal he's about to shut me down again.

I adjust my expression, inserting concern into my voice. "Listen, I got wind of a situation with Ghost. That's why he's refusing to see me."

The guard's brow furrows in confusion. "What kind of situation?"

I hesitate, just long enough to make it seem like I'm reluctant to divulge sensitive information. "I can't go into detail. But it's the kind of thing that, if left unchecked, could be disastrous. And if that happens, it will impact the entire facility."

I catch the twitch in his lip, and the slight tilt of his head that signals intrigue. I've almost got him.

Shaw nods slowly. "Ghost has been threatening to kill more people…"

"More people?" I repeat, my stomach churning. "What are you talking about?"

Shaw sighs, his hand resting on the counter, his expression grim. "Ghost killed an inmate last night. Snapped his neck through the bars of the guy's cell. Just like that."

Shaw snaps his fingers, and I flinch.

He continues, lowering his voice. "After the fight, we tried to put Ghost in solitary, but it didn't go as planned. He maimed one of the guards—broke his wrist and dislocated his shoulder. The guy's lucky it wasn't worse."

"Oh, my God."

"He's still in there," Shaw says, "far from the other prisoners. He's isolated, but it's not doing much good. The tension's building in this place because Ghost doesn't make threats without intending to carry them out."

Ghost is escalating. Solitary confinement might keep him physically separate, but it's only fueling the turmoil inside him.

"You're right to keep him away from the others, but isolation won't de-escalate this," I say. "If anything, it's making him more volatile. He needs help."

"You think you can get through to him?"

"I know I can." I meet his gaze with unwavering confidence that's a testament of my acting skills. "I've done it before, haven't I?"

Shaw exhales heavily, his doubt evident, but I catch the flicker of consideration in his eyes. I seize the opening, wrapping my tone in urgency. "If you don't let me try, the alternative could be disastrous. Just let me do my job. I would hate to see you, or anyone else, get hurt."

Shaw's jaw tightens, his skepticism giving way to unease. "We've got measures in place for that kind of thing. Ghost knows the consequences if he steps out of line."

I nod, acknowledging his point, but press forward. "Measures are reactive, Officer Shaw. This needs to be handled proactively. You've read his file. He's not impulsive; he's calculated. If he's planning something, it'll start subtle, almost unnoticeable. But by the time anyone catches on, it could be too late."

Shaw studies me, tapping his fingers against the counter in a rhythmic pattern. Finally, he blows out a breath, fixing me with a pointed stare. "All right, Dr. Andrews, you can talk to him. But if anything feels off, I'm pulling you out immediately."

I keep my expression composed and professional, despite my knees getting weak with relief. "I understand. Thank you, Officer."

He grabs his keys and motions for me to follow. "This way."

The walk through the plain hallways is agonizingly familiar. Each step feels heavier than the last, my resolve wavering with every turn. What in the hell am I going to say to Ghost? Will he even listen?

Shaw leads me deeper into the prison, past corridors I've walked countless times. The further we go, the more oppressive the atmosphere becomes. The lights overhead do nothing to erase the shadows in every corner.

"This area's been cleared out," Shaw says over his shoulder, his voice echoing in the empty space. "Only a skeleton crew assigned here. Too dangerous to keep him anywhere else."

I nod silently. The usual low hum of voices, the clang of cell doors, and the muted shuffle of inmates are missing. The silence is unnerving, punctuated only by the buzz of electricity and the faint sound of our footsteps.

We stop at a heavy steel door marked with bold yellow letters: **SECURED ISOLATION UNIT. AUTHORIZED PERSONNEL ONLY.**

Shaw punches in a code, and the lock releases with a heavy click. "Stay behind me," he says firmly, stepping through first.

The air here is colder. My eyes are immediately drawn to the thick yellow line painted on the floor, running parallel to the rows of reinforced bars. Shaw points to it with his flashlight.

"That's the safe zone," he says.

I stop just short of the line, my toes an inch away.

"Don't get too close to the bars," he continues, his tone leaving no room for argument. "Ghost is smart. And fast. If he gets his hands on you…" Shaw trails off, his meaning clear.

I force myself to nod again, even as my pulse races.

The guard leads me down the row, past empty cells that remind me of hollowed-out tombs. The walls here are thicker, the bars reinforced and the floors spotless. This place has been stripped of humanity, designed solely for containment.

Shaw stops in front of a cell, his hand resting on the baton at his hip as he glances at me. His expression is unreadable, but his posture radiates caution. "Dr. Andrews, I'll be right down the hall. If you yell, I'll hear you."

I nod, my throat dry. "Understood."

"Don't cross the line," Shaw reminds me, his voice low but firm.

I don't respond. My attention is locked on the man in the cell, his presence filling the space like a tangible force. The echo of Shaw's footsteps fades into the background, leaving me alone with Ghost.

CHAPTER 46

GENEVA

Ghost is sitting on the edge of the small cot, his elbows resting on his knees, his hands clasped loosely together. He doesn't look up, his focus fixed on a point on the floor.

"Ghost," I say softly, my voice trembling.

He doesn't respond. Doesn't move.

"Ghost," I try again, louder this time.

Still nothing. His posture doesn't change, but the tension lining his shoulders is unmistakable. As is the muscle flickering along his jaw every so often.

"I know you're angry," I say, taking a small step closer, careful to stay behind the yellow line on the floor. "And you should be."

His fingers twitch, but it's enough to make my stomach tighten. He heard me. He's listening.

I take another tentative step closer, my heart hammering in my chest. "I'm sorry."

He finally looks up, his eyes locking onto mine. There's no smirk, no spark of amusement. Just an empty void. This isn't the Ghost who risked his life to protect me. This man is a stranger.

"Why are you here, Dr. Andrews?"

His voice is low, rough, and colder than I've ever heard it. The sound of it makes me wince.

"Because I wanted to talk to you."

He waves a hand in dismissal. "Then talk, 'cause I don't have a fucking thing to say to you."

I rear back as though he's slapped me; the pain of his words lingers, harsh and distressing. My nails dig into the palms of my hands as I search for the right thing to say, something that will cut through the barriers he's built between us—which is ironic because until today, the only thing I've done is create walls between us.

"Ghost, I know I hurt you. And I don't know how else to express my regret, other than saying how sorry I am."

"You shouldn't have come."

"I know." I take another step forward, clutching the hem of my shirt. It's a telltale sign of my nervousness, but I can't make myself stop. No more than I can stop my attraction to Ghost. "But you needed to hear my apology."

My heart stutters in my chest when he slowly gets to his feet and walks up to the bars. His face is a mask, his expression unreadable, but his eyes burn with something volatile. "Get the fuck out."

I stand there, frozen, unable to move, the weight of his words pinning me in place.

"I said, get the fuck out."

The command guts me. I turn away, blinking back the tears threatening to spill, but something makes me stop. The question gnawing at the edge of my mind, the one that still needs an answer.

Why.... It's *always* why.

"Why are you here?" I ask, slowly turning back to face him.

For a moment, I think he won't answer, that he'll keep his silence just to punish me.

"You think you're so fucking smart, don't you, Doc? Always trying to analyze everything. If you haven't figured me out by now, you never will."

I take a step closer, standing on the yellow line. "I think you want me to. I think you're waiting for me to figure it out…And you didn't answer my question. Why, Ghost?"

His smirk fades, his jaw clenching, elongating the scar on his face. He leans forward, his fingers curling around the bars like they're the only thing keeping him from reaching for me. "Stop wasting my time."

"You knew I'd come," I whisper, more to myself than him. "Why else would you still be here?"

His expression hardens, his grip on the bars tightening until his knuckles blanch. "I have no idea what the fuck you're talking about."

"You can leave whenever you want. Yet you're here. You stayed. You were waiting for me. Why?" I begin pacing as the pieces of the puzzle fall into place. The process is slow and mentally taxing, but it's fitting together nonetheless. "You've been provoking me since the moment I walked in here. Pushing me, waiting to see if I'd stay."

"I don't give a shit."

He lets out a bitter laugh, shaking his head as though the very idea is ridiculous. But he hasn't denied it. At least, not in a way that I believe.

"But you do," I whisper. "Which means this is a test."

I stop pacing and turn to face him. Ghost's smirk is gone, replaced by a hard, unyielding expression that does nothing to hide the strain radiating from him. His hands tremble around the bars, and for a moment, I imagine him snapping them in half. Or wrapping them around my neck.

"A test?" he repeats, his voice low and mocking. "You're so fucking full of yourself, Geneva. Not everything is about you."

"Actually, it is. All of this is for me. *Because* of me."

His callous attitude hides the manipulation that began before I arrived. Ghost knew I'd come after he broke me last night. He knew I'd be vulnerable.

Anger surges inside me, burning away all caution and all composure. I march up to the bars and jab my finger in his chest.

"You don't get to test me," I say, my voice trembling with rage. "You don't get to play with my fucking emotions."

Ghost doesn't flinch at my outburst. He doesn't even blink. His eyes, bright and unrelenting, never leave mine. Instead of backing off, he gets closer, his body a wall of tension, his voice a low, dangerous drawl.

"If that's true, then why did I do it?"

I lift my chin. "You want to know if I'll stay, if I'll fight for this—whatever this is between us."

Ghost's lips curl into something between a smile and a snarl, his breath warm against my face as he leans even closer, the bars barely keeping us apart. "And what's the verdict?" he asks. "Are you going to stay and admit that you feel something for me? Or are you going to run like you always do?"

"Fuck you, Ghost."

I spin on my heel and barely take a step before a hand shoots out through the bars, gripping my throat with brutal precision. With great force, he jerks me toward him, slamming my back against the cold, unyielding metal. The air leaves my lungs in a rush, and for a moment, all I can focus on is the searing pressure of his fingers around my throat.

His face is mere inches from mine as he tightens his grip, squeezing until I gasp from pain. "Say it again," he growls, his voice a low, dangerous rumble that vibrates through my body. "Say it, Geneva. I fucking dare you."

My pulse hammers against his palm. The heat of his body bleeds through the steel bars separating us, seeping into my back. None of that stops my anger from surging to the forefront and drowning out the instinct to be afraid.

"Fuck you," I say on a wheeze.

"Thank you for the invitation, love."

Ghost snakes his free hand under my shirt, his palm hot against my stomach, his touch firm. My skin comes to life when he cups my breast, tugging at the nipple, and I press my lips together to keep from moaning. It's increasingly harder to act unaffected when his fingers expertly tease my sensitive skin, squeezing gently, and then more firmly, as if testing my reactions.

Ghost loosens his hold on my throat just enough for me to draw a shallow breath. Then he tightens it again, causing a fresh wave of adrenaline to sweep through me. The heat he ignited with his touch coils low in my stomach, a betrayal of my own traitorous desires.

"Let go of me," I wheeze.

When he doesn't listen, I reach up with both hands and yank on his wrist. It's like trying to move steel. In response, he grips my throat harder.

His breath is warm against my cheek. "You came to me. Now you'll come *for* me."

I rail against his hold, unable to admit how much I want his touch. How much I want him. My struggle results in me gasping, and my hair coming loose from its messy bun. Ghost gently runs his fingers through the strands, with the same hand that he used to murder someone last night.

"You're so fucking beautiful it kills me," he whispers, his voice a mixture of anger and awe.

Ghost shoves his hand under the hem of my skirt before he circles the entrance of my pussy, his fingers coming away drenched. Then he brings them to my clit, stroking me slowly, over and over.

I can't breathe and my wild thrashing subsides. Immediately, he releases his grip on my throat, and the air rushes into my lungs. My knees buckle, but Ghost is there, holding me up by the throat, his other hand gripping my pussy.

"You're a fucking mess, aren't you, Doc?"

I shake my head in what looks like a silent plea for him to stop, but it's really me unable to form coherent words. And because I'm enjoying what he's doing to me. I just won't admit it.

"I love watching you fight me," he says. "It's fucking delicious to watch."

"You're sick."

"And you're wet."

He thrusts a finger inside my pussy, and my body tightens at the sensual invasion. When he inserts two more, I can't hold back the moan that escapes my lips. He uses his thumb to circle my clit, while curling his fingers inside me, and I sag in his embrace, unable to take what he's doing to me.

And he doesn't stop.

Ghost keeps fucking me with his fingers, the strokes hard and fast. I bite my lip to keep from crying out. His fingers are relentless, stroking and demanding, driving me higher and higher. I'm getting close.

"Stop," I say, the lie a mere whisper.

Ghost chuckles. "Your pussy is saying otherwise, Geneva."

He releases his grip on my throat to slide his hand up to grip my jaw, forcing me to look back at him. "Are you finally ready to stop lying about us? About my feelings for you?"

I shake my head. With a growl he finger fucks me until I'm moving with him, following the punishing rhythm he's set. He knows exactly how to touch me, how to bring me right to the edge.

Then he stops.

I whimper at the loss, the ache excruciating. He slides his hands away from me and steps back, putting space between us. I sag against the bars, the adrenaline draining away, leaving me weak and shaky. I can't look at him yet. Not after what just happened.

After gathering my composure, I walk over to the opposite wall, needing to lean on it for support. And trying to put as much distance between us as possible.

"Look at me," he says. When I shake my head, he growls. "Look. At. Me."

I lift my head, narrowing my eyes at him. In return, Ghost studies me, his gaze roving over every inch of my body, lingering on the places where his hands had just been.

"I need to know if you're running or willing," he says.

I stiffen.

He steps closer, gripping the bars once more. "Are you willing to risk everything to be with me?"

I stare at him, unable to speak, my mind reeling.

"I want a fucking answer, Geneva."

CHAPTER 47

GHOST

GENEVA STARES AT ME WITH A BEWILDERED EXPRESSION, LUST making her eyes bright. "Why did you do that to me?"

"Because you needed to be taught a lesson."

Her expression shifts, anger flashing across her face. "Which is?"

"Actions have consequences, Doc. You think you can lie to me and get away with it?" I shake my head. "I know you have feelings for me. Just fucking say it."

"You don't deserve my answer," she snaps.

"Don't I? Remember that the next time you make yourself come, knowing it should've been me."

Her eyes narrow to little more than slits. She opens her mouth to respond and clamps it shut. Then something slides across her features, giving her a fierce expression.

She lifts her chin in pure defiance, right before she hikes up her skirt. I watch her, mesmerized, as she reaches down and begins to stroke herself.

"Fuck," I growl, the word ripped from my throat.

She watches me with those intense eyes, her movements enticing.

327

Then she widens her legs, and I can see her slick pussy, glistening with wetness. My mouth waters. I need to taste her.

"That's right," she murmurs, her voice sultry. Lusty. "It's *my* hand. Not yours."

The words are like a blow, hitting me in the chest. She's going to punish me for denying her an orgasm. But more importantly, for daring her to acknowledge her feelings.

"*Geneva*," I whisper, the word a warning.

Her hand moves faster, the rhythm frantic, along with her hips as they seek out her touch. I'm hypnotized, unable to tear my eyes away from the sight of Geneva pleasuring herself.

"Yes," she moans.

I grip the bars, my knuckles whitening, and grit my teeth. I can't fucking take it. But I can't tell her to stop.

"Ghost, I'm coming," she says, her voice a broken gasp.

"Fuck!"

Her eyes fly open, and she stares at me, her gaze locked on mine. Then she arches her back and her body convulses. I groan when she cries out, her pussy gushing. The sight is enough to push me over the edge.

I grab my dick and squeeze it before I come, refusing to give her more power over me. I release a harsh groan, the sound torn from my chest as pain shoots along my cock. I rest my forehead against the bars, the metal cool against my skin. We're both breathing heavily, one fulfilled, and one frustrated.

"Don't ever fuck with my emotions," she says, her voice soft and deadly.

She pushes off the wall, heading for the door, and I can't stand the sight of her walking away from me.

"Geneva!" I shout.

She stops, turning to face me, her expression cold. "Go fuck yourself, Ghost."

"You will admit it. This isn't over."

She stares at me for a long moment, her eyes burning with fury. Then she turns and walks out the door.

~

Hours later, I'm still leaning against the cold bars, my grip so tight my knuckles ache. Geneva's scent lingers in the air, faint but enough to taunt me. I can't get her out of my fucking head. Her words replay on a loop, torturing me.

The test wasn't just about breaking her or seeing how far I could push. It was about loyalty. About feelings.

Hers. And mine.

It's what fuels my obsession, the one that's been eating me alive every second she's not in my sight. I challenged her, forced her to confront what this thing between us really is. Will she give in and admit the truth?

What if she never does?

The thought twists my gut. For all my confidence, doubt creeps in, whispering that I went too far.

"Bullshit," I mutter under my breath, dragging a hand through my hair.

Geneva isn't weak. She's a fighter, just like me. She wouldn't have stood there, touching herself just to fuck with me if I broke her. I punished her and she retaliated.

Geneva won that round.

Pulling the phone from my pocket, I unlock it with a swipe, my thumb moving on autopilot. I immediately check the camera feed. Geneva's pacing her apartment, her movements agitated but purposeful. She's trying to think her way out of whatever emotions I've forced her to confront.

God, she's mesmerizing.

Her hair tumbles over her shoulder as she spins on her heel, her lips moving like she's talking to herself. Maybe she's cursing me, calling me every name in the book. I wouldn't blame her. But even through the screen, I can see the flush on her cheeks, the lingering heat from earlier. She's trying to fight it, but the pull between us is undeniable.

It always will be.

A notification pops up on my screen, pulling me from my reverie.

Alert: Motion detected on fire escape.

Adrenaline surges, cold and swift, as I open the live feed. Someone's climbing the fire escape outside her building. The hood obscures his face, but his movements are predatory. Focused.

I zoom in, my fists clenching when I recognize the figure. Skinner. One flight away from Geneva's bedroom window.

"What the fuck?" I grit out.

How did he find her?

How the fuck did he get out of prison?

My muscles tighten, the sight of him sparking a rage I can barely contain. Skinner doesn't just kill. He enjoys it. Thrives on it. And now he's outside her building, his vendetta against me written all over him.

"Fuck," I mutter, my mind racing. Panic claws at my chest, sharp and unfamiliar. This isn't like the prison riot. That was my chaos. My plan. I orchestrated every second of it. Well, mostly.

But this? This is chaos I can't control.

Skinner is pure violence, and for him to be free means someone wanted him out. Someone wanted to set him loose.

The Malones? No. They wouldn't cross me like this.

My need to protect Geneva, a primal instinct etched into my psyche, surges forward. I glance back at the camera feed inside her apartment. She's still pacing, completely unaware.

I call her. And she doesn't answer. I do it three more times, and she ignores them all. Then puts her phone face down on the coffee table.

I send a quick text, a fucking Hail Mary at this point.

> **Unknown:** Skinner is outside your apartment. Get out of there!

She doesn't look at her phone. She doesn't stop pacing.

"Damn it, Geneva," I mutter, my jaw clenching as I switch back to the other feed. Skinner is closer now, his hand gripping the railing just below her bedroom window. My blood boils as I imagine his hands on her, the sick grin he'd wear while he—

No.

Not fucking happening.

> **Unknown:** Hold on. I'm coming for you.

ACKNOWLEDGMENTS

To my Lord and Savior, Jesus Christ:

I'm *still* a hot mess and You *still* love me anyway, so thank You.

To my family:

I love you so much. You're the reason I'm writing this acknowledgment.

To my author friends:

Thank you for your unwavering support and loyalty. I couldn't do this without you.

To my editor, Sabrina Flemming:

Thank you for putting so much time and energy into my books. I truly believe you've been essential in making them something we can both be proud of. I love the friendship that we've created, and I can't imagine working with anyone else.

To the Forever team, thank you for the work you've put into my books:

Daniela Medina and Silviya Andreeva, cover designers; Carolina Martin, digital advertising manager; Bob Castillo, production editor; Emily Baker, production coordinator; Maisa Nammari, manufacturing coordinator; Taylor Navis, interior designer; Lynne Cannon Menges, copy editor.

To my agent, Jessica Alvarez:

Thank you for representing me and helping me achieve success in the world of traditional publishing.

To my readers:

I wouldn't be an author without you. I'll say this until the day I die.

ABOUT THE AUTHOR

USA Today bestselling author **Morgan Bridges** is a lover of anti-heroes, beautifully written words, and bedroom scenes that are so hot she blushes. She lives with her family near Dallas, TX.

You can find out more at:

Authormbridges.com
TikTok @morganbridgesauthor
Instagram @mbridges_author
Facebook @morganbridgesauthor